GEORGE ELIOT: ROMANTIC HUMANIST

GEORGE ELIOT: ROMANTIC HUMANIST

A Study of the Philosophical
Structure of her Novels

K. M. NEWTON

© K. M. Newton 1981

First published 1981 by
THE MACMILLAN PRESS LTD

First published in the USA 1981 by
BARNES & NOBLE BOOKS
81 Adams Drive
Totowa, New Jersey, 07512

Printed in Hong Kong

British Library Cataloguing in Publication Data

Newton, K M
  George Eliot
  1. Eliot, George – Criticism and interpretation
  823'.8   PR4688

MACMILLAN ISBN 0–333–28101–2

BARNES & NOBLE ISBN 0–389–20081–6

Contents

Acknowledgements

I would like to thank the following people for reading all or part of this study at one stage or another of its composition and for making helpful suggestions for its improvement: Mr Geoffrey Carnall, Professor K. J. Fielding, Catriona Newton, Professor J. Norton-Smith, Dr J. A. Sutherland and Mr R. J. C. Watt. Thanks also to Dr D. C. Gervais for useful general discussions.

I am grateful to the editors and publishers of the *Durham University Journal*, *Neophilologus* and the *Journal of Narrative Technique* for permission to reproduce some material from articles originally published in their journals.

K. M. N.

1 Introduction: George Eliot and Romantic Thinking

George Eliot has a strong claim to be the most important and interesting of English philosophical novelists. By calling her a philosophical novelist I mean not merely that certain ideas find expression in her fiction, or that her work reflects a particular philosophy, but that she uses her fiction as a means of thinking about philosophical and moral issues. Previous critical studies of the intellectual aspect of her fiction have tended to see her as passively incorporating a moral or humanist philosophy into her work and have attempted to analyse the underlying beliefs and assumptions of that philosophy. But this is to present her as an ideologist or moralist rather than as a philosophical novelist who is concerned to think about and work out in concrete and dramatic terms problems of a broadly philosophical and moral nature. It is arguable that George Eliot is the only English novelist who deserves comparison with major European philosophical novelists such as Tolstoy, Dostoevsky or Mann. Modern criticism has, however, been inclined to neglect this aspect of her work in favour of a more formalistic approach, and most of the claims that have been made for her as a major novelist have placed more emphasis on formal and artistic than on philosophical consider-ations.[1] This study tries to restore the balance by showing that the philosophical aspect of her work is not only an integral part of the structure of her novels but central to her literary achievement.

Most critical studies of George Eliot as a novelist concerned with ideas have given greatest emphasis to her connection with nineteenth-century rationalism and positivism.[2] In this study I shall argue that her fiction can be better understood if she is related to a Romantic tradition of thinking. It is not my intention to discuss fully her relation to Romanticism in general, which would require a different kind of study, but to suggest that she should be seen as an advanced Romantic in the philosophical sense. Commentators on the more philosophical side of Romanticism have stressed its radical anti-metaphysical impli-· cations. For example, Morse Peckham writes:

> Men have always had world-views, or metaphysics. . . . But such metaphysics had been unconscious; that is, there had been no language in which to discuss them. There were arguments about this or that view of the world as it affected some aspect of human behavior; but these were arguments about metaphysics as truths which described the character and structure of the world. But the new way of thinking, the Romantic way, looked at itself from right-angles; saw itself as creating a world-view because the very character of the mind's relation to the world required it to have a metaphysic. At the same time, however, there was a conviction, at first but faint though deeply disturbing, that any world-view told the mind nothing about the world, but merely told it something about the mind. Any metaphysic was seen not as derived from the nature of the world but rather derived from the nature of the mind and projected onto the world. A single step was taken, and all the world was changed. All previous world-views had assumed that the mind had access, whether through revelation from God or from study of the world, to the real nature and character, the true essence, of what was not the mind; and this assumption was unconscious.[3]

Sir Isaiah Berlin has taken a similar view of Romanticism:

> Whatever the differences between the leading Romantic thinkers—the early Schiller and the later Fichte, Schelling and Jacobi, Tieck and the Schlegels when they were young, Chateaubriand and Byron, Coleridge and Carlyle, Kierkegaard, Stirner, Nietzsche, Baudelaire—there runs through their writings a common notion, held with varying degrees of consciousness and depth, that truth is not an objective structure, independent of those who seek it, the hidden treasure waiting to be found but is itself in all its guises created by the seeker.[4]

In this study, I shall try to show that George Eliot belongs to a Romantic tradition of thinking in the sense described above, and indeed that she was an advanced Romantic who developed the anti-metaphysical implications of Romantic thinking to an extreme. For the advanced or later Romantic, subject and object, mind and world, exist in an asymmetrical relation; as Peckham puts it in a later essay: 'to the later Romantic the imagination, the unavoidable essence of man, constructs the object and relates the subject to the object but cannot comprehend or encompass the object; to the later Romantic the imagination reveals the anti-thesis of subject and object'.[5] Thus for the advanced Romantic, subject and object always exist in a state of tension which can never be fully overcome. In order to support my view that George Eliot is best classified as an advanced or later Romantic, I shall look at her relationship to the thought of two philosophers, Feuerbach and G. H. Lewes.

The general influence of Feuerbach on George Eliot has been discussed in detail by previous critics.[6] Here I wish only to stress Feuerbach's break with earlier metaphysical or rationalist ways of looking at religion. In his view religious beliefs are the projection into objective form of man's own feelings, desires and hopes, ordinary believers being unconscious of this projection. Some quotations from George Eliot's translation of *The Essence of Christianity* will illustrate the asymmetrical form of Feuerbach's thought which links him with advanced Romantic thinking:

In the object which he contemplates . . . man becomes ac-quainted with himself; consciousness of the objective is the self-consciousness of man. We know the man by the object, by his conception of what is external to himself; in it his nature becomes evident; this object is his manifested nature, his true objective *ego*. And this is true not merely of spiritual, but also of sensuous objects.

Hence the historical progress of religion consists in this: that what by an earlier religion was regarded as objective, is now recognised as subjective; that is, what was formerly con-templated and worshipped as God is now perceived to be something *human*.

Man—this is the mystery of religion—projects his being into objectivity, and then again makes himself an object to this projected image of himself thus converted into a subject.[7]

Feuerbach's anti-metaphysical view of Christianity must apply logically to all transcendent beliefs. If theology is really only the projection into objective form of psychological states, then all metaphysical systems which posit the existence of some transcendent reality must similarly be the projection of human subjective feelings into objectivity.

In a letter George Eliot expressed her agreement with Feuerbach—'With the ideas of Feuerbach I everywhere agree'[8]—and the influence of his view of religion is apparent throughout her work. Any antagonism that she had previously felt towards Christianity disappeared, for it was now unimportant to her whether or not religions were true. She had no interest in undermining religious belief from a rationalist standpoint,[9] and regretted that people were 'so incapable of comprehending the state of mind which cares for that which is essentially human in all forms of belief'.[10] Her attitude to Christianity emerges clearly in a letter to François D'Albert-Durade: 'I have not returned to dogmatic Christianity—to the acceptance of any set of doctrines as a creed, and a superhuman revelation of the Unseen—but I see in it the highest expression of the religious sentiment that has yet found its place in the history of mankind, and I have the profoundest interest in the inward life of sincere Christians in all ages.'[11] It is not the objective truth of religion that is important to her, but its embodiment of valuable human feelings and ideals. She believes the individual must integrate the essential human content of religion into his life if he is to maintain what she regards as a truly human identity. In *Daniel Deronda*, Deronda feels able to commit himself strongly to his Jewish heritage with its religious background without giving any indication of accepting Judaism as objectively true, a point I shall discuss more fully later.

George Eliot's attitude to philosophical systems is similar to her view of religion. Though sympathetic to much of the content of Comte's and Spencer's philosophies, she was decidedly sceptical about the truth of philosophical systems. She makes this plain in a letter to Sara Hennell about Spencer's philosophy:

I wish you did not find yourself so repelled by Herbert Spencer's writing. He has so much teaching which the world needs, and with all systems one is justified in doing what Goethe mentions satirically in relation to dramatic or other art as the universal practice of audiences—'If you give them a whole they will straightway take it to pieces. Each seeks what is adapted to him.'[12]

This way of looking at religions and systems of thought differs markedly from the rationalist–Enlightenment tradition of thinking, which believed in objective truth. In contrast, for George Eliot it was the essential human content of religions and systems that was important and not their objective truth.

It is, I believe, possible to illuminate further George Eliot's thinking by looking at her relationship to the philosophy of George Henry Lewes, with whom she lived for more than twenty years. Previous critics have disagreed over the relevance of Lewes's ideas to George Eliot. George Willis Cooke, a nineteenth-century critic, took the view that Lewes was a major influence: 'There was an almost entire unanimity of intellectual conviction between them, and his books are in many ways the best interpreters of the ethical and philosophical meanings of her novels.'[13] But Cooke also believed that George Eliot had as great an influence on Lewes as he had on her. P. Bourl'honne, however, in his study of her intellectual background, believed that Lewes's thought had little effect on her mind or her novels.[14] In my view, there are strong grounds for believing that George Eliot was in general agreement with Lewes's philosophical position. From her letters it is clear that she read his writings with great interest, and after his death she organised his notes into the last two volumes of his *Problems of Life and Mind*. She herself said there was 'thorough moral and intellectual sympathy'[15] between them, and a letter to Harriet Beecher Stowe shows her keen interest in his work and her sense of intellectual partnership with him:

When we come back from our journeying I shall be interesting myself in the MS.S and proofs of my husband's third volume of his Problems. . . . My studies have lately kept me away from the track of my husband's researches and I feel behindhand in my wifely sympathies. You know the pleasure of such interchange—husband and wife each keeping to their own work, but loving to have cognizance of the other's course.[16]

Though Lewes's mature philosophy was not written until the 1870s, many of his most important ideas are already present in his book *Aristotle*, published in 1864, which George Eliot read before publication and which gave her 'great delight'.[17] It is justifiable, therefore, to see his philosophy influencing her thinking during most of her career as a novelist. One should not, however, forget Cooke's point that George Eliot may also have influenced Lewes's philosophy since she was interested in the subject and had read Feuerbach before she met Lewes.

Though Lewes has been generally considered to be a Comtean positivist or a disciple of Spencer, in my view he is best seen as a philosopher who belongs to a Romantic tradition of thinking and who attempts to develop the extreme anti-metaphysical implications of that tradition. He opens the second volume of his *Problems*, for example, in the following manner: 'The Universe is mystic to man, and must ever remain so; for he cannot transcend the limits of his Consciousness, his knowledge being only knowledge of its changes.'[18] All through his writings, particularly from *Aristotle* onwards,[19] one of Lewes's major concerns is to show that what we take to be objective reality is an interaction between the mind and otherness. Knowledge of the world does not derive from passive description and observation of external reality; the mind plays an active role in the relation between mind and world:

> Psychological investigation shows that the objects supposed to *have* forms, colours, and positions within an external hemisphere, have these only in virtue of the very feelings from which they are supposed to be separated. The *visible* universe only exists *as seen*: the objects are Reals conditioned by the laws of Sensibility. The space in which we see them, their geometric relations, the light and shadows which reveal them, the forms they affect, the lines of their changing directions, the qualities which distinguish them,—all these are but the externally-projected signs of feelings. They are signs which we interpret according to organised laws of experience; each sign being a feeling connected with other feelings.[20]

A passage in his *History of Philosophy* shows his connection with Romantic thinking more directly in its rejection of the idea that the mind is a mirror:

> The radical error of those who believe that we perceive things *as*

they are, consists in mistaking a metaphor for a fact, and believing that a mind is a mirror in which external objects are reflected. . . . Consciousness is no mirror of the world; it gives no faithful reflection of things as they are *per se*; it only gives a faithful report of its own modification as excited by external things.[21]

This general philosophical position had an important effect on Lewes's view of science, with which George Eliot can be shown to be in agreement. The orthodox view of science in the nineteenth century was that it describes the true structure of the reality that exists independently of the human mind; it finds an order in the world which is prior to perception and language. This view of science naturally brought consolation to many, for even if there was no supernatural order, scientific laws gave order and meaning to the external world. But though Lewes was one of the strongest advocates of science and scientific method, his conception of science was quite different. He rejects the view that science is the simple description of the structure of the external world. Science, he says, is 'no transcript of Reality, but an ideal construction framed out of the analysis of the complex phenomena given synthetically in Feeling, and expressed in abstractions', and 'its truths are only truths of symbols which approximate to realities'.[22] In *Aristotle* he denies that there is any fundamental difference between science and metaphysics: 'a theory may be transferred from Metaphysics to Science, or from Science to Metaphysics, simply by the addition or the withdrawal of its verifiable element'.[23] It is a mistake to believe 'that Science deals solely with facts, and Metaphysics with ideas. Both deal largely with both. The difference lies in the *authenticity* of the Method by which the facts are collected, and co-ordinated.'[24] He asserts that the basic ideas of science are as transcendental as metaphysical ideas: 'The fundamental ideas of modern science are as transcendental as any of the axioms in ancient philosophy. Who will say that the Law of Causation, or the Laws of Motion, although *suggested* by experience, and found to be *conformable* with it, do not transcend it?'[25] Even in science there is a tendency to anthropomorphise nature: 'We animate Nature with intentions like our own. We derive our ideas of Cause, and Force, from our own experience of effort; and the changes we observe are interpreted as similar in origin to the changes we effect.'[26]

In *Problems of Life and Mind* these ideas are taken further. He regards certain scientific hypotheses, which he calls 'auxiliary hypotheses', as fictional creations: '*An Auxiliary Hypothesis* is a conscious fiction by which Imagination pictures what would be the effect of a given Agent, or Agency, *if present.*'[27] Though he regards verification as basic to science, he denies that it can necessarily prove the truth of a hypothesis: 'A hypothesis may be false, yet help us to a truth; but no demonstration of the truth of any process proves that the hypothesis which explains the process is true. . . . This caution is the more needful because of our tendency to consider the verification of a result as a proof of the independent truth of the hypothesis.'[28] He admits that the atom may be an indispensable conception for physicists but regards this as no proof of its objective existence: it is 'only an artifice, by which we introduce congruity into our symbols, and bring a variety of phenomena under one set of quantitive dynamic symbols. The utility of such hypotheses is not affected by any scepticism as to the reality of atoms.'[29]

We can infer George Eliot's agreement with Lewes's view of science from the following quotation, the epigraph to the first chapter of *Daniel Deronda*:

> Men can do nothing without the make-believe of a beginning. Even Science, the strict measurer, is obliged to start with a make-believe unit, and must fix on a point in the stars' unceasing journey when his sidereal clock shall pretend that time is at Nought. His less accurate grandmother Poetry has always been understood to start in the middle; but on reflection it appears that her proceeding is not very different from his; since Science, too, reckons backwards as well as forwards, divides his unit into billions, and with his clock-finger at Nought really sets off *in medias res*. No retrospect will take us to the true beginning; and whether our prologue be in heaven or on earth, it is but a fraction of that all-presupposing fact with which our story sets out.[30]

Here we can see strong similarities between George Eliot's view of science and Lewes's, for example her reference to make-believe and pretence in science is obviously similar to his emphasis on the role of conscious fiction and artifice. The connection she sees between science and poetry is also an idea which can be found throughout his writings. The influence of Lewes's view of science is particularly clear in *Middlemarch*. Lydgate's scientific practice corresponds closely to Lewes's conception of the scientist's procedure. The scientist for Lewes imaginatively creates his hypothesis, his 'ideal construction', and then devises rigorous tests for it to pass. In the sixteenth chapter of *Middlemarch* we see Lydgate 'combining and constructing with the clearest eye for probabilities and the fullest obedience to knowledge; and then, in yet more energetic alliance with impartial Nature, standing aloof to invent tests by which to try its own work'. George Eliot even uses the phrase 'ideal construction', so often used by Lewes to define scientific procedure, in drawing an ironic contrast between Lydgate's approach to science and his unscientific attitude where women are concerned: 'The reveries from which it was difficult for him to detach himself were ideal constructions of something else than Rosamond's virtues' (Chapter 27).[31]

If George Eliot agreed with Lewes's view of science, it seems very likely that she would also have accepted the philosophical premises, deriving I believe from advanced Romantic thinking, on which it was based. One can see more clearly the radical nature of Lewes's philosophical position in his disagreement with John Stuart Mill over causality and the laws of nature. In *Aristotle* Lewes had questioned the tendency even in science to turn 'cause' into a metaphysical concept: 'The metaphysical conception of a cause, the *producer* of effect, needs limitation.'[32] He sees cause as a purely mental concept which is useful for understanding phenomenal processes: 'we say the earth's attraction *causes* the weight of the apple; but the weight *is* the attraction: they are two aspects of one unknown reality'.[33] In his disagreement with Mill in *Problems of Life and Mind* he argues that 'the common distinction between a cause and conditions is to be accepted only as a logical artifice, which throws especial emphasis on *one* out of many co-operants'.[34] He similarly attacks metaphysical thinking in questioning the notion that every process is governed by laws: 'The law *is* the process; and there is no other *must* in the case than is involved in the identical proposition that the process must be the process.' He regards Mill's 'Ultimate Laws' as 'subjective constructions having no corresponding objects'.[35] His difference from Mill emerges clearly in the following comment: 'We are not to suppose that Law is an objective real acting in phenomena. . . . The invariability we find in Nature is what we

have put there.'[36] It is interesting to compare these ideas of
Lewes, with which it is reasonable to believe that George Eliot
agreed, since they follow logically from his philosophy of science,
with the following passage from Nietzsche, probably the most
radical of advanced Romantic thinkers:

> One should not mistakenly *objectivize* 'cause' and 'effect' in the
> manner of the natural scientists (and whoever else nowadays
> naturalizes in his thinking). . . . One should make use of
> 'cause' and 'effect' only as pure *concepts*, i.e. as conventional
> fictions for the purpose of designation and mutual understand-
> ing, *not* for explanation. . . . there *is* no 'law' which rules
> phenomena. It is *we*, we alone, who have dreamed up the
> causes, the one-thing-after-anothers, the relativity, the con-
> straint, the numbers, the laws, the freedom, the 'reason why',
> the purpose. And when we mix up this world of symbols with
> the world of things as though the symbols existed 'in them-
> selves', then we are merely doing once more what we have
> always done: we are creating myths.[37]

This is more strongly stated than anything to be found in Lewes
but is fundamentally similar.

The connection that can be drawn between the thought of
Lewes and George Eliot and that of Nietzsche shows the potential
dangers of advanced Romantic thinking, since Nietzsche was able
to use such thinking to undermine the basis of Christian moral
values and to support nihilistic and anti-moral views. Even if
George Eliot had no knowledge of the writings of Nietzsche, she
must have been aware that the ideas she accepted as valid could
have dangerous implications and that these implications were
perhaps the most obvious ones. Yet she is rightly recognised as
one of the most morally responsible and socially concerned of
nineteenth-century writers. How can these two sides of George
Eliot be reconciled? Does she choose to ignore the dangerous and
subversive potential of advanced Romantic thinking or does she
believe that it can be reconciled with the moral and social values
to which she was so deeply committed? I hope to show that the
latter is the case and that this makes her one of the most
significant writers in the Romantic tradition.

There are two important elements or tendencies that one can
discern in the Romantic tradition as it develops through the

nineteenth century, what one may call the 'egotistic' and the 'organicist' sides of Romanticism. It is not possible to place every Romantic writer precisely in either one category or the other: many writers seem to occupy a position between the categories or to move from one to the other and then back again. But it is nevertheless useful to employ these terms to define a tension which was always present in the Romantic tradition. Though all the Romantics accepted with varying degrees of consciousness that the ego played an active role in the relation between mind and world and recognised the tension that was always part of that relation, the 'egotistic' side of Romanticism laid greatest stress on the role of the ego and refused to accept that anything beyond the ego, in either the spiritual or the material world, could claim superiority and could thus impose definition on it. The 'organicist' side of Romanticism, on the other hand, attempted to move beyond the nihilism and assertive egotism associated with egotistic Romantics such as Byron and searched for a positive philosophy or belief which could provide the ego with definition. The move from an egotistic to an organicist position receives classic formulation in the three chapters of Carlyle's *Sartor Resartus* entitled 'The Everlasting No', 'The Centre of Indifference' and 'The Everlasting Yea'. Other figures one could describe as organicist Romantics would be Wordsworth, Coleridge, Schelling and Schleiermacher, while the egotistic Romantic tradition would include, in addition to Byron, Chateaubriand, Lenau, Stirner and Nietzsche.[38] But the development of advanced Romantic thinking, as Nietzsche's philosophy shows, seemed to support the egotistic Romantic tradition rather than the organicist one. Given their metaphysical basis, it was difficult to reconcile the positive philosophies of organicist Romanticism—for example the nature philosophies of Wordsworth and Schelling or the various attempts to combine Romanticism and Christianity—with advanced Romantic thinking which was radically anti-metaphysical. What makes George Eliot a particularly important figure in the Romantic tradition, in my view, is that she is an advanced Romantic thinker who sympathises almost entirely with the aims and values of the organicist Romantics, and what makes her a major philosophical novelist is that her work can be seen as an attempt to support much of the positive philosophy of the organicist Romantic tradition from an advanced Romantic standpoint.

I shall try to show that George Eliot has two main aims as a philosophical novelist: first, to attack the nihilistic and egotistic philosophies that could be derived from the set of ideas that she herself accepted, and, second, to support a humanist philosophy similar in many respects to the moral and social thought of the organicist Romantics without denying that set of ideas. In the earlier chapters of this study, '*Romola* and Nihilism' and 'Egotism and Sublimation', I discuss the negative side of her aim, and in the following three chapters, on 'Feeling', 'The Organic Society', and 'Memory and *The Mill on the Floss*', I discuss the positive side. The final chapters, on *Middlemarch* and *Daniel Deronda*, look more broadly at what are probably the two most important of her works in the light of the issues raised in the previous chapters.

Although my prime concern in this study is with the philosophical structure of George Eliot's novels, it is not my intention to neglect more purely literary issues. Her intellectual concerns had both good and bad effects on her as a novelist. When she succeeded in integrating her interest in philosophical and moral issues with convincing dramatic presentation, the result was a remarkable intellectual and artistic achievement, as *Middlemarch* testifies. But when she was not as successful in achieving this integration, though the results are always intellectually interesting, the artistic achievement was of course less. In my view, though George Eliot was strongly committed both to her philosophical interests and to the art of the novel, the former had priority. She was not the kind of intuitive writer who would allow a novel to develop according to its own logic with the exertion of little conscious control on her part. As a result, at times one feels her intention is achieved at the expense of art. In this study I shall discuss where I think this happens and why. However, in my view she has sometimes been unfairly criticised because of a failure to grasp the philosophical or moral structure of a novel, and I shall discuss this also.

2 *Romola* and Nihilism

I

Romola cost George Eliot greater efforts than any of her other novels. According to J. W. Cross she said of it: 'I began it a young woman, – I finished it an old woman';[1] and in a letter to Alexander Main she wrote that it 'was an intense occupation of my feeling as well as thought for three years before it was completed in print'.[2] Her journal of the early 1860s records her despairing state of mind as she struggled with her subject, for example the following entries from 1862: 'it is impossible to me to believe that I have ever been in so unpromising and despairing a state as I now feel'; 'I ask myself, without being able to answer, whether I have ever felt so chilled and oppressed. I have written now about sixty pages of my romance. Will it ever be finished? Ever be worth anything?'; 'I am extremely spiritless, dead, and hopeless about my writing.'[3] After she had finished *Romola*, an entry in her journal of 17 July 1864 refers to 'Horrible scepticism about all things paralysing my mind.'[4] This suggests something more than the depression she usually suffered from while she was writing a novel. In an essay on George Eliot during the 1860s, Miriam Allott has argued that this state of mind was the result of George Eliot's increased awareness of the implications of her own views.[5] It seems likely that it was during the early 1860s that George Eliot realised most clearly the challenge presented to the values she believed in by the very ideas she accepted as valid, for example that there is no transcendent significance or purpose in life, no God or divine providence, no objective order in the world, no authority beyond the human for morality. Such ideas could clearly be used to justify the rejection of traditional values and to support egotistic philosophies of self-interest or nihilism.

Romola is, I think, centrally concerned with this issue, which partly explains the immense effort George Eliot put into writing it. In her study of the nihilistic Tito, one can see her confronting the potentially dangerous and subversive consequences of her own views, and in her characterisation of Romola she tries to show how the moral and social values she believed in can be justified on a purely human, non-metaphysical basis. I shall discuss the latter aspect of the novel in the chapter on 'Feeling', but in this chapter I shall concentrate on George Eliot's critique of the nihilism and scepticism of Tito.

Although *Romola* is of great interest as a philosophical novel, it has been argued by most critics that it is nevertheless a failure in artistic terms. This can be attributed to its being conceived more as a novel of ideas than any of George Eliot's other novels. In a letter to R. H. Hutton in response to his essay on the novel she refers to 'the imperfect degree in which I have been able to give form to my ideas',[6] which suggests that ideas were the starting point for her in this work. But it is likely that she always had ideas very much in mind when she wrote all of her novels, and that this therefore cannot account wholly for the artistic weaknesses of *Romola*. It seems to me that a more important reason for these artistic weaknesses lies in the fact that *Romola* was designed as an historical novel. Although George Eliot did a great deal of work to try to establish the historical authenticity of the Florentine background, it is doubtful if her real interest was in the historical situation as such. The novel seems rather a vehicle for embodying issues which interested her in the present. As a result the Florentine dimension fails to come to life. It is also difficult to believe in Tito or Romola as fifteenth-century characters: their consciousnesses seem too modern. It is interesting to note that though Browning admired *Romola*, he was finally disappointed in it because the historical aspect was not sufficiently developed:

> I told you what I thought of the *two* first volumes of *Romola*: as honestly, I add now that I was much disappointed in the third & last: there was too much dwelling on the delinquences of the Greek after he had been done for, and might have been done with, as a pure and perfect rascal—while the great interests, Savonarola and the Republic, which I expected would absorb attention and pay for the previous minutenesses, dwindled strangely.[7]

But despite its artistic weaknesses, *Romola* is a work of considerable interest that deserves to be much more widely read today.

II

The setting of *Romola*, late fifteenth-century Florence, is that of a city in a state of crisis, and George Eliot probably chose it because she saw parallels with the sense of crisis in her own society. The Florentine situation could be used as a means of treating indirectly nineteenth-century problems. The death of Lorenzo de' Medici has ended a period of order and stability in Italy; this creates in Florence a society divided into contending political parties and interest groups engaged in a struggle for power. The structure of the novel can be illuminated if we consider the response of the major characters to the disorder in Florence. Tito Melema is an extreme sceptic who believes in no divine purpose or moral order in the world. I shall suggest that his symbolic role in the novel is to represent the type of person who could emerge as a result of the subversive interpretation of ideas George Eliot herself accepted as valid. Rejecting the belief that there is any supreme external authority or any immanent meaning in the world, he sees no reason to accept moral claims which interfere with his personal gratification. He views the situation in Florence with its conflicts and contending parties as an environment he can exploit for his own advantage. He uses his scepticism about traditional religious and moral claims to justify a nihilistic world-view and amoral conduct. In contrast to Tito, Savonarola sees the crisis in Florence in the light of his religious idealism. God is at last interfering in the affairs of the world to re-impose moral order. For Savonarola, the world exhibits the order and purpose of the divine will and this conviction is the basis of his absolute assurance in the Christian faith. In his symbolic role in the novel, he is a pre-Romantic figure; he assumes there is a symmetrical relation between subject and object. Meaning for him is not a human creation but is immanent in the world. This belief underlies his devotion to the Christian faith and his effort to redeem religious and social life in Florence. Between these contrasted world-views stands Romola, who struggles to find a tenable position which will be independent of the assumptions of both Tito and Savonarola.

For my present purpose, Tito is the most important character in the novel. In rejecting the traditional bases of religion and morality he is able to reason away any limitations on self-interest. The question the novel implicitly raises is whether the way of life into which this leads him is tenable for a human being and whether such a man can be expected to thrive in his environment. The word 'chance' is frequently used in connection with Tito's view of life, which suggests that he sees no order in the world that has any relation to human hopes and desires: 'life was taking more and more decidedly for him the aspect of a game in which there was an agreeable mingling of skill and chance' (Chapter 35). He believes that because he is not restricted by any set of principles or values, he can exploit chance and circumstances for his own selfish purposes. His attitudes are the product not only of intellectual analysis but also of his background and upbringing. The word 'alien' is often used of him, and he is an alien in several senses. Religion has never had any serious influence on his life and he has never identified himself with any country or any moral beliefs. He possesses 'the unimpassioned feeling of the alien towards names and details that move the deepest passions of the native' (Chapter 22). He is not an Iago-like villain who enjoys inflicting pain and suffering on others but a sceptical nihilist who can see no reason why he should not place self-interest before all other considerations. His decision not to go in search of his benefactor Baldassarre seems to him intellectually justified: 'He would rather that Baldassarre should not suffer: he liked no one to suffer; but could any philosophy prove to him that he was bound to care for another's suffering more than for his own?' (Chapter 11).

It is the disordered situation in Florence that seems to give him great advantages in the struggles among the various factions. Though he has nothing but intellectual contempt for the beliefs and values of the contending parties, he pretends to serve the interests of several of these parties while in reality serving only his own interests:

> He managed his affairs so cleverly, that all results, he con-
> sidered, must turn to his advantage. Whichever party came
> uppermost, he was secure of favour and money. That is an
> indecorously naked statement; the fact, clothed as Tito habitu-
> ally clothed it, was that his acute mind, discerning the equal
> hollowness of all parties, took the only rational course in
> making them subservient to his own interest.   (Chapter 46)

The means he adopts to accomplish this is role-playing. By

playing a different role on each significant occasion he thinks he can exploit every situation for his own advantage. He comes to believe that this strategy will enable him to gain power: 'such power as is possible to talent without traditional ties, and without beliefs. Each party that thought of him as a tool might become dependent on him. His position as an alien, his indifference to the ideas or prejudices of the men amongst whom he moved, were suddenly transformed into advantages' (Chapter 39). He is also capable of almost any action to protect himself if threatened. When Baldassarre seems on the point of exposing him, in order to seize 'the chance of escape', the narrator asserts, 'he would have been capable of treading the breath from a smiling child for the sake of his own safety' (Chapter 39). He regards the various roles he plays as having no defining influence on his identity. He thinks he can behave like an actor in the theatre who knows the parts he plays are quite separate from his real self: 'Could he not strip himself of the past, as of rehearsal clothing, and throw away the whole bundle, to robe himself for the real scene?' (Chapter 57).

George Eliot brings the way of life which is the product of Tito's attitudes into confrontation with the reality of human and social experience in the novel. She cannot resort to mere moral condemnation of him. Her own philosophical position would make it difficult for her to do this in simple terms, for she cannot accuse him of offending against moral absolutes. She attacks him in an indirect way by showing that his nihilism cannot be reconciled with a human identity. Only someone almost completely dehumanised could live his kind of life.

In intellectual terms, however, Tito is certainly right in believing that there is no moral order or divine purpose in the world. Opposed to him in the novel is Savonarola, who sees divine providence guiding the development of the world. But the novel undercuts this belief, and the moral position based on it becomes caught up in ambiguities. There is no going back to religious or metaphysical ideas to refute Tito's nihilism. For Savonarola what is happening in Italy is providential. The invasion of the French he sees as 'in a peculiar sense the work of God' (Chapter 21). God is acting directly in the world to punish the wicked and to root out corruption: 'From the midst of those smiling heavens he had seen a sword hanging—the sword of God's justice—which was speedily to descend with purifying punishment on the Church and the world.' He sees the purification of the Church as the first step in the domination of the world by Christianity. He believes in his moral ordering of the world with such intensity that he sees visions. But it is made clear that his prophetic visions are unconscious mental projections: 'But the real force of demonstration for Girolamo Savonarola lay in his own burning indignation at the sight of wrong; in his fervent belief in an Unseen Justice that would put an end to the wrong, and in an Unseen Purity to which lying and uncleanness were an abomination.'

The narrator is repeatedly ironic about Savonarola's vision of the French as the instruments of divine purpose: 'it was satisfactory to be assured that they would injure nobody but the enemies of God!' (Chapter 26), and the King of France, considered by Savonarola to be a modern Charlemagne, would have fitted his role better if he 'had looked more like a Charlemagne and less like a hastily modelled grotesque'. Machiavelli forecasts that once his prophetic visions fail to fit the facts, his power will crumble. As the reality of the situation in Florence becomes more intractable and entangled, so his fanaticism increases and he is forced to rely more and more on prophecies to enforce his authority, which makes him vulnerable if these prophecies conflict with the facts. He also cannot logically reject the prophetic visions of others of his own party like Camilla: 'he was fettered inwardly by the consciousness that such revelations were not, in their basis, distinctly separable from his own visions' (Chapter 52).

Savonarola is presented as a tragic figure: a man who possesses a noble vision but by basing it on the untenable assumption that God is directing the world in accordance with his divine purpose, is defeated by the disorder of events. Though Romola finally breaks with him she learns to sympathise with the ideal that inspires him. His was 'the struggle of a mind possessed by a never-silent hunger after purity and simplicity, yet caught in a tangle of egoistic demands, false ideas, and difficult outward conditions, that made simplicity impossible' (Chapter 59). The 'eyes of theoretic conviction' (Chapter 61) with which he views the world cannot cope with a reality in which there is no order or purpose that takes account of human desires and hopes.

Tito is right, then, to see chance and disorder as characterising the external world. There is no sign of any moral order or divine purpose which the ego must recognise. In his view there is nothing to restrain him from devoting himself utterly to self-interest through his life of role-playing, concealing his real motives so that he can exploit every situation for his own advantage. The novel examines the effects of this on both his outward and his inward life. Is he less vulnerable to events than men who live in accordance with a firm and unchanging set of values, and is he more capable of coping with life in his disordered society? What also are the psychological effects of leading this kind of life? It is in its treatment of the latter question that the novel is particularly interesting.

III

An important passage describes Romola's feelings when, on the point of leaving Tito for the first time, she takes off her wedding ring:

> Romola's mind had been rushing with an impetuous current towards this act, for which she was preparing: the act of quitting a husband who had disappointed all her trust, the act of breaking an outward tie that no longer represented the inward bond of love. But that force of outward symbols by which our active life is knit together so as to make an inexorable external identity for us, not to be shaken by our wavering consciousness, gave a strange effect to this simple movement towards taking off her ring—a movement which was but a small sequence of her energetic resolution. It brought a vague but arresting sense that she was somehow violently rending her life in two: a presentiment that the strong impulse which had seemed to exclude doubt and make her path clear might after all be blindness, and that there was something in human bonds which must prevent them from being broken with the breaking of illusions.   (Chapter 36)

The phrase 'external identity' is significant. Romola feels intuitively that her external identity must be directly connected with her innermost feelings, the shaping memories of her life, and those acts to which she feels she has committed her whole self. In taking off her ring and thus repudiating her marriage, she experiences a sense of self-division and her sense of identity comes under stress, though her will still urges her to rebel.

Tito, in contrast, in the parallel case when he sells the ring Baldassarre had put on his finger, is eager to be rid of a symbol which created an external identity for him: 'The ring had helped towards the recognition of him. Tito had begun to dislike recognition, which was a claim from the past' (Chapter 14). The significance of the ring is rationalistically dismissed as superstition. The idea that he could possess an external identity which expresses his inner being is quite alien. For him his external identity is only a role which he can perform as long as it serves his personal interests, and then give up whenever he likes without feeling that his actions have had any defining influence on what he thinks of as his real self. While Romola experiences the need for a sense of continuity between her inner self and the outward form of her life, for Tito there must always be discontinuity between the two.

When Romola nevertheless decides to leave Tito, she disguises herself as a nun in order to escape from Florence, a role which, in the manner of Tito, she thinks she can dispense with as soon as it has served its purpose. But she is confronted by Savonarola, who denies that one can wilfully choose to reject the claims and duties of the past. She must accept a higher authority than her own will: 'You are seeking some good other than the law you are bound to obey. . . . It is not a thing of choice; it is a river that flows from the foot of the Invisible Throne, and flows by the path of obedience' (Chapter 40). Romola's feelings of guilt over what she has done finally compel her to submit to Savonarola. But Tito ·believes there is no higher authority which demands that he accept the claims of the past. He therefore considers himself free to choose self-consciously his outward identity. The novel examines the effects of this on both his external life and his inner self.

It is in the depiction of the human and psychological problems presented to Tito by role-playing that the novel becomes most interesting from a literary standpoint. George Eliot successfully conveys the psychological consequences of self-conscious role-playing on Tito and the process of dehumanisation which it sets in motion. Instead of possessing one firm external identity which he feels is the objectification of his inner self and past actions, he creates a number of roles which vary in relation to whatever persons and groups he comes in contact with. The Tito Romola knows differs radically from that known by Baldassarre or Tessa. The role he adopts with Savonarola and his supporters has nothing in common with the one he assumes when he is with Dolfo Spini. By playing a different role on each significant occasion, he thinks he can exploit all sets of circumstances for his advantage while remaining free and uncommitted in his inner self. He believes he will be less vulnerable to the disorder of events than those who possess a firm external identity which they feel expresses their whole selves and with which they confront all situations. How can such people possibly survive in the struggle of party and faction in Florence? But Tito finds that playing a variety of roles also has its disadvantages. There are serious weaknesses in his position which are eventually exposed.

Two important key words in *Romola* are 'dread' and 'crisis'. The word 'dread' expresses more than ordinary physical fear. Rather it denotes an individual's psychological anxiety when he feels that external reality is in conflict with his sense of identity and brings it under stress. When this conflict becomes particularly acute, 'crisis' occurs. Few of George Eliot's main characters are free from 'dread' but none experiences it as often as Tito:

The only thing he could regret was his needless dread.
(Chapter 17)

Tito shrank with shuddering dread from disgrace.
(Chapter 23)

The horrible sense that he must live in continual dread of what Baldassarre had said or done pressed upon him like a cold weight.   (Chapter 27)

. . . his heart palpitated with a moral dread, against which no chain-armour could be found.   (Chapter 32)

Likewise, no one suffers as many experiences of crisis as Tito:

He felt that a new crisis had come.   (Chapter 11)

. . . his intellect was urged into the utmost activity by the danger of the crisis.   (Chapter 32)

It was a fearful crisis for Tito.   (Chapter 39)

Though Romola and Savonarola must also cope with experiences of dread and crisis, neither is threatened as much as Tito, who thinks his way of life will make him the master of every situation.

The reason for this is obvious. Instead of confronting the world with a stable external identity, Tito changes his role to suit each set of circumstances. Since each role he plays is in contradiction and conflict with his other roles, he is continually being met with facts and placed in situations which threaten the credibility of the particular role he is playing in the eyes of other people. Self-interested role-playing is morally unacceptable to society and Tito knows this and fears being found out. For anyone to see through his mask would leave him vulnerable and exposed; thus he repeatedly suffers from 'dread' and, when seriously threatened, from 'crisis'. If Romola knew of his conduct towards Baldassarre, this would destroy her regard for him. In his political life, if any of the parties for which he works discovered his double-dealing, he would be placed in a dangerous situation. To prevent this happening he is prepared to resort to any means necessary to maintain his dominance and survive. But he soon finds that even in terms of his external life he is far from invulnerable.

This is clearly shown by reconsidering the subject of chance. It is one of his central assumptions that he can exploit chance and circumstances for his advantage since he has no allegiances or inner commitments, and is prepared to adapt himself to events in whichever way seems necessary, and he succeeds in this. But chance can as easily work against him as otherwise, for no amount of calculation can anticipate events. Tito is in effect gambling with experience and inevitably finds he must lose sooner or later: 'Life was so complicated a game that the devices of skill were liable to be defeated at every turn by air-blown chances, incalculable as the descent of thistle-down' (Chapter 47). All through the novel, this man who thinks he can exploit chance finds that he is also threatened by it. The chances seemed against Baldassarre ever finding him, but he turns up in Florence. By chance he meets Dolfo Spini in the street when walking with Romola, who knows nothing of his association with him, and suffers an agonising conflict of roles. This is one of the more successful scenes in the novel since George Eliot's criticism of self-conscious role-playing is expressed through the presentation of a humanly convincing incident. Tito is also unfortunate when the Medicean conspiracy comes to light, though he succeeds in avoiding complete ruin by being willing to give information. But it is the end of his political influence in Florence. He ac-knowledges his failure: 'things were not so plastic in the hands of cleverness as could be wished, and events had turned out inconveniently' (Chapter 57).

If it were only the unpredictability of events and unfortunate chance that ruin Tito, the novel would be less interesting than it is, for these external factors only partly account for his fall. Human feeling is more complicated than he supposes and cannot be controlled completely by narrow self-interest. This is part of the complexity of experience with which calculation cannot cope. For example, Tito has genuinely fallen in love with Romola though this does not serve his interest: 'His brilliant success at Florence had some ugly flaws in it: he had fallen in love with the wrong woman, and Baldassarre had come back under incalculable circumstances' (Chapter 57).

But Tito maintains to the last the belief that he can calculate on chance, and, fittingly, at least in relation to the novel's intellectual scheme, his death is the result of an unlucky chance. When he is threatened by the mob he thinks he can swim to safety as he had done before: 'It was his chance of salvation; and it was a good chance. His life had been saved once before by his fine swimming' (Chapter 67). Since he is 'less afraid of indefinite chances' he swims far so as to be quite sure of escaping. But again chance proves dangerous to calculate on, for by chance Baldassarre is on the river bank. At last chance favours Baldassarre after so many previous attempts to ruin or kill Tito, 'the hated favourite of blind fortune' (Chapter 38), had failed. Baldassarre asks: 'Could that be any fortunate chance for *him*?' (Chapter 67), and transforms his 'fortunate chance' into the belief that this is his 'justice on earth'. But this is an emotional projection; there is no justice which exists separate from human feelings: 'Who shall put his finger on the work of justice, and say, "It is there"? Justice is like the Kingdom of God—it is not without us as a fact, it is within us as a great yearning' (Chapter 67).

The consequences of Tito's self-conscious role-playing and calculation on chance are just as disastrous for his inner life, and George Eliot probably regards this as more important. Though he might have profited and survived in outward terms, the psychological effects of his way of life are inevitably damaging. In his personal life, he becomes increasingly alienated from others, most importantly from Romola. He cannot afford to let anyone, even his wife, see into his inner self since this would be a threat. The more he becomes caught up in activities he knows would be hateful to her, the more he must conceal his thoughts and feelings from her. This is not only because she might be a danger to him in political terms, but also because he knows she would despise his hidden actions and secret motives, and he still has sufficient inner feeling to be affected by this. The screen between self and role must be maintained at all costs, and the chain-mail he is forced to wear for his physical protection becomes an obvious symbol of his mental alienation from others. This barrier prevents any real tenderness or openness between him and Romola. He becomes more and more isolated with only the doe-like Tessa to provide relief. She is his only personal source of comfort, and ironically this is because she accepts him completely for himself, without asking questions. He has no need to act out a role with her, though even this relationship is rooted in the deception of a false marriage.

Even when Romola urges openness to break their alienation, he must refuse. Alienation from others is not only the consequence of his way of life, it must be actively chosen, since he cannot allow anyone to penetrate behind the mask he wears. Without this mask he feels vulnerable in both an outward and an inward sense. The more he becomes committed to role-playing and calculation, the more he must choose alienation and the concealment of his inner self from others.

Tito's mistake is to think that his inner self owes nothing to others, that his identity exists independently of their judgements of him. As the narrator comments in *Middlemarch*: 'Who can know how much of his most inward life is made up of the thoughts he believes other men to have about him, until that fabric of opinion is threatened with ruin?' (Chapter 68). The very fact that he puts on various masks to hide what he feels to be his real self is a tacit admission that he fears what other people will think of his secret motives and feels guilty. In creating a disjunction between his external identity and his inner self, he leaves his inner self exposed and vulnerable to the judgement of others if they see through the mask: 'He shrank from condemnatory judgments as from a climate to which he could not adapt himself' (Chapter 57). He cannot help but feel ashamed when exposed, no matter how hard he tries to rationalise away such feelings. Thus the psychological effect of Baldassarre clutching him outside the Duomo: 'He wondered at the power of the passionate fear that possessed him. It was as if he had been smitten with a blighting disease that had suddenly turned the joyous sense of young life into pain' (Chapter 23). His acts are defining him despite his refusal to admit that they can. He is always conscious of what the attitudes of others would be to his actions, and though he tries to reason away shame and guilt, his inner self is affected nonetheless. The Dorian Gray-like picture Piero di Cosimo paints of him brings out the traumatic psychological consequences of his way of life.

Tito thinks that his real self exists apart from his actions instead of being expressed in action, that action is merely a function of role which can be self-consciously chosen. At the time of his death he is planning to leave Florence and start a new life elsewhere which will take no account of his life in Florence. But in separating his actions from his sense of self and thus rejecting the self-definition action can offer if the self chooses to identify with it, he both denies himself the possibility of realising himself through action and allows himself to be defined completely by others' judgements of his actions. Instead of possessing almost total freedom to define himself, which he believes he has, he loses his freedom. His actions are not designed as expressions of what he feels to be his real self, but they nevertheless allow other people to judge him, and he cannot help but be affected by this. He also finds that his choices and actions in the past lead to impulsive behaviour in the present in which the self is conscious of having little choice; his character is being shaped despite his belief that action relates to role and not to self: 'Tito was experiencing that inexorable law of human souls, that we prepare ourselves for sudden deeds by the reiterated choice of good or evil which gradually determines character' (Chapter 23). Men like Savonarola and Bernardo are destroyed by the disorder of events in Florence, but unlike Tito they committed themselves to beliefs and actions with which they completely identified. They are convinced that their lives have meaning and value even in death. But Tito, never having identified with any beliefs or actions which he felt had any meaning or importance in themselves, has never really lived. His death has no meaning or significance in his own terms since it expresses nothing of himself. The judgement of others is all that remains; Tito himself was an emptiness, a vacuum.

In neither an outward nor an inward sense, then, is Tito's life of nihilistic self-seeking successful. For man as a social animal, such a form of existence proves untenable. His behaviour becomes increasingly characterised by animal-like egotism in which self-gratification and the urge to survive predominate over all other considerations. But a man's relation to the social medium is utterly different from an animal's relation to nature because man's consciousness has been transformed by social influences. This makes it impossible for Tito or for anyone who preserves some form of human identity to live a completely egotistic life. The individual human consciousness is in a large degree a social product: social life, particularly language, has created its very being. The human individual, then, can never think of himself in isolation from others as an animal can, since thought and language are necessarily shared. Tito's nihilistic way of life cannot be lived openly, but only be deceiving others and by refusing to acknowledge that his actions have any real meaning. In George Eliot's view, the individual can never wholly separate himself from social life or from the moral considerations that are part of its fabric. These moral considerations, she believed, do not have their basis in religious doctrine but are an inevitable and intrinsic part of the human and social context. Even the ideas Tito uses to justify his nihilism have emerged from a particular social and cultural context. His actions and his awareness of how other people will judge them necessarily build up an individual sense of identity which he cannot reject or deny completely, and the attempt to do so ultimately proves to be disastrous. It leads to the negation of human identity and involves a degree of isolation that must finally prove unbearable.

The most important point in George Eliot's critique of Tito is that she does not suggest he is wrong to see no order of meaning in the world, or to reject an external moral authority, or even to believe that self and role are separate. She tries to show, however, why it is wrong to go on to use these beliefs as the justification for a life of nihilistic self-seeking. In her view, the Christian morality and values which Tito's way of life rejects must be preserved, but they must be based on non-metaphysical principles. Christianity saw morality as being guaranteed by the existence of God and of a divine meaning and purpose in the universe. The Enlightenment tended to think that morality could be justified in purely rational terms. But, for George Eliot, morality was rather a natural product of the social life of man; its basis was in human feelings which had become transformed into moral ideas through the interaction of men and society. I shall discuss this point in detail later. Nevertheless, Tito illustrates her fear that human egotism could become allied with intellectual scepticism and undermine all moral ideas. Her concern with egotism, however, is much more far-reaching than this, and deserves a chapter to itself.

3 Egotism and Sublimation

I

Though almost all writers on George Eliot have recognised her concern with egotism, she is not generally considered among those nineteenth-century writers who had an interest in the aspects of egotism which figure prominently in the work of the Romantics. Among the most notable of these aspects are Byronic egotism, demonic forces in the self, and impulse. I shall try to show that all of these have an important place in her work. The Byronic egotist is, I think, of particular importance. This was the character who had emerged from Gothic literature and the *Sturm und Drang* and who plays a central role in many works of Byron. The Byronic egotist is found throughout nineteenth-century literature and was used mainly to represent rebellion or a purely egotistic desire for self-realisation. Perhaps his fundamental attribute is that he refuses to recognise any external source of authority that claims to be superior to the self. He either defies such authorities, like Byron's Manfred, or else he thinks he can create his own values by an act of will quite independently of all generally accepted moral sanctions.[1]

A reading of the novels alone might suggest that George Eliot was not greatly interested in Byronic egotism, though there are several characters who possess Byronic features. The weight of realistic detail in the novels, however, tends to make these features appear relatively insignificant. But Byronic elements are clearly present in her poetry which, despite its limited artistic merit, reveals George Eliot's interest in the Byronic and gives one a better understanding of the significance of Byronic egotism in her novels. *The Legend of Jubal*, for example, makes use of the Cain myth as Byron does in *Cain*. But George Eliot's poem is set after Cain has been 'driven from Jehovah's land' and is concerned with the need of 'the tribe of Cain' to come to terms with the realisation that they live in a world where death is inevitable. Two

contrasting responses emerge in the poem. Tubal-Cain adopts a
Byronic philosophy based on belief in his own strength of will,
which

> urged his mind through earth and air to rove
> For force that he could conquer if he strove,
> For lurking forms that might new tasks fulfil
> And yield unwilling to his stronger will.   (p. 10)[2]

He offers men a power philosophy to help them overcome 'the
blank of death'. By controlling fire 'He was the sire of swift-
transforming skill,/Which arms for conquest man's ambitious
will' (p. 15). Tubal-Cain is contrasted with Jubal, who seeks a
different way of reconciling men to their situation. He creates
music which draws men together and makes them experience the
value of their new life without exerting their will against it:

> The generations of our race shall win
> New life, that grows from out the heart of this,
> As spring from winter, or as lovers' bliss
> From out the dull unknown of unwaked energies.
> (p. 19)

This contrast between Tubal-Cain and Jubal can be understood
in terms of the conflict between the egotistic and the organicist
sides of Romanticism. There is no doubt where George Eliot's
sympathies lie.

A more directly Byronic poem is *Armgart*, written in 1870. The
work is of interest not only for its own sake but because its heroine
has strong affinities with the Princess Halm-Eberstein in *Daniel
Deronda*. Armgart is an opera singer who glories in the power of
ego she can experience through her art. Nothing must stand in the
way of her own self-realisation. But while Byron was clearly on
the side of his egotists in their defiant assertion of will and their
refusal to submit to either human or divine authority, even in the
face of death, George Eliot takes an extremely critical view of her
Byronic egotists. The only value Armgart recognises is self-
created. Her art is not important to her for its own sake but is
the vehicle for her egotistic energies: it is her means of discovering value in pure self-expression and imposing her will on the
world:

> She bears
> Caesar's ambition in her delicate breast,
> And nought to still it with but quivering song!   (p. 73)

Without the self-fulfilment she achieves through her art, the
egotistic forces in her nature would have

> Made her a Maenad—made her snatch a brand
> And fire some forest, that her rage might mount
> In crashing roaring flames through half a land.   (p. 75)

In Byronic fashion she celebrates the will and despises any
compromise of it. She rejects with contempt the woman's role of
wife and mother and regards love as mere submission. For this
reason, she rejects defiantly a proposal of marriage:

> Whom I refuse to love!
> No; I will live alone and pour my pain
> With passion into music, where it turns
> To what is best within my better self.   (p. 102)

Armgart is clearly the embodiment of Byronic attitudes: self-
assertion, defiance, the refusal to recognise any authority as
superior to the self, adherence to her own self-created values.

   In the fifth scene she has lost her singing voice through illness.
But she reacts to this situation with Byronic rebellion:

> An inborn passion gives a rebel's right:
> I would rebel and die in twenty worlds
> Sooner than bear the yoke of thwarted life,
> Each keenest sense turned into keen distaste,
> Hunger not satisfied but kept alive
> Breathing in languor half a century.   (pp. 127–8)

This marks the turning point in the poem. Her servant Walpurga
turns against her and assails her position. She stresses the
privileged nature of Armgart's situation. Her freedom was
dependent on the service of others and her rebellion implies that
she despises other sufferers. Walpurga's most sustained attack on
Armgart is also George Eliot's own humanist criticism of the
Byronic egotist:

... you claimed the universe; nought less
Than all existence working in sure tracks
Towards your supremacy. ...
For what is it to you that women, men,
Plod, faint, are weary, and espouse despair
Of aught but fellowship? Save that you spurn
To be among them?   (p. 133)

Armgart is moved to accept renunciation and looks beyond herself to others' needs. She vows to take humble work teaching.

Though the moral development of this poem is predictable, it is interesting that even as late as 1870, while working on *Middlemarch*, George Eliot could take the trouble to write a poem attacking Byronic egotism. Why at this late date does she feel the need to repudiate Armgart's assertion of the primacy of the ego? And this attack is continued in *Daniel Deronda* in the portrait of the Princess Halm-Eberstein who shares Armgart's attitudes. It is important, I think, to try to suggest why George Eliot concerned herself with the subject of Byronic egotism during this period, even though she had very little sympathy with Byron and the subject itself might have seemed of little relevance in the later nineteenth century.[3]

In the early Romantic period the Byronic egotist was used to symbolise revolt against a universe which was, as Carlyle put it in *Sartor Resartus*, 'all void of Life, of Purpose, of Volition, even of Hostility: it was one huge, dead, immeasurable Steam-engine, rolling on, in its dead indifference, to grind me limb from limb' (Book II, Chapter 7). Against this the egotist had asserted his 'Everlasting No'. The early organicist Romantics and Carlyle were subsequently able to transcend such egotistic defiance, most closely associated with Byron's heroes, primarily by discovering the presense of God in an organic universe. When Carlyle's Teufelsdröckh experienced nature as the 'Living Garment of God', Byron could be renounced: 'Close thy *Byron*; open thy *Goethe*' (Book II, Chapter 9).

But the dead, indifferent universe associated with the scepticism and pessimism of the late Enlightenment and which had called forth Carlyle's defiance was even more powerfully present in the second half of the nineteenth century as a result of developments in science and philosophy which had taken place since the period of the earlier Romantics. In the light of Darwin it was difficult to regard nature as the 'Living Garment of God'. Should one therefore re-open one's Byron? It is a significant feature of Byron that he refused to give up his scepticism and defiance and accept any positive belief. Some of his more recent critics have stressed this aspect of him and have seen him as surviving better than the other Romantics in consequence. Peter L. Thorslev, for example, argues that it was Byron's view that man is free in an amoral, alien universe:

> In this sense Byron is closer to us than any of the English Romantics. Wordsworth's vision of an organic and morally-centered universe suffered from a long Victorian disillusionment. . . . Shelley's vision of a divine 'kingdom of love', for all its spiritual nobility, seems almost pathetically utopian; and we can no longer see with Coleridge or Carlyle the natural universe as the garment of God. But Byron's skeptical vision of an alienated universe which takes no reckoning of man or of his hopes and infirmities is a universe in which we can, I think, feel quite uncomfortably at home.[4]

The influence of Byron on the nineteenth century was, of course, immense, but many later figures went much further than he did in their egotistic philosophies. George Eliot's concern with this was perhaps heightened by the fact that in Germany the work of David Strauss and especially Feuerbach, both of whom she had translated, had influenced subversive and extreme egotistic views. According to F. A. Lange, the nineteenth-century German historian of ideas and philosopher, 'intelligent opponents have often urged it against Feuerbach that his sytem must morally lead necessarily to pure Egoism'.[5] George Eliot, who was very familiar with German intellectual life, may have been aware of this. It may also be significant that the most uncompromising expression of egotism in the nineteenth century was strongly influenced by Feuerbach's philosophy. In a study of Max Stirner, whose most important work, *Der Einzige und sein Eigentum*, was first published in 1844, R. W. K. Paterson writes:

> . . . it may be said that from one point of view Stirner's achievement was to carry Feuerbach's religious critique to its logical conclusion by demonstrating *all* religion, whether theological or anthropological, to be essentially a dispossession

of the only reality there is—the reality of the private, unique self, which is indefinable because he is without an 'essence' of any kind. . . . It was ultimately from his study of Feuerbach, therefore, that Stirner was brought to recognize himself as a nihilistic egoist and to state his protest in the grim and exultant language of nihilistic egoism.[6]

George Eliot would surely have been worried at such a development of ideas which she had accepted and helped to promulgate, and which led Stirner to proclaim the following egotistic philosophy:

As *own* you are *really rid of everything*, and what clings to you *you have accepted*; it is your choice and your pleasure. The *own* man is the *free-born*, the man free to begin with . . . he does not need to free himself first, because at the start he rejects everything outside himself, because he prizes nothing more than himself, rates nothing higher, because, in short, he starts from himself and 'comes to himself'.[7]

Stirner's assertion that all values stem from the self finds support in Nietzsche, an admirer of Byron's *Manfred*: 'The distinguished type of human being feels *himself* as value-determining; he does not need to be ratified . . . he knows that *he* is the something which gives honor to objects; he *creates values*.'[8]

The organicist and egotistic sides of Romanticism agreed that the ego played an active part in the relation between mind and world, but organicists like Wordsworth, Schelling, or Carlyle rejected the Romantic egotist's assertion that the ego had supremacy and instead sought a new means of self-definition and a new basis for a social vision. George Eliot is clearly in sympathy with organicist aims and rejects Romantic egotism. But what distinguishes her from such writers as Wordsworth or Carlyle is that she also rejected any metaphysical basis for organicism. She herself had ceased to believe in a transcendent reality and therefore cannot refute the Byronic egotist's claim that in an amoral universe the individual is free to rebel or assert his chosen values by proclaiming, like Carlyle, that nature is the 'Living Garment of God'. We see her awareness of the value of religion in her praise for religious assemblies because their very nature expressed 'the recognition of a binding belief or spiritual law which is to lift us into willing obedience and save us from the slavery of unregulated passion or impulse'.[9] But it was impossible for her to argue that the truth of religion supported Christian morality and contradicted the egotist's claim that there is no moral order that can define the self. For her, the moral order to which the self must submit must first be discovered within the self as feeling. This could then act as the foundation for a larger social and moral vision. Even if the universe was amoral and Godless, the egotist could not simply dismiss all moral and religious sanctions and adhere to his own chosen value.

The work in which George Eliot asserts this most clearly and which contains one of her most notable characterisations of the Romantic egotist is *The Spanish Gypsy*. This dramatic poem, written in the mid-1860s, is her most direct treatment of Byronic egotism and a work she regarded highly.[10] The work is similar to *Romola* in that it is predominantly concerned with ideas and is set in a fairly remote historical period, 'that moment in Spanish history when the struggle with the Moors was attaining its climax'.[11] Though a failure in dramatic terms, the poem illuminates her ideas and preoccupations and is of considerable help in interpreting some aspects of her novels.

The dominating character of the poem is Don Silva, a Spanish knight who is disillusioned with the world and with his country because of the nature of the war against the Moors and the activities of the Inquisition:

> Death is the king of this world; 'tis his park
> Where he breeds life to feed him. Cries of pain
> Are music for his banquet; and the masque—
> The last grand masque for his diversion, is
> The Holy Inquisition.   (p. 193)[12]

He feels therefore that Spain has no claim on him, and though he still serves the Spanish cause, he regards himself as free to rebel against it any time he chooses. Having lost faith in his Spanish heritage, he creates his own personal value out of love. The Gypsy Fedalma becomes his substitute for the values he has lost; in her 'Silva found a heaven/Where faith and hope were drowned as stars in day' (p. 178). In a world he believes meaningless and valueless, love becomes his subjective creation of value to overcome despair. When Fedalma submits to her father's appeal and chooses to unite herself with her gypsy people, Silva decides to forsake Spain and follow her. He claims that his personal value of love is superior to all past duties. It is his means of self-realisation and he will let nothing stand in the way of his will:

> I will elect my deeds, and be the liege
> Not of my birth, but of that good alone
> I have discerned and chosen.   (p. 299)

The poem tests Silva's Byronic philosophy against experience.

Silva claims that he has the right to make a purely personal choice. For him the will is absolute:

> You may divide the universe with God,
> Keeping your will unbent, and hold a world
> Where He is not supreme.   (p. 177)

George Eliot criticises this philosophy by showing that such elevation of the will is not a purely personal choice but has been socially determined. Silva is a Spanish aristocrat and he is merely transforming aristocratic values to serve the interests of will and ego: 'What could a Spanish Noble not command?/He only helped the Queen, because he chose' (p. 175). Silva's Byronic philosophy which leads him to rebel against his Spanish past has been shaped by that past. In the words of the narrator of *Felix Holt*: 'there is no private life which has not been determined by a wider public life' (Chapter 3). In George Eliot's view, Silva's rebellion against the country which has conditioned his identity is a mistake. For her, the self's need for a sense of meaning and value is projected outwards onto the traditions, institutions and customs of a country or people, and if these become moribund or corrupted, their essential content, which corresponds to this need within the self, must be reformulated. But Silva makes no attempt to do this. Instead of trying to create new forms for the valuable content of his heritage or acting against corrupt forces within it, he constructs a self-created philosophy of the will. The poem shows that this philosophy offers him no possibility of finding a stable identity.

When the Spanish town of Bedmár is taken by the gypsies, with many deaths among the Spaniards, Silva realises that his Spanish past cannot be rejected by an act of will; it is a fundamental part of his being. He repudiates the gypsy role he has chosen and kills Zarca, the gypsy leader and Fedalma's father. The poem shows that the valuable content of Silva's past life must provide the basis for his identity, otherwise he will suffer an intolerable sense of self-division. It is the misfortune of both Silva and Fedalma that neither of them can whole-heartedly accept the tradition and heritage they belong to. Though Fedalma chooses to return to the gypsies, she derives no happiness from this choice. Having been brought up apart from the gypsies, she has little sense of tribal consciousness. It is probable that George Eliot intended to suggest through her characterisation of Silva and Fedalma, the alienation of the modern consciousness from its past heritage. They are contrasted with Silva's uncle, the Prior, and Zarca who, in different ways, are utterly sure of their identities, the Prior because of his total belief in his religion and Zarca because of his complete identification with his race. But the poem suggests that the Prior and Zarca are less modern in their sensibilities than Silva and Fedalma who are unable to feel such total commitment. In consequence Silva and Fedalma suffer from extreme self-consciousness and the lack of a secure sense of identity.

The Byronic egotism which Silva embraces in response to alienation from his Spanish heritage is one manifestation of what one might term 'negative egotism'. Though George Eliot is widely regarded as an opponent of egotism, her opinion on this subject needs to be carefully defined. It is a mistake, in my view, to believe that she rejects egotism in favour of 'transcendence of self' or 'objectivity'.[13] Almost all of her most positive characters have strong egos but they are able to redirect or sublimate their egotistic energies. She attacks egotism only when it becomes allied with narrow self-interest or expresses itself purely impulsively, and she places high value on a strong ego. In *The Spanish Gypsy*, for example, Zarca's egotistic energies are at least as strong as Silva's. He is a Carlylean hero-figure who uses all the power of his ego to serve his race, and he is clearly treated as a positive character. The gypsies have no great tradition or religion to build on, and they will achieve nationhood only if Zarca is strong enough to hold them together and can bear the guilt of such acts as killing the Spaniards who stand in their way:

> The Zincali have no god
> Who speaks to them and calls them his, unless

I, Zarca, carry living in my frame
The power divine that chooses them and saves.   (p. 325)

Egotism can be sublimated if the self can find an authority or
ideal in relation to which it can positively direct egotistic energies.
Negative egotism emerges when the self lacks or perverts such an
authority or ideal. It is perhaps useful to try to categorise the main
forms of negative egotism that are to be found in George Eliot's
work. It is to her credit as an artist that one cannot easily classify
her characters into egotistic types. Few of them possess only one
form of egotism; rather they exhibit a number of egotistic
tendencies. I think one can distinguish five important categories
of negative egotism. I have already discussed Byronic or wilfully
assertive egotism in considering such characters from her poems
as Armgart and Silva. Obviously in the novels, the need for
psychological realism requires a less openly Byronic treatment,
but clearly the Princess Halm-Eberstein in *Daniel Deronda* has
many Byronic features as do Gwendolen Harleth in the same
novel and Mrs Transome in *Felix Holt*. Traces of the Byronic can
also be found in Lydgate in *Middlemarch*, though the strong
social emphasis in that novel tends to conceal them. The other
main negative egotistic categories are the following: the drive for
self-gratification, the drive for mastery and domination, complete
commitment to a belief or cause that leads to the belief that acts of
evil become good if they further the cause, and debilitating self-
consciousness that paralyses action. For example, Tito in *Romola*
and Lapidoth in *Daniel Deronda* are amoral seekers after
gratification; Featherstone in *Middlemarch* and Grandcourt in
Daniel Deronda are men who thrive on an almost sadistic
domination of others; the Prior in *The Spanish Gypsy*, a supporter
of the Inquisition, believes any means becomes good if it allows
his religion to triumph, and Savonarola in *Romola* and Bulstrode
in *Middlemarch* are also attracted to this kind of reasoning; and
the narrator of the short story 'The Lifted Veil' and Casaubon in
Middlemarch are men who are alienated by almost pathological
self-consciousness.

Though I have called these egotistic tendencies negative, they
are not necessarily negative in themselves, but only become so
when they predominate over other qualities in the self. Almost
every human being possesses several of them in some degree.
Those of George Eliot's characters whom one can describe as

negative egotists fail to exercise control over their egotistic drives
with the result that self-interest almost eradicates moral and
sympathetic feeling, or else they are particularly subject to
impulses of the moment, and in extreme cases there can be a build-
up of egotistic energy which can issue in a demonic act like
murder. I have mentioned particular characters as exhibiting one
egotistic tendency, but they also display others on occasion. This
prevents George Eliot's characterisation being one-dimensional.
Though Tito, for example, is generally a seeker after self-
gratification, he is also capable of succumbing to the drive for
power and mastery: 'The husband's determination to mastery,
which lay deep below all blandness and beseechingness, had risen
permanently to the surface now, and seemed to alter his face, as a
face is altered by a hidden muscular tension with which a man is
secretly throttling or stamping out the life from something feeble,
yet dangerous' (Chapter 48). Such tendencies can also find
expression in indirect ways: for example, in *Middlemarch*
Rosamond masters Lydgate without exerting her will in any
obvious sense.

What distinguishes such characters as Romola, Felix Holt,
Dorothea, or Deronda from the negative egotists is not that they
possess less basic egotism. They are able to find a form for their
lives which enables them, to a great extent, to sublimate their
egotistic energies. Often they are in danger of allowing a negative
egotistic tendency to gain control of the self and have to struggle
hard against it, and like the negative egotists they must learn that
external reality remains indifferent to the human will. But unlike
them, they are eventually able to accept the limits placed on the
ego but yet are not discouraged from devoting their energies to
moral or social ideals. However, the comparative failure of most
of George Eliot's positive characters in artistic terms indicates the
difficulty of dramatising sublimated egotism, a point I shall return
to later.

It is worth pointing out that those characters of George Eliot
who are comparatively lacking in egotism, though they may be
worthy and moral, are often shown by her to be ineffectual. A
notable example of such a character is Seth Bede in *Adam Bede*.
Seth is easily able to avoid the problems created by the strong
egotistic forces in his brother Adam's nature. One cannot
imagine, for instance, Seth like Adam surrendering to a violent
impulse when Adam and Arthur fight 'with the instinctive

fierceness of panthers' (Chapter 27). But it is clear that Adam's strength of character and many of his most positive qualities also derive from the power of his egotistic energies. Mr Farebrother in *Middlemarch* is another character who possesses comparatively little egotistic drive. Though he is one of the most likeable characters in the novel, George Eliot implies that his lack of egotistic energy has limited his potentialities. He says to Lydgate: 'The world has been too strong for *me*, I know. . . . But then I am not a mighty man—I shall never be a man of renown (Chapter 18). Irony is directed against Lydgate in this exchange since he is convinced he suffers from no such 'pitiable infirmity of will' and is later crushed, but one also feels that Farebrother's renunciation is made too easily.

Though it has been said that George Eliot's work lacks any heroic dimension, her work reveals that she did believe in, and valued highly, spiritually superior qualities and that the source of these is a strong basic egotism. The following passage from the final volume of Lewes's *Problems*, which George Eliot revised, clearly states that man's best and most moral qualities are created not by eradicating egotistic impulses but by sublimating them:

All emotions in the beginning are egoistic, and their root-manifestation is probably a form of Fear, which in the reaction of its relief is the initiation of that emotional ease called gladness or joy. In the collision of appetites, whether of hunger or sexuality, arise the aggressive and defensive impulses, which would remain fiercely and solely egoistic but for that sense of dependence on individual beings or other-selves which lies implicitly in the sexual or parental relations. With the enlargement of the mental range in the human being, and under that influence of the social medium which raises emotions into sentiments, the consciousness of dependence is the continual check on the egoistic desires, and the continual source of that interest in the experience of others which is the wakener of sympathy; till we finally see in many highly wrought natures a complete submergence (*or, if you will, a transference*) of egoistic desire, and a habitual outrush of the emotional force in sympathetic channels. True, the same enlargement of perception and imagination brings with it more elaborate forms of egoism, and civilised man is still a beast of prey directing murderous artillery for the satisfaction of his more highly differentiated greed. Appetite is the ancestor of tyranny, but it is also the ancestor of love. The Nutritive instinct, which urged the search for prey, has ended in producing an industry and ingenuity of device which is its own delight, a conversance with the external universe which is sublimely, disinterestedly specu-lative; the Reproductive instinct has ended in producing the joys and heroism of devoted love, the sacred sense of duty towards offspring; and both instincts have been at work together in the creation of the sentiments which constitute our moral, reli-gious, and aesthetic life.   (my italics)[14]

George Eliot's concern with egotism and sublimation could be illustrated from almost any of her works, but it emerges particularly clearly in *Felix Holt*, which I shall now discuss in some detail. The novel also features prominently those aspects of egotism most closely associated with the Romantics: the defiant or rebellious will, demonic forces in the self, and strong impulse. George Eliot shows that the energies which are the source for these must be sublimated or, if this is not possible, consciously renounced. She is also aware of the dangerous psychological consequences that can result from such energies being repressed.

II

Felix Holt

Egotism plays a more important structural role in *Felix Holt*, perhaps, than in any of George Eliot's other novels, and an understanding of this can help overcome some of the problems critics have raised about its structure. It has been argued, for example, that George Eliot fails to reconcile her interest in the political and social with her study of character: 'Is this to be a novel about Radicalism or a novel about Mrs. Transome? The logic and structure of the book point in one direction, the emotional engagement of the author in the other.'[15] The setting of *Felix Holt* in a period of political crisis and the narrator's statement that 'there is no private life which has not been determined by a wider public life' might appear to suggest that George Eliot intended to concentrate more on the novel's social and political aspects than on the problems of individuals. But there is not, I think, any such division of interest, since her aim is to show the connections between egotism and political and social attitudes. Egotism is an intrinsic part of human nature and thus prior to the social life into which an individual is born, but the form an individual's egotism will take is largely determined by society. In *Felix Holt* political action and social behaviour have their basis in egotism.

As in all of her later novels, George Eliot creates an elaborate formal structure based on a double plot in which there are numerous parallels and thematic links between the characters and situations of each plot. Both plots exist within a world of social division and political crisis, one in which traditional values and the frameworks which formerly supported and directed the ego are coming under stress. Egotism thus becomes a danger at both an individual and a social level. It is interesting, for example, that George Eliot does not present the riot, the culmination of the political crisis in the novel, as the outcome of social conflict but focuses on the egotistic motives of the individuals involved: 'the multitudinous small wickednesses of small selfish ends, really undirected towards any larger result' (Chapter 33). The political and social life of the novel lacks, except for Felix Holt and Mr Lyon, who have little general influence, any larger aim or ideal which can direct egotistic energies and create a sense of corporate identity. This results in wilful self-assertion, struggles for power and dominance among individuals, and conflict among social groups united only by self-interest.

The dominating egotist in *Felix Holt*, though she has a comparatively small part to play, is Mrs Transome. She possesses many of the attributes one associates with the Romantic egotist. Convinced of her natural superiority and rejecting all moral claims that restrict the ego, she has allowed will and impulse to govern her life. Her presence 'would have fitted an empress in her own right, who had to rule in spite of faction, to dare the violation of treaties and dread retributive invasion, to grasp after new territories, to be defiant in desperate circumstances, and to feel a woman's hunger of the heart for ever unsatisfied' (Chapter 1). All her life has been devoted to seeking satisfaction for her 'hungry much-exacting self' and 'imperious will'. Her adulterous affair with Jermyn had been a surrender to a dominant impulse and a refusal to let moral or social considerations stand in her way. She created her own personal value out of passionate love, but this failed because the relationship degenerated into a contest of wills which she lost. She herself has quite crushed the will of her husband, whom she despises.

Having failed to find satisfaction for her will in her affair with Jermyn, she devotes her energies wholly to Harold, the child of her passion. We see the demonic forces in her nature almost finding expression in her desire that her first child by her husband die: 'a hungry desire, like a black poisonous plant feeding in the sunlight,—the desire that her first, rickety, ugly, imbecile child should die' (Chapter 1). There is a suggestion that she would have been capable of murdering him to achieve her desire. Harold becomes her means of vicariously obtaining satisfaction for her will, and when he disappoints her she is left only with frustration and the 'dread' that her past will be discovered. Her frustrated will, deprived of any outlet for its energies, makes her inner life a misery, and since there is no one in whom she can confide, she grows more and more isolated.

Despite the novel's criticism of Mrs Transome's egotistic philosophy, however, it is recognised that, in contrast to Jermyn, she possesses a heroic quality that must be respected: 'There is heroism even in the circles of hell for fellow-sinners who cling to each other in the fiery whirlwind and never recriminate' (Chapter 42). Jermyn, who is described as 'beneath her in feeling' (Chapter 9), devotes his egotistic energies to achieving self-gratification in the most materialistic sense and to the sadistic pleasure of dominating others. He possesses a combination of the qualities of Tito in *Romola* and Grandcourt in *Daniel Deronda*, though he is less extreme than either. Like Grandcourt he had a brief passionate phase, but his strongest pleasure now is having people in his power, and like Tito he believes he can adjust to any set of circumstances so as to serve his self-interest. But both he and Mrs Transome find that a life devoted to ego and will leads to conflict with the reality of human and social experience.

George Eliot's critique of her egotists, however, is not directed only at the failure of their egotistic philosophies to survive in confrontation with the complex nature of life in the human and social world. She also shows that Mrs Transome's belief in the superiority of her will is not freely chosen on her part but in large measure socially determined. The fact that she belongs to an upper class which has become socially anachronistic is an important factor in her devotion to will and ego. Social change in

Treby Magna has deprived the Transomes of an authentic role in the community. Harold Transome has recognised that the way of life and the values of Transome Court are no longer socially relevant and has rejected his mother's Toryism for Radicalism: 'the Radical sticks are growing, mother, and half the Tory oaks are rotting' (Chapter 1). Mrs Transome's determination to find satisfaction for her will is in part a response to this social alienation, and her belief in the primacy of her will is only a transformation into personal terms of the aristocratic values she has been brought up to believe in, as with Don Silva. Her exercise of her superior social position is no longer naturally accepted by the community, so that her behaviour seems tyrannical. The social superiority which had served a social function in the past and been accepted by the community degenerates into a personal love of power: 'she liked every little sign of power her lot had left her. She liked that a tenant should stand bareheaded below her as she sat on horseback. She liked to insist that work done without her orders should be undone from beginning to end' (Chapter 1).

Thus even while she ostensibly rejects the moral and social values of her class in favour of her own will, her belief in her own superiority has its roots in her upbringing as part of the upper class. She is, however, quite unaware of how her philosophy of will and ego has been socially determined. She believes the superior status she enjoys is something fixed and immutable; it implies no community acceptance or responsibility, and therefore she feels no sense of contradiction in being proud of her genealogy yet committing acts which offend against its basic values. George Eliot implies that the only remedy for her condition and that of the upper class she represents is to recognise the need to play an authentic role in the changing society of nineteenth-century England. If this does not happen, the upper class will eventually become moribund and obsolete, or corrupted from within like life in Transome Court.

Jermyn's egotism is likewise related to his social situation. He is a representative of a materialistic middle class which has developed without having any social philosophy or any concept of the social good other than its self-interest. Jermyn is thus prepared to use any dubious means to make money and ascend the social scale; he had 'no glimpse of an endurable standing-ground except where he could domineer and be prosperous according to the ambitions of pushing middle-class gentility'

(Chapter 42). Both his and Mrs Transome's social attitudes also threaten the social structure by inviting reaction from other sections of society. The novel shows a society in danger of splintering into factions determined to think only of their own interests and indifferent to any concept of the general social good.

In contrast to Mrs Transome and Jermyn, Felix Holt and Mr Lyon direct their egotistic energies to purposes which transcend their own egos. They are also characters with strong egos but the egotistic forces in their nature are sublimated rather than expressed in negative form. The presence of Mr Transome in the novel shows that to lack force of ego can be almost as bad as being completely dominated by it. His spirit has been crushed by his inability to resist his wife's stronger will: 'To Esther the sight of this feeble-minded, timid, paralytic man, who had long abdicated all mastery over the things that were his, was something piteous' (Chapter 40). The use here of the word 'mastery' in a positive context is significant and contrasts with its uses in negative contexts elsewhere in the novel, as I shall show later in discussing Harold Transome. This indicates that the quality is not a bad one in itself, indeed that it is intrinsic to the ego's existence.

Felix Holt is not intended to be the ideal character that most critics have seen him as being, but the fact that he has been interpreted so often as an ideal figure is an indication of George Eliot's failure to dramatise convincingly sublimated egotistic energies. Though Felix possesses similar egotistic tendencies to Mrs Transome's, the moral and social vision which directs his life has enabled him to control them and use them to generate the energy needed to fight for his beliefs:

> It is just because I'm a very ambitious fellow, with very hungry passions, wanting a great deal to satisfy me, that I have chosen to give up what people call worldly good. . . . It all depends on what a man gets into his consciousness—what life thrusts into his mind, so that it becomes present to him as remorse is present to the guilty, or a mechanical problem to an inventive genius.   (Chapter 27)

But if his directing social vision broke down, he would be as capable as Mrs Transome of succumbing to pure impulse:

> When once exasperated, the passionateness of his nature threw

off the yoke of a long-trained consciousness in which thought and emotion had been more and more completely mingled, and concentrated itself in a rage as ungovernable as that of boyhood. . . . Felix had a terrible arm: he knew that he was dangerous; and he avoided the conditions that might cause him exasperation, as he would have avoided intoxicating drinks if he had been in danger of intemperance.   (Chapter 30)

Since he is in possession of an ideal which gives shape to his life, Felix can, in contrast to Mrs Transome, sublimate the potentially demonic forces in his nature.

The connection, however, between Felix's egotistic energies and his social idealism exists only at the level of statement. Most of the time the reader forgets about the link between the egotistic and the idealistic sides of Felix because George Eliot fails to integrate them convincingly in her dramatic presentation of the character. The problem of dramatising sublimated egotism was never fully overcome by George Eliot. She probably comes closest to success in *Middlemarch*, particularly with Dorothea, both by maintaining a certain ironic distance between the narrator and the character and by showing egotistic motives informing apparently altruistic actions. But little of this is to be seen in her characterisation of Felix.

The novel encourages us to compare Felix Holt with Harold Transome, who at first sight also seems to have sublimated his egotistic energies in his devotion to a political and social ideal. But this is not a true sublimation. Harold's egotistic energies are only disguised, not sublimated. He still longs like his mother for personal dominance. He embraces radicalism because he knows his mother's Toryism is now outdated, but his real desire is for power. He wants to dominate the radical movement by the force of his own will and personality. He was

fond of mastery, and good-natured enough to wish that every one about him should like his mastery; not caring greatly to know other people's thoughts, and ready to despise them as blockheads if their thought differed from his, and yet solicitous that they should have no colourable reason for slight thoughts about *him*. The blockheads must be forced to respect him.   (Chapter 2)

His view is not far from his uncle's that 'If the mob can't be turned back, a man of family must try and head the mob.'

Not only can Felix sublimate his egotistic energies, he is also capable of renunciation. Both he and Harold fail in political terms, but while this is a great blow to Harold's masterful will, Felix feels no sense of frustration at the outcome of events. His social vision acts as a means of self-definition, even when reality contradicts his hopes:

> But I'm proof against that word failure. I've seen behind it. The only failure a man ought to fear is failure in cleaving to the purpose he sees to be best. As to just the amount of result he may see from his particular work—that's a tremendous uncertainty: the universe has not been arranged for the gratification of his feelings. As long as a man sees and believes in some great good, he'll prefer working towards that in the way he's best fit for, come what may.   (Chapter 45)

This conscious acceptance of the ego's limitations prevents Felix from feeling, like Mrs Transome, that his suppressed egotistic desires are violating his inner self. He is also protected from a build-up of resentment which could eventually find expression in an uncontrollable impulse.

The importance of the sublimation of egotistic energies is also shown through a comparison between Mr Lyon and Mrs Transome, Mr Lyon having been tempted like her by impulse and by demonic forces in the self. This comparison is somewhat contrived, for while these qualities seem a natural part of Mrs Transome's character, one feels that they are added artificially to Mr Lyon's. As with Felix Holt, the egotistic side of Mr Lyon exists only at the level of statement and is not made an integral part of his character. It is George Eliot's intention, however, to show that Mr Lyon is able to sublimate the egotistic forces in his nature, for example in his religious work: 'The good Rufus had his ire and his egoism; but they existed only as the red heat which gave force to his belief and his teaching' (Chapter 4). We are also to believe that he was impulsively carried away by passion just as Mrs Transome was in her affair with Jermyn: 'he had been blinded, deafened, hurried along by rebellious impulse; he had gone astray after his own desires, and let the fire die out on the altar' (Chapter 15). His desire for Annette tempts him to reject his position as a Christian minister, to cast aside the beliefs which have defined his life, and to live only for passion: 'He was as one who raved, and knew that he raved. These mad wishes were irreconcilable with what he was . . . they were irreconcilable with that conception of the world which made his faith' (Chapter 6). To give way to these forces within him would be to act in a way alien to what he feels is his true self.

Unlike Mrs Transome, however, he struggles to keep some control over this animal passion. He does not, like her, accord it absolute value. Though it urges him to scepticism and the rejection of his faith, 'Yet he never ceased to regard it as the voice of the tempter: the conviction which had been the law of his better life remained within him as a conscience' (Chapter 6). Through refusing to surrender to his impulse and through the renunciation of selflessly tending Annette during a long illness, he is able eventually to achieve a feeling for her as an independent person and in turn to discover a more authentic relation to his vocation. By overcoming the desire to regard her only as the means of satisfying his passion, he discovers a human love for her based on a respect for her 'equivalent centre of self', to quote *Middlemarch*.

A comment by Lewes on the relation between the animal and the human illustrates his view and also, I feel sure, George Eliot's, that a human being can overcome even the strongest animal impulse by sublimating it into a truly human emotion: 'All the animal Impulses become blended with human Emotions. In the process of evolution, starting from the merely animal appetite of sexuality, we arrive at the purest and most far-reaching tenderness.'[16] This is no doubt what George Eliot is intending to suggest in her treatment of Mr Lyon. His experience gives him a new self-understanding which allows him to reassume his role as a minister with greater security. Previously he had tended to suppress the egotistic forces in his nature in a mechanical devotion to duty instead of truly sublimating them. But now that he has become aware of these forces in himself, he is able to use his religious faith as a means both of exerting control over them and of giving positive direction to the energies they generate. He is thus able to discipline and redirect his egotistic and impulsive tendencies and also to avoid the psychological effects of repression. While Mrs Transome must suffer the traumatic effects of having her egotistic desires trapped within, Mr Lyon is able to channel his energies in the service of society: 'What if he were inwardly torn by doubt and anxiety concerning his own private relations and the facts of his past life? That danger of absorption within the narrow bounds of self only urged him the more towards action which had a wider bearing, and might tell on the welfare of England at large' (Chapter 15). Part of Mrs Transome's tragedy is that she has no such outlet.

Felix Holt shows, then, that though egotism cannot be avoided, the energies it generates need not find expression in impulsive or self-interested behaviour but can be redirected to purposes beyond the desire for power or gratification. The ideal to be aspired to is proclaimed in the episode concerning the rebellious choir, which is symbolically related to the novel's concerns. Even a church choir is vulnerable to rebellious impulse: '[it] had declined to change the tunes in accordance with a change in the selection of hymns, and had stretched short metre into long *out of pure wilfulness and defiance*'. (Chapter 13; my italics). When Felix humorously defends the choir, Mr Lyon reproves him and makes the following speech:

> You yourself are a lover of freedom, and a bold rebel against usurping authority. But the right to rebellion is the right to seek a higher rule, and not to wander in mere lawlessness. . . . I apprehend that there is a law in music, disobedience whereunto would bring us in our singing to the level of shrieking maniacs or howling beasts: so that herein we are well instructed how true liberty can be nought but the transfer of obedience from the will of one or of a few men to that will which is the norm or rule for all men. And though the transfer may sometimes be but an erroneous direction of search, yet is the search good and necessary to the ultimate finding. And even as in music, where all obey and concur to one end, so that each has the joy of contributing to the whole whereby he is ravished and lifted up to the courts of heaven, so will it be in that crowning time of millennial region, when our daily prayer will be fulfilled, and one law shall be written on all hearts, and be the very structure of all thought, and be the principle of all action.   (Chapter 13)

This is clearly an ideal and unattainable in real terms, as the religious language and the word 'millennial' suggest. Nevertheless, George Eliot believes it is important for such an ideal to be present in human consciousness. It helps order an individual's existence by channelling positively his egotistic energies and giving his life a sense of meaning and direction. If such an ideal is not present, she implies, there is a danger that many men will live only for self-gratification, like Christian or Jermyn in *Felix Holt*, and easily succumb to their strongest impulse or to demonic forces in the self, like Mrs Transome. There is also the danger of social breakdown since individuals or social groups will not be restrained from seeking their own interests and might reject the larger social good, and one sees the potentiality for this in the political and social world of *Felix Holt*. There would then be no social harmony, no continuity with the past, no aim to work towards in the future. It may be an illusion to believe in the truth of such ideals, but this is no criticism of their value, as the narrator indicates: 'For what we call illusions are often, in truth, a wider vision of past and present realities—a willing movement of a man's soul with the larger sweep of the world's forces—a movement towards a more assured end than the chances of a single life' (Chapter 16). Lewes's view on the value of ideals perhaps provides further insight into George Eliot's attitude:

> They are not the laws by which we live, or can live, but the types by which we measure all deviations from a perfect life. The mind which has once placed before it an ideal of life has a pole-star by which to steer, although his actual course will be determined by the winds and waves. . . . Our passions and our ignorance constantly make us swerve from the path to which the pole-star points; and thus the ideal of a Christian life, or the ideal of Marriage, are never wholly to be realised, yet who denies that such ideals are very potent influences in every soul that has clearly conceived them?[17]

Felix Holt and the other works I have discussed in this chapter illustrate George Eliot's deep concern with egotism. The fact that Romantic aspects of egotism feature prominently in her works and are subject to criticism suggests that she believed that the attack by earlier organicist Romantics on the 'cult of the ego' associated with Byron and other figures needed to be re-formulated. As I have tried to show, the critique of such egotists as Tito Melema, Don Silva, or Mrs Transome makes subtle use of psychological and sociological argument. One can see some similarity between George Eliot's critique of egotism and that of Marx and Engels in their attack on the egotistic philosophy of Max Stirner in *The German Ideology*. Like George Eliot, Marx and Engels cannot refute the views of someone like Stirner by appealing to moral absolutes or religious doctrine. Their attack must try to expose the inner contradictions of Stirner's philosophy and undermine it by psychological and sociological analysis, a similar strategy to that adopted by George Eliot in her study of her negative egotists. The fact that Stirner, like Marx and Engels themselves, had been considerably influenced by Feuerbach perhaps explains why they see Stirner as such a threat and why he is treated at such great length in *The German Ideology*. This would, of course, be a further similarity with George Eliot, also influenced by Feuerbach and perhaps concerned about the subversive use that might be made of this philosophy.

Though George Eliot and Lewes were unbelievers, they clearly recognised that one of the great values of Christianity was its power to make men live their lives in relation to an ideal standard which helped to control or direct the egotistic drive for self-gratification and strong impulse. One notes Lewes's reference in the passage quoted above to 'the ideal of a Christian life', and of course George Eliot's Christian characters are treated with great sympathy. Christianity also, by providing people with a set of beliefs and a code of ethics that had wide social acceptance, helped support the structure of society. In the undermining of Christian belief and religious faith generally, which George Eliot had been involved in through her translations of Strauss and Feuerbach, lay great danger to both the self and society. The ego would no longer possess the unquestioned external authority which acted as a control on its energies and social values would become problematic. It is clearly one of the major philosophical concerns of George Eliot's fiction to face this problem. It was of crucial importance to her to show that even if the moral and social values associated with the Christian tradition could no longer find metaphysical justification, these values could be justified in purely humanist and non-metaphysical terms. In the next chapter I shall try to show the importance she attaches to feeling in her belief that Christian moral values can be preserved on a non-metaphysical basis.

4 Feeling

An obvious criticism that can be made of George Eliot's humanism is that it retains Christian morality even though it discards the metaphysical beliefs of Christianity. It could be argued that the humanist philosophy embodied in her novels is weakened by this apparent contradiction, and indeed this is the view of Nietzsche in his criticism of her in *Twilight of the Idols*:

> *G. Eliot*—They have got rid of the Christian God, and now feel obliged to cling all the more firmly to Christian morality: that is *English* consistency, let us not blame it on little bluestockings *à la* Eliot. . . . When one gives up Christian belief one thereby deprives oneself of the *right* to Christian morality. For the latter is absolutely *not* self-evident: one must make this point clear again and again, in spite of English shallowpates. Christianity is a system, a consistently thought out and *complete* view of things. If one breaks out of it a fundamental idea, the belief in God, one thereby breaks the whole thing to pieces: one has nothing of any consequence left in one's hands. . . . If the English really do believe they know, of their own accord, 'intuitively', what is good and evil; if they consequently think they no longer have need of Christianity as a guarantee of morality; that is merely the *consequence* of the ascendancy of Christian evaluation and an expression of the *strength* and *depth* of this ascendancy. . . . For the Englishman morality is not yet a problem . . .[1]

For Nietzsche, George Eliot is philosophically naive in believing that Christian morality can be retained even if Christian belief is given up. In this chapter I shall try to show that her position is not a naive one, but one which tries to counter the kind of objections that Nietzsche makes. For her it was possible validly to re-

construct Christian morality on a non-metaphysical basis, and
the key to this was feeling.

One of the prime beliefs one finds in the work of the early
Romantics, particularly the English Romantics, is that feeling can
be a direct means of knowledge. They saw it as not merely
supporting reason but as superior to it. Lilian R. Furst writes:

> On the whole . . . the Romantics envisaged the heart not only,
> or even primarily, as the fountainhead of happiness and
> sorrow, but particularly as an organ of knowledge. As a
> corollary to the rejection of rationalism, the mind was demoted
> from its controlling position and replaced by the heart as the
> means of perception: 'The feelings will set up their standard
> against the understanding, whenever the understanding has
> renounced its allegiance to the reason', to use Coleridge's
> words. 'Only what we feel, we know' could well have been the
> motto of the Romantics; the heart must be believed before the
> reason because here lies that essential part of man wherein he is
> linked to the universal spirit.[2]

This calls to mind an exchange between Ladislaw and Dorothea
in Chapter 22 of *Middlemarch* in which he asserts that a poet's
soul is one 'in which knowledge passes instantaneously into
feeling, and feeling flashes back as a new organ of knowledge', to
which Dorothea replies: 'I understand what you mean about
knowledge passing into feeling, for that seems to be just what I
experience.'

The idea of feeling as an 'organ of knowledge' is fundamental
to George Eliot's thought. But as a later Romantic, she could not
merely accept this idea in the intuitive way of many of the earlier
Romantics. It needed philosophical or scientific support and the
difficulties of some of its implications had to be faced. I shall first
of all try to reconstruct her position on feeling and then discuss its
importance in the philosophical structure of some of her novels.

Nietzsche in the passage quoted above takes the view that
Christianity is a system which collapses if belief in God is removed
from it. The morality which has been based on it then has
no foundation. But George Eliot took a different view of
Christianity. Following Feuerbach she believed that Christianity
consisted essentially of human content which man had projected
outside himself. God was the projection into objectivity of certain

human feelings. Even if God was rejected as an objectively existing being, these feelings remained. One could then argue that it was not the existence of a divine being which was the basis of Christian morality; the human feeling underlying the concept of God was the real basis. There are numerous passages in Feuerbach in which Christian concepts are interpreted as projections of human feeling:

> God suffers, means in truth nothing else than: God is a heart. The heart is the source, the centre of all suffering. A being without suffering is a being without a heart. The mystery of the suffering God is therefore the mystery of feeling, sensibility. A suffering God is a feeling, sensitive God. But the proposition: God is a feeling Being, is only the religious periphrase of the proposition: feeling is absolute, divine in its nature.[3]

What the fundamental idea of Christianity, God is love, really means, says Feuerbach, is that 'feeling is the God of man, nay, God absolutely, the Absolute Being. God is the nature of human feeling, unlimited, pure feeling, made objective.'[4] George Eliot, like Feuerbach, was aware of the dangers if feeling operated without any restraint, but she believed that properly controlled and directed it could serve as the basis for a humanism which would preserve the moral content of Christianity.

There are numerous passages in George Eliot's writings which illustrate her view that feeling could be a direct means of knowledge, superior to reason or to religious systems. In her essay on the theological views of Dr Cumming, for example, she asserts that moral actions are the product of spontaneous moral feelings, not of mechanical obedience to Christian theological concepts, as Cumming had claimed: 'A man is not to be just from a feeling of justice; he is not to help his fellow-men out of good-will to his fellow-men; he is not to be a tender husband and father out of affection: all of these natural muscles and fibres are to be torn away and replaced by a patent steel-spring—anxiety for the "glory of God".'[5] She goes on to argue that 'The idea of God is really moral in its influence . . . only when God is contemplated as sympathizing with the pure elements of human feeling'. Her essay on the poet Edward Young attacks his view that it is only Christianity as a religious system that makes men moral. She refers to Young's 'utter want of moral emotion'[6] and argues that justice and benevolence are direct human feelings and not the product of a moral system; a man who would act against the rights of his fellow-men if he disbelieved in a future life would be 'wanting in the genuine feelings of justice and benevolence'.[7]

The influence of Romantic ideas is evident in the following passage in which she sees an affinity between art and morality:

> Now, the products of Art are great in proportion as they result from the immediate prompting of innate power which we call Genius, and not from laboured obedience to a theory or rule; and the presence of genius or innate prompting is directly opposed to the perpetual consciousness of a rule. The action of faculty is imperious, and excludes the reflection *why* it should act. In the same way, in proportion as morality is emotional, *ie.*, has affinity with Art, it will exhibit itself in direct sympathetic feeling and action, and not as the recognition of a rule. Love does not say, 'I ought to love'—it loves. Pity does not say, 'It is right to be pitiful'—it pities. Justice does not say, 'I am bound to be just'—it feels justly. It is only where moral emotion is comparatively weak that the contemplation of a rule or theory habitually mingles with its action.[8]

This rejection of rules in both art and morality is obviously related to the Romantics' dismissal of mechanical conceptions. For George Eliot morality is not a given set of rules governed by a religious system; it emerges naturally from the encounter between human feeling and the world.

One also sees a Romantic influence on George Eliot in her belief that there are people with higher natures who possess a superior quality and intensity of feeling and are able to call forth nobler feelings in others. In her novels, characters like Dorothea Brooke and Felix Holt are clearly of this type. In 'Leaves from a Notebook', in a section entitled ' "A Fine Excess" Feeling Is Energy', she enlarges on the role of such persons: 'One can hardly insist too much . . . on the efficacy of feeling in stimulating to ardent co-operation.' Quoting Fedalma's 'The grandest death! to die in vain—for Love/Greater than sways the forces of the world', she goes on:

> I really believe and mean this,—not as a rule of general action, but as a possible grand instance of determining energy in

human sympathy, which even in particular cases, where it has only a magnificent futility, is more adorable, or as we say divine, than unpitying force, or than a prudent calculation of results. . . . But the generous leap of impulse is needed too to swell the flood of sympathy in us beholders, that we may not fall completely under the mastery of calculation, which in its turn may fail of ends for want of energy got from ardour.[9]

The use of the word 'ardour' suggests a parallel with Dorothea in *Middlemarch*, whose key word is 'ardour'. One is reminded of how her ardent feeling liberates Rosamond, even if only temporarily, from her calculating egotism.

The lack or misdirection of feeling can present a danger to morality. This danger is especially great in the case of Tito in *Romola* since he both lacks strong feeling and has rejected Christianity or any form of religious belief. He finds it easy to dismiss in rational terms all forms of moral action and to justify a life of total self-seeking. He illustrates the moral danger that may arise if Christianity ceases to function as a system. But for George Eliot no person can be completely lacking in human feeling; the lack is only comparative. Even Tito cannot entirely rid himself of feelings of guilt. With Hetty Sorrel in *Adam Bede*, narcissistic self-absorption prevents feeling being shaped morally by experience. Children and animals which would normally call forth human feeling arouse little other than irritation in her. Mrs Poyser is critical of her for this reason: 'there's nothing seems to give her a turn i' the' inside, not even when we thought Totty had tumbled into the pit. . . . It's my belief her heart's as hard as a pebble' (Chapter 15). It is only with 'The shattering of all her little dream-world' (Chapter 31) that her 'pleasure-seeking nature' (Chapter 15) is forced into intense confrontation with external experience, which makes it possible for her egotistic, animal emotions to be transformed into moral and sympathetic feeling. The guilt feelings she experiences in abandoning her child break down her egotism and self-absorption, and she eventually needs to share these feelings with another human being, with Dinah in the scene in the prison.

While Hetty possesses 'the lower nature' in which egotistic emotions are only to a very limited extent transformed into moral feelings, Dinah Morris is of 'the higher nature' (Chapter 15) in which this sublimating process takes place to a high degree. Dinah, however, like Mr Lyon, has a religious faith which controls and morally directs strong feeling. But George Eliot also recognised that certain forms of religion encouraged over-subjective feelings: 'in proportion as religious sects exalt feeling above intellect, and believe themselves to be guided by divine inspiration rather than by a spontaneous exertion of their faculties—that is, in proportion as they are removed from rationalism—their sense of truthfulness is misty and confused'.[10] Though she greatly values feeling, it needs to be directed and controlled.

But it is clear throughout George Eliot's writings that she believed that in moral terms feeling is prior to the intellect. Rational thought supported feeling rather than the reverse. It is perhaps here that one can distinguish her from her contemporary Mill, who also laid great stress on feeling.[11] It is unlikely that Mill would have gone as far as George Eliot in claiming that feeling could be a direct means of knowledge. It is arguable that for him feeling supported rational thinking and was not prior to the intellect. A commentator on Mill writes: 'Wordsworth's poems did indeed offer Mill the "culture of the feelings" he had desired; but nowhere does he suggest that they offered any kind of imaginative truth, or made possible any grasp of reality not available to the ordinary, logical intellect.'[12] But there are obviously difficulties in making feeling the most important element of morality, and one of the main interests of George Eliot's moral thought is how she tried to overcome these.

II

Even if feeling as a means of moral knowledge is shaped by objective experience or subject to rational criticism, this still leaves certain problems. One may experience, spontaneously, 'moral' feelings of pity, justice, or benevolence, but what about the direct prompting of impulsive, violent, or rebellious feelings? Feeling and egotism cannot be completely separated. Many emotions become fused with the egotistic drives I discussed in the previous chapter and this fusion creates feelings which obviously must be distinguished from the feelings which George Eliot believed could form the basis of a purely humanist morality. To classify certain feelings as moral and to reject others would seem to necessitate moving beyond feeling to some implicitly normative standpoint outside feeling. Christianity had been able to provide an external authority which exercised some control over the excesses of feeling since certain moral values were an intrinsic part of it. But if Christianity as a system was rejected, on what grounds could one classify certain feelings as moral and others as immoral? It might seem that George Eliot, in believing that feeling was the true basis of Christian morality, was covertly clinging to Christianity as a system in claiming that certain feelings were moral, as Nietzsche had suggested in his attack on her. Another important difficulty of her moral position is how it is possible for moral feelings of justice, benevolence and so on to be spontaneously generated when human beings confront the world. Is she suggesting that moral feelings are an innate part of the organism? This could be seen as lapsing back into metaphysical ideas.

George Eliot was, I believe, aware of these problems. For her, as a later Romantic, the idea of feeling as an 'organ of knowledge' had to be separated from the metaphysical formulations that earlier Romantics had tended to use and supported on solid philosophical or scientific grounds. We can understand better how she tried to provide her moral position with this kind of support and to overcome some of its difficulties by relating her views on feeling to those of Herbert Spencer and G. H. Lewes.

Spencer's *Principles of Psychology* is probably the most useful of his works for understanding some of George Eliot's ideas about feeling, especially with regard to the origin of moral feelings. She had many discussions with him about it and it is likely that she had some influence on his views. Spencer believed that men inherited tendencies of potentially moral feeling:

> Given a race of organisms habitually placed in contact with any complex set of circumstances . . . there will slowly be established in them a co-ordination of these compound impressions corresponding to this set of circumstances. The constant experiences of successive generations will gradually strengthen the tendency of all the component clusters of psychical states to make one another nascent. And when ultimately the union of them, expressed in the inherited organic structure, becomes

innate, it will constitute what we call an emotion or sentiment, having this set of circumstances for its object.[13]

The adjustment between organism and environment through countless generations has made tendencies of potentially moral feeling an inherent part of human nature, so that certain feelings are spontaneously generated when human beings confront any suitable set of circumstances. We cannot help but respond, for example, to another's suffering or to injustice.

That George Eliot agreed with Spencer is suggested in her poem of intellectual debate, 'A College Breakfast-Party'. Her representative, Guildenstern, claims that

> God, duty, love, submission, fellowship,
> Must first be framed in man, as music is,
> Before they live outside him as a law.   (p. 246)[14]

This is possible because she believes, like Spencer, that certain tendencies of feeling have become instinctive in man in the course of evolution through the confrontation between human consciousness and the resistant otherness of the world

>   whose unconquerable sway
> Resisted first and then subdued desire
> By pressure of the dire Impossible
> Urging to possible ends the active soul
> And shaping so its terror and its love.   (pp. 245–6)

In George Eliot's view human beings do not need to justify morality by reference to an external source; morality originates in the tendencies of feeling which are part of human nature. Guildenstern argues that a morality based on feeling must be an integral part of the structure of any community. Even if human beings must live in a recalcitrant world, they can still

>   take their common sorrows for a rock,
>   On it erect religion and a church,
>   A worship, rites, and passionate piety.   (p. 248)

The relationship between George Eliot's argument in this poem and the thought of Spencer shows how she attempts to provide intellectual justification for the Romantic view that feeling could spontaneously create moral knowledge. Both Spencer and Lewes had broken with the pure empiricist position that knowledge is derived solely from individual sense experience, and it seems certain that George Eliot agreed with them. They adopted a partially Kantian epistemology in believing that knowledge of the world was conditioned by the innate structure of the perceptual and cognitive faculties. This is particularly true of Lewes, one of whose main concerns was to account for the Kantian categories which condition human knowledge in evolutionary and bio- logical terms, thus effecting a reconciliation between Kantian thinking and empiricism. We can see Spencer attempting some- thing similar in the following account of how inherited tendencies of feeling are gradually given form in the course of human experience, an account George Eliot would very likely have accepted:

As the forms of thought, or the accumulated and transmitted modifications of structure produced by experience, lie latent in each newly-born individual, are vaguely disclosed along with the first individual experiences, and are gradually made definite by the multiplication of such individual experiences; so the forms of feeling likewise lying latent, are feebly awakened by the first presentations of the external circumstances to which they refer, and gradually gain that degree of distinctness which they are capable of, through oft-repeated presentations of these circumstances. Thus the infant, as soon as its perceptions are developed enough to allow of even an imperfect discrimination of faces and of sounds, is made to smile automatically by the laughing face and tender tones of its mother or its nurse. An organized relation has been established in the race between the perception of this natural language of kind feeling and the subsequent experience of benefits from those who manifest it.[15]

Lewes's views on feeling are similarly useful in helping one understand George Eliot's attempt to reconcile Romantic ideas with later nineteenth-century philosophical and scientific thought. He himself suggests her agreement with his belief that Kantian thinking can be reconciled with empiricism. After the following passage: 'The Mind is built up out of assimilated experiences, its perceptions being shaped by its pre-perceptions, its conceptions by its pre-conceptions. Like the body, the Mind is shaped through its history', Lewes refers to George Eliot in a footnote:

> George Eliot in *The Spanish Gypsy* expresses a profound truth in saying:–
>
> > 'What! Shall the trick of nostrils and of lips
> > Descend through generations, and the soul
> > That moves within our frame like God in worlds,
> > Imprint no record, leave no documents
> > Of her great history? Shall men bequeath
> > The fancies of their palates to their sons,
> > And shall the shudder of restraining awe,
> > The slow wept tears of contrite memory,
> > Faith's prayerful labour, and the food divine
> > Of fasts ecstatic—shall these pass away
> > Like wind upon the water tracklessly?'[16]

This is from a speech of the Prior relating to Fedalma and her gypsy ancestry. It also has an obvious relevance to Daniel Deronda's decision to serve his Jewish heritage even though he has not been brought up as a Jew.

It would be a mistake, however, to conclude that Lewes and George Eliot believed that specific racial or moral feelings could be inherited. Deronda thinks that his strong desire to serve the Jewish cause his grandfather devoted his life to has its basis in 'an inherited yearning' (Chapter 63). But this yearning in itself has no form. What he inherits is a tendency of feeling for which he must find a form. Though George Eliot believes that such tendencies of feeling can be inherited, a form for them can be supplied only by one's social and cultural situation. Conceivably Deronda might have found a non-Jewish form for his 'inherited yearning'. Lewes uses an analogy from music to illustrate this. We can, he says, inherit a musical aptitude, but we cannot inherit particular musical knowledge. Our moral sense is similar to this; we have certain moral predispositions but we have no specific ideas of what is right or wrong. These are supplied by the social context:

> But if we take the term Moral Sense to mean the power of discerning right and wrong, this is as impossible to an animal as

the power of discerning arithmetical proportions. . . . Even in man this moral sense cannot properly be said to be connate otherwise than as a musical sense is connate: it no more brings with it conceptions of *what* is right, *what* wrong, than the musical aptitude brings with it a symphony of Beethoven. What it carries are certain organised predispositions that spontaneously or docilely issue in the beneficent forms of action which the experience of society has classified as right.[17]

Lewes avoids saying that men are innately moral in their feelings. Instead he argues that man inherits animal emotions which constitute a rudimentary moral sense which 'the social life has developed into devoted affection, passionate sympathy, and self-denying forethought'.[18]

An interesting aspect of Lewes's thought is the importance he places on language in man's moral development: 'Language enables man's intelligence and passions to acquire their peculiar characters of Intellect and Sentiment. And Language is a social product of a quite peculiar kind.'[19] George Eliot's characterisation of Harold Transome's young son Harry in *Felix Holt* suggests that she believed that until a human being acquired language he was little different from an animal:

This creature, with the soft broad brown cheeks, low forehead, great black eyes, tiny well-defined nose, fierce biting tricks towards every person and thing he disliked, and insistence on entirely occupying those he liked, was a human specimen such as Esther had never seen before . . . [he] stared at this new-comer with all the gravity of a wild animal. . . . But what old Mr Transome thought the most wonderful proof of an almost preternatural cleverness was, that Harry would hardly ever talk, but preferred making inarticulate noises, or combining syllables after a method of his own. (Chapter 40)

The strongest emphasis in both Lewes and George Eliot, then, is not on man being innately moral but on the interaction of inherited tendencies of potentially moral feeling with acquired social characteristics, particularly language. These inherited tendencies of feeling take on a specifically human form in the social community, so that moral feelings become almost instinct-ive in men as social animals. Since social influences transform man's animal nature, it is possible for him to sublimate animal energies and impulses and impossible for him to act with the single-minded egotism of an animal.

There are still, however, some difficulties with the view that morality does not need transcendent justification but is the product of inherited tendencies of feeling taking on moral form in a social context. How does one decide which feelings are moral and which are not? Lewes is aware of this problem and faces it in a section of *Problems of Life and Mind* entitled 'The Place of Sentiment in Philosophy', in which he tries to create the basis for a 'Moral Science'.[20] He regards feelings 'of awe, tenderness, and sympathy' as 'ultimate facts of Feeling which we simply accept'. We possess moral and aesthetic instincts which are 'facts of the human organism'. He thinks it impossible to convince anyone on purely rational grounds that he ought to feel morally, but no human being is entirely devoid of moral feelings: 'There are only men who feel less vividly than others; none are wholly without the feelings. And it is on this foundation that a Moral Science is possible.'

Lewes appreciates that feelings are diverse and unstable and often over-subjective. The problem is how to control and discipline irrational or impulsive feelings. He argues that there must be a method of investigating the validity of a feeling. For example, if one feels a sense of repulsion to social change, one should ask 'What are the experiences organised in that repulsion?' The feeling of repulsion in itself is not conclusive:

> unless it springs from one of the deep-seated instincts which express the moral experiences of the community, it is no more than an indication; and even then, we must bear in mind that our moral experiences widen with advancing civilisation, the deep-seated instinct of the community of today will not correspond with the enlarged social experiences of to-morrow, for there is evolution of the Moral Instincts no less than of the Rational Judgments.

Feeling, Lewes believes, must be capable of being shared before it has any claim to general validity, and though feeling is always necessary as an inspiration, it must be 'controlled by verification'. One can see Lewes here endeavouring to bring feeling under the control of a scientific method. He ends by saying that he must devote his second volume of *Problems of Life and Mind* to the question of the 'tests of certitude' by which one will be able to verify feelings in scientific terms.

Lewes's 'Moral Science' is, in effect, an attempt to reconcile Romantic and scientific thinking. In Romantic thinking, human subjectivity as expressed in feeling and imagination are central in any knowledge we have of the world, while science demands that all ideas and theories be submitted to empirical tests. Lewes believes that in science itself the greatest subjectivity is manifested in the construction of theories but this is controlled by the necessity of testing and verification: 'I venture to affirm that the wildest flights of Imagination consciously sweeping round the circle of Experience, and alighting where it pleases, are legitimate tentatives of scientific Research, if these only submit to the one indispensable condition (unhappily too often neglected) of ultimate verification'.[21] Lewes hopes that it will be possible to formulate a moral science that will be capable of testing and verifying feelings. Though it is probable that George Eliot was in general agreement with Lewes's aim, *Middlemarch* nevertheless suggests that with regard to the practical problems that face the individual in the course of his life, the verification of feelings had only a limited role to play, a point I shall discuss later.

This attempt by Lewes to combine Romantic thinking with scientific method helps one understand how George Eliot could adhere to the Romantic view that feeling was an organ of knowledge which could directly form moral ideas, and reconcile it with an acceptance of science and scientific practice, which on the surface seem opposed to the subjectivity of Romantic thinking. Both she and Lewes believed that feeling could not be allowed completely free expression even though it was the basis of moral knowledge. Over-subjective feeling had led to the excesses of egotistic Romanticism, for example. Feeling needed, then, to be subject to some form of objective control. But it is here that the comparison between conventional science and 'moral' science becomes difficult. The object to which scientific theories could be submitted for testing and empirical verification was the external world. If a scientific theory fails to withstand testing against data derived from external reality it must be modified or rejected. If feelings are to be tested for validity in accordance with scientific method, as Lewes had urged, what was the object they were to be tested against? Is there an objective world of feelings similar to the

objective physical world assumed by science? It seems clear from
certain of his statements that Lewes believed that the best values
and traditions of existing society provide a kind of objectivity
which subjective feelings must confront. In the extracts quoted
earlier Lewes had referred to 'the beneficent forms of action which
the experience of society has classified as right', and had stated
that repulsion to social change was valid only if it sprang 'from
one of the deep-seated instincts which expresses the moral
experiences of the community'. That George Eliot shared Lewes's
view is suggested by the following passage: 'All human beings
who can be said to be in any degree moral have their impulses
guided, not indeed always by their own intellect, but by the
intellect of human beings who have gone before them, and created
traditions and associations which have taken the rank of laws.'[22]

For Lewes and George Eliot, feelings become moral only if
they are directed by or can be tested against something which can
exert authoritative control over them. Religion or metaphysical
systems had provided this authority for feeling in the past. But
they could no longer believe in such absolute authorities. They
attempted to find some non-metaphysical equivalent for them in
the objectification of the valuable feelings of the past preserved in
the traditions and values of societies which exist or have existed.
Although these could not be taken as absolutes, they did provide
an object of some kind against which feeling could be tested. For
this reason George Eliot thought great care must be taken before
rejecting tradition: 'a mind at all rich in sensibilities must always
have had an indefinite uneasiness in an undistinguished attack on
the coercive influence of tradition'.[23]

One can perhaps understand George Eliot's moral thought
more clearly if one regards the feeling which she believes forms the
basis of morality as a kind of language which all members of a
community have in common. Spencer had used such phrases as
the 'language of the emotions' and 'the natural language of the
feelings'. For George Eliot, moral feeling develops in human
beings in a similar way to language. We possess its basic
principles, its grammar as it were, as innate human instincts, but
we must learn its vocabulary and certain rules from social
experience. Everyone who is brought up in a social community
naturally learns the language of feeling, and thus everyone comes
to share the basis of a common morality, one which does not need
to rely on religious systems for support, but is the product of

tendencies of feeling taking on moral form in a social context. As our social experience becomes more complex, so the language of moral feeling becomes more developed. There can be shared moral values because everyone in the community will have learned this language of moral feeling. It can help both to unify the community and to create a sense of continuity with the past.

It is because George Eliot saw morality as a kind of natural language of the feelings intrinsic to man as a social animal that she believed that Christian morality could be retained even if one rejected Christianity as a system. Behaving justly to others or relieving suffering did not require external justification but were feelings built into the personality. Though egotism could undermine such feelings, they could not be completely eroded as long as man continued to use language in a social environment. Even her most egotistic characters experience guilt or shame, though perhaps only intermittently, as a result of rejecting morality for their own selfish ends. If morality is seen as a kind of language, this also implies that it does not need to be rigidly rule-governed. Like ordinary language it is capable of constantly varying to cope with changing circumstances, but at the same time there is an underlying set of finite principles, a grammar as it were, that must be preserved. For George Eliot, a person who thought he could totally reject the morality of society and create his own personal morality would be acting like someone who rejected the language of society and decided to speak his own personal language.

Since moral feelings are internalised in anyone brought up in a human community, to violate such a feeling on egotistic grounds is tantamount to betraying a deep instinct and could have disastrous psychological consequences. This means that human beings cannot adapt themselves to external circumstances in any way that would assure their personal advantage. Certain limits are built into the human personality as a result of moral feeling being almost instinctive in man as a social animal. It is this which crucially separates man from the animals. Characters like Tito in *Romola* and Jermyn and Christian in *Felix Holt*, who are prepared to adapt themselves to any set of circumstances or situation for their own advantage, risk losing human status and reducing themselves to the level of animals.[24]

It is by thinking of morality as a language of the feelings that George Eliot tries to overcome one of the most serious difficulties raised by her moral position: the problem of impulse. How can

moral control be exerted over powerful feelings of the moment
which are stronger than the more stable feelings and which urge
action before the rational side of the self has time for reflection?
One can find many examples in her fiction of the word 'impulse'
being used negatively to refer to animalistic feelings of which she
clearly disapproves. For example, in *The Mill on the Floss* when
Stephen Guest's sexual passion for Maggie Tulliver overcomes
his powers of resistance: 'A mad impulse seized on Stephen; he
darted towards the arm, and showered kisses on it, clasping the
wrist' (Book VI, Chapter 10). But there are also many occasions
in which 'impulse' is used positively to describe strong feelings of
which George Eliot approves. In *Middlemarch* Dorothea's 'effort,
nay, her strongest impulsive prompting, had been towards the
vindication of Will from any sullying surmises' (Chapter 77). It
might appear that George Eliot has no coherent position on
impulse, but this, I think, would be a mistaken view.[25] In her
judgement the only valid impulse is one which is the expression of
the whole personality and which therefore will embody feelings
that do not merely belong to the moment but can be integrated
with the social and cultural influences that have shaped the self. I
shall consider her concept of whole self more fully later in dealing
with memory and *The Mill on the Floss*. In such impulses the
strongest feeling finds moral direction. For George Eliot, an
individual with a clear sense of continuity of self intuitively knows
when an impulse stems from his whole self and when it is the
product of a purely temporary state of feeling. One of the most
interesting aspects of her presentation of feeling in her novels is
the treatment in dramatic terms of the problem of impulse, as I
shall try to show.

III

Romola

Feeling plays an important part in all of George Eliot's novels,
but *Romola* is particularly important because it contains probably the most coherent working out of her moral position. In
Romola we see George Eliot thinking concretely about the moral
problems I have discussed in this chapter, and though the novel
achieves only limited artistic success in its dramatic presentation,

it illuminates considerably the role of feeling in the moral structure of her work as a whole. The three main characters represent opposed moral positions: Tito, having rejected metaphysical beliefs, regards morality as having no valid basis; Savonarola bases his moral certainty on his belief in a divine order in the universe; while Romola, whom I shall concentrate on, struggles to find a moral orientation which is not dependent on metaphysical beliefs and which can exert control over the instability created in her life by impulsive feeling.

Romola is endowed with exceptional strength of feeling, but her feelings have been relatively little shaped by confrontation with the external world, especially with the complexities of social experience. The nature of her upbringing with her father has restricted her life and provided her with only a narrow outlet for feeling. She has had little experience of meeting people outside her immediate family and had almost no contact with anything in the outside world which might have had a shaping influence on her. This has had the effect of making her feelings intensely subjective, relatively uninfluenced by external factors apart from love for her father, Bardo. The first serious consequence of this is that she falls in love with Tito, the first attractive man she has met, and marries him. It is not surprising that her feelings, having been so restricted in their outlet, should immediately respond to his surface attractions. But this is also an indication that strong subjective feeling has its dangers and requires some means of being controlled and disciplined. One of the major problems the novel is concerned with is where such control and discipline can come from.

Romola has also been strongly influenced by the attitudes of her father, a man of defiant and rebellious nature. Bardo has sought self-realisation through scholarship. He believes in the power of the personal will and praises Romola's expression of 'Promethean' sentiments (Chapter 5). Like her father she has a strong tendency to rebel against any authority that sets itself up in opposition to her personal will and subjective feelings, as is apparent in her first meeting with Savonarola. Her father has brought her up to be contemptuous of the Church or of any external authority which might provide control and guidance for her strong subjective feelings.

When her father dies and she is given an insight into Tito's true nature, an extremely dangerous situation arises for her. Her father is no longer present to direct her, which leaves her at the mercy of her impetuous feelings. When she discovers that Tito has sold her father's library, she has an 'impulse of fury': 'her whole frame seemed to be possessed by impetuous force that wanted to leap out in some deed' (Chapter 32). Her love for Tito quickly changes into rejection of him. There are no external forces which can help guide her feelings. She can only respond to this crisis in the manner of her father since she recognises no authority beyond her personal feelings: she asserts her will; she chooses to be true to her dominant feeling, rejects her marriage and leaves Florence. This leads to her encounter with Savonarola in which he repudiates her claim to be subject to no authority but her own will. He overcomes her resistance to him by making her feel guilty about wearing a disguise and forsaking the duties which marriage imposes, guilt which she has already experienced intuitively when she takes off her betrothal ring. This time her strongest feeling urges her to obey Savonarola: 'her impulse now was to do just what Savonarola told her' (Chapter 40). His religious and moral certainty leads her to accept the authority of the Church as the means of providing moral form for her life. For Savonarola, moral right and wrong are absolutely defined by the divine truths of Christianity, and Romola, otherwise at the mercy of extreme oscillations of impetuous feeling, resolves to be guided by him. But it is clear that she cannot whole-heartedly accept Christian theology; it is the personal influence of Savonarola which is her main support.

She now devotes herself to moral actions since her newly-accepted religion demands this, though she avoids thinking about religious doctrine. She is uneasy in her submission and unhappy, yet without religion she would again be subject to the instability of her impulsive feelings. She is not at this stage performing charitable work because her feelings demand it of her but because it is her religious duty. Thus her whole self cannot fully identify with it. This is not to say that feeling is not present in these moral actions, but if she had no authority beyond feeling to justify the performance of them she would then have no means of resisting a more powerful personal feeling which urged her to behave rebelliously or impulsively. Her mind and feelings are not at one, and the price she must pay for having an authority which can control and discipline her feelings is a sense of self-division.

Her greatest crisis occurs when she loses her faith in Savonarola and with it her acceptance of religious authority. This takes place not because of an intellectual decision to reject him but because a strong feeling tells her he is wrong in his belief that five Mediceans, including her godfather Bernardo, should be executed. She had been prepared previously to submit to him despite intellectual doubts and the pressure this placed on her repressed feelings, 'But now a sudden insurrection of feeling had brought about that collision' (Chapter 52). Feeling is her ultimate source of knowledge and it finally cannot be ignored. The authority provided by religion is too separate from feeling to be stable. But in rejecting religious authority she is again subject to impulsive and rebellious feelings. Her life seems to have no centre or direction. Thus the undermining of Savonarola's influence 'was an illumination that made all life look ghastly to her' (Chapter 52).

At the same time as feeling forces her to reject Savonarola because of his belief that evil ceases to be evil if it promotes what he regards as the good, she is once again led into rebellion against her role as a wife on learning the full extent of Tito's treachery. As before, impulsive feeling leads her to reject both Florence and her marriage: 'The impulse to set herself free had risen again with overmastering force' (Chapter 61). Romola's feelings are right in their spontaneous opposition to the actions of both Savonarola and Tito, but Thomas Pinney over-simplifies when he writes: 'Romola is right to rebel against Tito and Savonarola.'[26] Her rebellion is mistaken as it was before, when she left Florence and asserted that she needed no authority other than her personal will. Rebellion is an important theme in the novel and concerns both Romola and Savonarola, who is in revolt against the leaders of the Church. But both these rebellions have serious dangers: Romola is in despair and Savonarola could undermine religion itself, a greater evil than corruption in the Church. What they both need to learn is Mr Lyon's lesson in *Felix Holt* that 'the right to rebellion is the right to seek a higher rule'.

Romola again adopts a disguise and leaves Florence. Religion has failed to solve the problem of where she is to find an authority which her feelings can accept and which can guide her life. Her rebellion has only a negative force. With her life devoid of purpose she succumbs to despair: 'What force was there to create for her that supremely hallowed motive which men call duty, but which can have no inward constraining existence save through some form of believing love?' (Chapter 61). Deprived of anything to sustain or direct her existence, she feels no real sense of identity. This crisis is more dangerous than her last because, with the loss of her faith in Savonarola, there seems no possibility of finding any external support. Being true to the knowledge communicated by feeling seems only to have led to despair.

One of the most important concerns of the novel is how Romola can find a moral frame or authority which is not separate from feeling and which can interact with it, making use of its power and energy, but not be swept away by its intensity or instability. Savonarola's religious authority was too divorced from Romola's personal feelings to offer her security. But rejecting him seems to have deprived her life of all moral form, and left her with the insecurity of the oscillations of personal feeling. The narrator, however, regards her reaction against Savonarola as over-subjective: 'And if such energetic belief . . . is often in danger of becoming a demon-worship . . . tender fellow-feeling for the nearest has its danger too, and is apt to be timid and sceptical towards the larger aims without which life cannot rise into religion. In this way poor Romola was being blinded by her tears' (Chapter 61). Her feelings are too personal, too little controlled by a larger vision. But where can she find such a vision which would not, like her previous acceptance of a religious authority, separate her from her feelings? This situation leads to her despair: 'She read no message of love for her in the far-off symbolic writing of the heavens, and with a great sob she wished that she might be gliding into death.'

It is only after Tito's death and Savonarola's fall that the novel again focuses on Romola. At this point all of the three major characters have failed. None of them had a philosophy of life which could withstand confrontation with the world. But now Romola emerges as the character who is able to survive this experience and goes on to discover a positive philosophy which can sustain a strong sense of identity. She finds the authority she has been searching for which can interact with feeling and give her life meaning and purpose. Instead of submitting feeling to an external authority separate from it, which had been the main difficulty during her Christian period, she discovers that in feeling itself she can find the basis for the larger moral vision she has been seeking.

She has drifted into a village where she thinks 'she might rest and resolve on nothing'. A crucial passage follows:

> She had not been in this attitude of contemplation more than a few minutes when across the stillness there came a piercing cry; not a brief cry, but continuous and more and more intense. Romola felt sure it was the cry of a little child in distress that no one came to help. . . . But it went on, and drew Romola so irresistibly, seeming the more piteous to her for the sense of peace which had preceded it, that she jumped on to the beach and walked many paces before she knew what direction she would take.   (Chapter 68)

Hearing this cry makes Romola's feelings immediately and spontaneously project themselves morally outwards. Moral feeling is instantly created by this direct confrontation with another's suffering. No external authority is necessary to justify acting to help others. Experience itself, she finds, transforms feeling into moral response and creates moral knowledge. She has discovered the basis of creating her own moral language, out of personally generated feelings. She thus feels no need of an external authority to act as a support in helping others, as had been the case when she was in Florence. The religious authority she had accepted had justified such acts on doctrinal grounds, not on the grounds of human feeling, which was of secondary importance. But now in the village, direct feeling calls on her to act morally. She realises that confronting the needs and sufferings of the world with natural human potentialities of feeling creates moral knowledge. This gives form to an individual's existence, but a form which emerges from within the self. An authority external to feeling is no longer needed.

Though this episode is in many ways the culminating experience of the novel, it also illustrates the work's artistic weakness. Despite its central importance in the philosophical. structure, the episode has little human reality. It works only in symbolic terms, as George Eliot was aware. In a letter to Sara Hennell she confessed that 'The various *strands* of thought I had to work out forced me into a more ideal treatment of Romola than I had foreseen at the outset', and said that Romola's drifting and the plague-ridden village scenes 'were by deliberate forecast adopted as romantic and symbolical elements'.[27] This suggests that she was determined to express the ideas which are embodied in these scenes even if this involved the sacrifice of realistic presentation. The ideas she was concerned with were more important to her than achieving artistic success, as her letter to R. H. Hutton implies:

> I can well believe that the many difficulties belonging to the treatment of such a character [Romola] have not been overcome, and that I have failed to bring out my conception with adequate fulness. I am sorry she has attracted you so little; for the great problem of her life, which essentially coincides with a chief problem in Savonarola's, is one that readers need helping to understand. But with regard to that and to my whole book, my predominant feeling is,—not that I have achieved anything, but—that great, great facts have struggled to find a voice through me, and have only been able to speak brokenly.[28]

In *Romola* George Eliot is prepared to pay an artistic price to write a philosophical novel.

It seems clear that the village is symbolic of an imperfect world in its suffering and need. The whole world is metaphorically plague-ridden in that human effort is required to alleviate suffering and to make life better. Plague, in this symbolic sense, existed in Florence, but Romola's over-subjective feelings prevented her seeing it with sufficient intensity and clarity. But her experience of the child crying creates this insight in the form of a feeling as intense as any of her purely personal impulses, and this feeling urges direct moral action to help others. This provides her with the foundation of a wider perspective which is the objectification of such feelings and which can direct personal feeling and control its instability. She is now capable of understanding that Savonarola's ideal vision is itself the objectification of human feelings, and thus has value even if he believed it had a theological source she cannot accept. Religion itself is the objectification of such human feelings, as Romola realises in taking on the role of 'Holy Mother' to the villagers.

Her despair in the boat she now regards as mere egotistic complaint; it disintegrated as soon as she heard the child's cry:

> . . . but from the moment after her waking when the cry had

drawn her, she had not even reflected, as she used to do in Florence, that she was glad to live because she could lighten sorrow—she had simply lived, with so energetic an impulse to share the life around her, to answer the call of need and do the work which cried aloud to be done, that the reasons for living, enduring, labouring, never took the form of argument. (Chapter 69)

In other words, moral action is the outcome of direct, spontaneous feeling and not of rational judgement or theological justification. In Florence she had felt self-divided because her charitable acts were motivated by something external to feeling. But in the village her whole self is expressed in acting to relieve the villagers' suffering. After her work in the village is over, she can see her relationship to Florence in a new light. She can now establish a proper relationship between herself and her own community: 'the emotions that were disengaged from the people immediately around her rushed back into the old deep channels of use and affection'. Her whole self can identify with action to serve the community of Florence as it had done with the village community.

Her relationship with Tito is still a problem for her, and here one detects a blurring of the issue by George Eliot. The novel gives no clear indication as to what she should do about having Tito as a husband. In all of the unfortunate marriages in George Eliot's fiction, the unions are too conveniently ended by death, with the exception of Lydgate and Rosamond's marriage in *Middlemarch*, and there it could be argued that the egotistic Lydgate partly deserves his fate. The importance George Eliot attaches to continuity and responsibility for one's actions makes any unfortunate marriage a problem for her, but that between Romola and Tito raises particular difficulties. Romola's rejection of Tito as a husband would clearly be wrong, in George Eliot's terms, since her marriage is an aspect of her past that cannot be eradicated. Yet to return to him as his wife knowing of his treachery and unfaithfulness is surely impossible. Tito is, however, planning to leave her, which would make a decision by her unnecessary, and his death solves her problem finally. But this still leaves the deeper moral issue of how Romola should act in this situation unresolved.

Romola's relationship to Florence, in contrast, presents no

problems to her. She realises that it must be the centre of her life
and have the strongest claims on her feelings: 'Florence, and all
her life there, had come back to her like a hunger; her feelings
could not go wandering after the possible and the vague: their
living fibre was fed with the memory of familiar things' (Chapter
69). Although life there is 'a web of inconsistencies', she identifies
with Savonarola's ideal of Florence as 'a pure community,
worthy to lead the way in the renovation of the Church and the
world' (Chapter 35). This is the larger vision for which she has
been searching. Service to such a vision or ideal which is itself the
objectification of moral feeling and aspiration can direct her life,
interact with the energies of personal feeling but at the same time
prevent it becoming over-subjective in expression. It can channel
the energy generated by impulse and also control its instability.
She finds new sympathy and respect for Savonarola because she
now understands that his vision was fundamentally a social one,
though for him it had a religious justification. Her experience in
the village has enabled her to discover the human truth underlying his vision. Though still conscious of his errors, she knows how
much she is indebted to him. And unlike Savonarola, she is able to
maintain her social vision even in the face of disorder. For her, his
ideal of Florence is something to be worked towards; it is not
providentially guaranteed to become real. The fact then that
disorder continues to characterise Florence is not a cause for
despair, nor is she tempted into believing, as Savonarola was, that
all means are justified to achieve the ideal.

In contrast to Romola, all of Tito's attitudes derive from his
comparative lack of feeling and his intellectual refusal to let what
feeling he has influence his behaviour. He does feel 'inward
shame' at his decision not to go in search of Baldassarre, but his
'unimpassioned' mind soon reasons such feelings away. He is also
free from religious belief or from any firm social connections
which might exert moral control over his actions. He knows
society would disapprove of his seeking his own pleasure at
Baldassarre's expense, but it is easy for him to dismiss such
considerations:

> That, he was conscious, was not the sentiment which the
> complicated play of human feelings had engendered in
> society. . . . But what was the sentiment of society?—a mere
> tangle of anomalous traditions and opinions, which no wise

man would take as a guide, except so far as his own comfort was
concerned. . . .

Having once begun to explain away Baldassarre's claim,
Tito's thought showed itself as active as a virulent acid, eating its
rapid way through all the tissues of sentiment.   (Chapter 11)

He also rationalistically dismisses the natural fear of wrong-doing
which exists in people. It is this kind of scepticism which George
Eliot considers particularly dangerous: 'Such terror of the unseen
is so far above mere sensual cowardice that it will annihilate that
cowardice; it is the initial recognition of a moral law restraining
desire, and checks the hard bold scrutiny of imperfect thought
into obligations which can never be proved to have any sanctity in
the absence of feeling.' It is apparent from this that George Eliot
rejects any purely rational ground for ethics. It is Tito's surrender
of feeling to rationalistic thought that leads him to a life of
calculation and role-playing in the pursuit of personal pleasure:
'arranging life to his mind had been the source of all his
misdoing' (Chapter 31). The more he becomes involved in this
way of life, the greater the necessity to suppress moral and
sympathetic feeling.

The human effects of this suppression of feeling are disastrous.
It leads to an almost total isolation from others since he must keep
his inner self concealed. Any deep contact with another person
might leave him vulnerable. Thus there is no possibility of any
proper relationship between him and Romola although she is the
only person he has ever respected or valued. By elevating the
sceptical intellect above feeling, he comes to the conclusion that
there is no point in serving anything other than one's own desire
for pleasure. But this has the consequence of making his life quite
empty and pointless. Men like Savonarola and Bernardo die, but
the principles for which they lived give their lives a value both to
themselves and to others even in death. But Tito refused to create
an identity for himself by revealing his inner self and feelings to
others or by identifying himself with anything but personal
gratification. At his death, then, nothing remains but fragments
of a life to which he refused to give form. Any meaning his life
possesses is supplied by others' judgements since his own actions
were not designed to express his own sense of self. In the view of
George Eliot, he rejected the opportunity to be truly human.

IV

Felix Holt

A brief look at Esther Lyon in *Felix Holt* illustrates well the Romantic nature of George Eliot's view of feeling and brings out clearly the contrast she sees between that aspect of Romanticism in which ego predominates and that in which feeling predominates, a subject she pursues also in *Middlemarch* and *Daniel Deronda*.

Esther Lyon develops from being someone with an attachment to egotistic Romanticism to being a Romantic who ascribes the greatest importance to feeling. At the beginning of the novel there are parallels between her and Mrs Transome. She admires the work of Byron and Chateaubriand and longs for an elevated social position in which she can assert what she feels is her natural right to superiority. However she differs from Mrs Transome in her openness to feeling: 'she hated all meanness, would empty her purse impulsively on some sudden appeal to her pity, and if she found out that her father had a want, she would supply it with some pretty device of a surprise' (Chapter 6), and 'Even in her times of most untroubled egoism Esther shrank from anything ungenerous' (Chapter 38). Such comments have the unfortunate artistic effect of making the change that takes place in Esther too predictable. In this novel, though perhaps to a lesser extent than in *Romola*, George Eliot has still not solved the problem of reconciling her philosophical and moral interests with convincing dramatic presentation.

Esther's development is related to the growth of feeling in her, partly owing to Felix's influence and his criticism of her egotism, and partly to experiences that call forth her sympathy, like her father's confession about his past life. Esther's strong Romantic tendencies of feeling eventually enable her to overcome her attraction to Romantic egotism. The best life, she declares, is 'that where one bears and does everything because of some great and strong feeling—so that this and that in one's circumstances don't signify' (Chapter 26). When she has the opportunity to live the same kind of life as Mrs Transome, she rejects it because for her it is not Romantic enough: it offers too little scope for feeling and imagination. To marry Harold Transome, whose belief in the power of his own ego resembles that of the Byronic heroes she had formerly admired, and to live the life of a lady in Transome Court would be to settle for a 'middle lot'. Her feelings in Transome Court are those of 'dread', but the similarity to Mrs Transome, who also experiences dread, is only ironic. For Esther's dread is 'what the dread of the piligrim might be who has it whispered to him that the holy places are a delusion, or that he will see them with a soul unstirred and unbelieving' (Chapter 45). It is the dread of one who feels that the world has cut her off from her greatest potentialities of feeling and imagination.

It is only through uniting herself with Felix Holt and his social vision that she can discover an outlet for the intense feeling which is part of her nature. The life of the ego and the will, exemplified by Mrs Transome, Harold, and the values of Transome Court, becomes for Esther a denial of her Romantic nature. It offers nothing to feeling and imagination, whereas Felix and his vision call forth all her powers of feeling, as her experience at his trial shows:

> When a woman feels purely and nobly, that ardour of hers which breaks through formulas too rigorously urged on men by daily practical needs, makes one of her most precious influences: she is the added impulse that shatters the stiffening crust of cautious experience. Her inspired ignorance gives a sublimity to actions so incongruously simple, that otherwise they would make men smile. Some of that ardour which has flashed out and illuminated all poetry and history was burning to-day in the bosom of sweet Esther Lyon. In this, at least, her woman's lot was perfect: that the man she loved was her hero; that her woman's passion and her reverence for rarest goodness rushed together in an undivided current. And to-day they were making one danger, one terror, one irresistible impulse for her heart. Her feelings were growing into a necessity for action, rather than a resolve to act.   (Chapter 46)

Like Romola in the plague-stricken village, Esther finds an outlet for her impulses with which her whole self can identify and which gives her life meaning and direction. There are also clear resemblances to Dorothea in *Middlemarch*—for example, the use of the words 'ardour' and 'current'—though such a comparison only highlights the superior artistry of the later novel, in which the heroine's ardour is treated much more ironically and with greater

control. But, as I shall try to show later, Dorothea is an equally Romantic figure, despite George Eliot's less idealised presentation. The passage also expresses George Eliot's belief that women possess exceptional powers of direct feeling and can encourage such feeling in others. Esther has undergone 'an inward revolution' (Chapter 49); the influence of Felix and her experience of life at Transome Court have overturned her former ideas. And the greatest loss she would suffer if she chose to remain with the Transomes would be 'the fatal absence of those feelings which, now she had once known them, it seemed nothing less than a fall and a degradation to do without'.

Esther, then, is characterised very much in Romantic terms. But for George Eliot as a later Romantic, intensity of feeling is not its own justification as it was for many of the earlier Romantics. The Romantic self must reject rebellion and pure impulse and socially direct its energies. What both *Romola* and *Felix Holt* show with regard to feeling is that it must be supported by a vision or an ideal aim if it is not to run the risk of being taken over by egotistic forces in the self. For George Eliot the best expression of such a vision in her time is the ideal of the organic society. She believed that this ideal could call forth the best qualities of human feeling and provide that feeling with direction and control. Characters like Romola and Esther Lyon not only possess great intensity of feeling but also, in committing themselves to a social ideal, discover a vision that shapes and guides their impulses. Without such a vision or ideal there was a danger that strong feeling and impulse could find negative expression in rebellion, the demonic, or despair, or could be transformed into the sick subjectivity of the alienated protagonist of 'The Lifted Veil'. The need to provide human beings with an organic social vision to which both the energies of the ego and the power of feeling could submit was one of George Eliot's central concerns and it is this that I now want to go on to discuss.

5 The Organic Society

I

George Eliot's commitment to the ideal of a spiritually organic society is an important part of her thought. Though the concept of an organic society had its origin before the Romantic period, it is extremely prominent in Romantic social thought, particularly among the German Romantics,[1] and it is very likely that George Eliot was influenced by Romantic formulations of it. Her organicist social views are most directly presented in her essays 'The Natural History of German Life' and 'Address to Working Men, by Felix Holt', the former being a very sympathetic review of the first two parts of *Naturgeschichte des Volks* by the German sociologist, W. H. Riehl, a writer clearly influenced by the social thought of the German Romantics.[2]

Since there has been a good deal of discussion of George Eliot's social views by other writers,[3] it will not be necessary for me to go into the subject in great detail. However, it does seem to me that one should look beyond the influence of a comparatively minor social thinker like Riehl to her affinities with a much more important figure, probably the major influence of Romantic organicist thought, J. G. Herder, who, as far as I am aware, has not been discussed in connection with her. There is no direct evidence of influence, but references to him in her essays 'Three Months in Weimar' and 'The Future of German Philosophy',[4] suggest that she knew his work and admired him.

The two most important affinities between Herder and George Eliot are their belief in the need for a society to possess a common culture and a sense of corporate consciousness, and their acceptance of cultural relativism. This last point is important, for it distinguishes Herder from those German Romantics who were attracted to ideas of racial or cultural superiority, and also from an English organicist such as Coleridge.[5] Though both Herder and George Eliot identified strongly with their respective nationalities and cultures, they recognised other nationalities and cultures as equal. This was probably an important reason for George Eliot's dislike of British imperialism, which is clearly expressed in her essay 'The Modern Hep! Hep! Hep!' in her last published work, *Impressions of Theophrastus Such*.

When George Eliot uses such phrases as 'the organic structure of society' and 'the organic constitution of society',[6] she is employing the term 'organic' in the sense derived from Herder. However, it is clear in her essays on social subjects, that she believed the sense of organic community in England had been undermined to a considerable extent: 'for though our English life is in its core intensely traditional, Protestantism and commerce have modernized the face of the land and the aspects of society in a far greater degree than in any continental country',[7] and this leads her to fear 'the decomposition which is commencing in the organic constitution of society'.[8] It is likely that she was aware of Herbert Spencer's different use of the organism as a metaphor for society in his essay 'The Social Organism', first published in *The Westminster Review* in 1860. Spencer sees society as resembling a living organism: all parts of it are organically connected and any change in one part will affect all the others. But while for Herder and Romantic organicists it was essential that society possess a sense of corporate consciousness, in Spencer's concept of the social organism this is not necessary and he denies that the metaphor is appropriate in this respect.

For Herder a society can be organic only if there is a consciousness of a shared culture and tradition. F. M. Barnard brings out clearly the contrast between Herder's organic community and Spencer's social organism when he writes that for Herder organic societies

> seek to maintain their sense of collective identity by treasuring and perpetuating the memory of a common past and all that this entails. They will extol the deeds of their forefathers, observe tribal customs and rituals, and, above all, preserve the distinctiveness of their own language.

It was these essentially spiritual elements which constituted for Herder the *organic* forces (*Kräfte*) of social and political cohesion, since they united men from *within*. He saw therefore in most of the contemporary dynastic states more artefacts, lifeless assemblies of aggregates whose parts, though they were functionally related like those of an organism, nevertheless depended in their operation on an *external* source of power. . . . A state can perish, but the *Volk* remains intact provided it retains the consciousness of its distinctive cultural traditions.[9]

Spencer's social organism has no sense of corporate consciousness and is composed of individuals with separate interests:

It is well that the lives of all parts of an animal should be merged in the life of the whole, because the whole has a corporate consciousness capable of happiness or misery. But it is not so with a society; since its living units do not and cannot lose individual consciousness, and since the community as a whole has no corporate consciousness. This is an everlasting reason why the welfares of citizens cannot rightly be sacrificed to some supposed benefit of the State, and why, on the other hand, the State is to be maintained solely for the benefit of citizens. The corporate life must here be subservient to the lives of the parts, instead of the lives of the parts being subservient to the corporate life.[10]

One of the social developments one can discern in George Eliot's fiction is the movement from organic societies in Herder's sense towards social organisms in Spencer's sense; that is, from societies with a high degree of corporate consciousness based on a shared culture and traditions to societies in which there are conflicts of interest, relativism of values, and atomistic individualism. It is in her later novels, *Felix Holt*, *Middlemarch* and *Daniel Deronda*, that we find the clearest examples of societies which exhibit many of the characteristics of social organisms. One can perhaps see these opposed social concepts being contrasted in the 'Prelude' to *Middlemarch*.

In the 'Prelude' the narrator states that there was 'no coherent social faith and order which could perform the function of knowledge for the ardently willing soul'. It seems very likely that what is meant here is that society is no longer organic in a spiritual sense. Middlemarch society is not completely fragmented, but the spiritual homogeneity associated with societies of the past which had been called organic is largely absent. The way gossip and rumour can sweep through the town shows that there still exists some sense of general consciousness, but there is no longer a unified community consciousness based on shared values and assumptions. There is little of the spiritual harmony which Romantic organicists valued. Middlemarch society is more like a Spencerian social organism in which corporate life is subservient to individual interests or to the interests of social groups, and Middlemarch is only reflecting tendencies present in England at large. This helps to explain why Dorothea, although possessing qualities similar to St Theresa of Avila, cannot play as great a role in her society, and must reconcile herself to influencing only a small number of people. In her modern society, there is much less possibility of a person of great spiritual qualities exerting a powerful influence because the lack of a generally accepted social faith necessarily fragments society. There is comparatively little sense of corporate consciousness based on shared values and assumptions, which could create an organic community. The traditional St Theresa was part of a society which did possess shared values and assumptions founded on a religion which penetrated every area of life, and which therefore could be said to be organic. This made it possible for her to enter into spiritual communication with the people of her society in general, and to use her natural gifts to influence their minds and feelings. But the world of a St Theresa or an Antigone, one of the complete spiritual harmony, no longer exists: 'the medium in which their ardent deeds took shape is for ever gone' (Finale). In a Spencer-like social organism of competing interests and relativism of values, such spiritual harmony can no longer be achieved. The modern Theresa can only operate, to continue Spencer's metaphor, as one cell in a complex organism made up of separate centres of consciousness without a 'coherent social faith and order' to create spiritual unity. She must therefore accept a less heroic role than might have been hers in different circumstances.

A major concern of George Eliot's is how the spiritual homogeneity that characterised certain societies in the past, like that of St Theresa, can be recreated in a new form in industrialised societies in which social and economic change was breaking up traditional social groupings and the power of religion was in decline. It was, of course, Thomas Carlyle who urged the necessity for this most strongly, and in my view he had a greater influence on George Eliot than most commentators have thought. It is interesting to note the Carlylean tone in George Eliot's letter to James Thomson, who had sent a copy of his poem of social alienation, 'The City of Dreadful Night', to both her and Carlyle: 'I trust that an intellect informed by so much passionate energy as yours will soon give us more heroic strains with a wider embrace of human fellowship in them—such as will be to the labourers of the world what the odes of Tyrtaeus were to the Spartans, thrilling them with the sublimity of the social order and the courage of resistance to all that would dissolve it.'[11] Though in *Sartor Resartus* Carlyle had shown Romantic egotism being overcome by the apprehension that nature was the 'Living Garment of God', a later work, *Past and Present*, was more concerned with the need to create an organic society in the present industrial age. In the 'Prelude' to *Middlemarch*, George Eliot was perhaps influenced by the comparison Carlyle drew in *Past and Present* between the medieval and the modern eras: 'We will now quit this of the hard, organic, but limited Feudal Ages; and glance timidly into the immense Industrial Ages, as yet all inorganic, and in a quite pulpy condition, requiring desperately to harden themselves into some organism!'[12]

Both Carlyle and George Eliot saw the problem of society in similar terms: how could a spiritually organic society be supported in the modern era subject to many fragmenting influences? For Carlyle a 'new Mythus' was necessary to act as the basis for a unified social consciousness,[13] a symbolic form that would express the essential human truths which in the past had been embodied in religion. Carlyle believed that Christianity was a dead form which could no longer support an organic society, as it had done in the Middle Ages. George Eliot had a less negative attitude to Christianity, many of her most positive characters being convinced Christians, but it seems clear from both her fiction and non-fiction that religion, in her view, can no longer provide the spiritual homogeneity needed for an organic society. Probably one of the major reasons for her interest in positivism was that Comte's system attempted to create the foundation for a spiritually unified society in the modern world. In his *History of Philosophy* Lewes writes: 'If the past points to the necessity for a homogeneous and all-embracing Doctrine, what indications are there in the present of a speedy realisation of that aim?' In his view, positivism 'is the only system which can embrace all tendencies and furnish a homogeneous Doctrine of the world, society, and man'.[14] However, both Lewes and George Eliot were unable to accept Comte's complete system. The furthest they were prepared to go was to regard it as expressing 'hypotheses carrying more or less of truth'.[15]

This illustrates the difficulty faced by George Eliot and Lewes. Though it might be necessary for society to possess a 'homogeneous Doctrine' if it was to be spiritually unified, was it possible finally to believe that such a doctrine was true? Was it not as liable to be undermined by scepticism as Christianity had been? And even if one could accept some system such as Comte's as a set of hypotheses or a symbolic form, this created the further problem of how one could adhere strongly to a doctrine if one was aware of its symbolic function. This is a problem I shall return to in my chapter on *Daniel Deronda*. But at this point it will be useful to look at George Eliot's presentation of organicist ideas in two of her earlier novels: *Silas Marner* and *Adam Bede*. In these works she depicts organic communities which belong to the past, and implicitly points a contrast with her contemporary society.

II

Silas Marner and *Adam Bede*

Raveloe in *Silas Marner* is the clearest example of an organic society in any of George Eliot's works. It is really the community of Raveloe that is the centre of the novel, since it is the acceptance of its way of life, its values and traditions, which cures Silas Marner of the alienation he suffers as a result of the breakdown of the rigid form of Christianity in which he had formerly believed. Raveloe is an example of a pre-industrialised organic community. It has preserved close links with the past, which means that mystery and superstition form part of its way of life. It is not George Eliot's intention to attack such beliefs, though the reader is made aware that some events which seem supernatural to the villagers, like the coming of Eppie into Silas's life, can be accounted for in normal causal terms. In a village like Raveloe, 'where many of the old echoes lingered, undrowned by new voices' (Chapter 1), supernatural explanations are inevitable. Myths and superstitions are the means by which people who live in such communities try to cope with the disorder of experience. Certain past events also take on a mythic function and become dramatisations of the underlying values of the community. The story of the Lammeter's wedding performs such a function. Everyone has heard it many times, but listening to it again creates in people a feeling which reaffirms their community values. It is akin to going to church and attending the New Year dance. These perform the ceremonial function of reinforcing the unity and the implicit values of the community, and are important in giving the people a sense of corporate identity. The individual is able to communicate with others at a deeper level than the merely verbal, since the existence of shared symbols and implicit values creates a deep sense of fellowship. Silas Marner eventually becomes integrated into this society and recovers from his mental crisis. The unified community consciousness is able to provide protection against the amoral otherness which resists human control and categorisation, and which is a potential threat to both the individual and society.

In Raveloe, religion is part of the social fabric and does not require the support of a rigid theology. This is in sharp contrast to industrialised Lantern Yard, where Silas lived originally, in which Christianity has taken the most rigid doctrinal form in the extreme providential beliefs of Silas's sect. People in Raveloe, however, are suspicious of the notion of beneficent providence. Their connection with older, almost pre-Christian traditions prevents such ideas gaining control; as the narrator puts it: 'the rude mind with difficulty associates the ideas of power and benignity' (Chapter 1). Religion, therefore, does not take the extreme forms common in industrialised towns, but the community is nevertheless able to absorb both good and bad fortune. It can accept that the appearance of Eppie apparently in place of Silas's gold has a more than natural meaning, but such a belief does not become hardened into rigid theological form. Raveloe can also accommodate the alternative rational explanation of reality, exemplified by Mr Dowlas in his difference with Mr Macey over whether a ghost or a tramp took Silas's gold. Both of them are wrong, but transcending their differences is the community's awareness of Silas's plight. Though Silas has been a recluse for fifteen years, they are willing to help him, and this, for George Eliot, is more important than differing interpretations of the nature of reality.

George Eliot takes care to portray the atmosphere and feeling of life in Raveloe in the style of the novel by giving the narrative something of the mythic and mysterious qualities of a fairy tale. It is possible that such features were incorporated into the work because she intended that life in Raveloe should serve a kind of mythic function for her own society. By creating the unified social life of Raveloe, she presents the reader with an image that embodies his own need of a similar organic relationship to his own society.

Raveloe is an example of a valuable social form which belongs to the past. George Eliot is not setting it up as a model to be imitated but using it as an example to the present. Carlyle employed a similar tactic in *Past and Present* in his description of an organic feudal society. Raveloe cannot be imitated, but the kind of social and human experience it made possible must be embodied in a new form in the present industrial age. Despite the value of the community life of Raveloe, it is nevertheless clear that it belongs to a time which is passing; the future belongs to industrialised societies like Lantern Yard. There is no going back to that particular form of rural community as a solution to the problems of modern society, but it is implied, I think, that life in an industrialised society needs to be organic in a similar way.

Adam Bede is another novel concerned with a rural community in which life is still to a large degree organic, though it is written in a more obviously realistic style with character and society analysed in greater depth. Again there is a contrast between the pre-industrialised and the industrialised society: Hayslope has been comparatively unaffected by industrialism in contrast to Snowfield. But Hayslope is experiencing more influence from these new external forces than Raveloe. Enthusiastic religion, for example, has made its presence felt. George Eliot regarded the development of enthusiastic forms of religion as a response to industrialism and the social life it generated, as the following comment in *Felix Holt* on the consequences of the industrialisation of Treby Magna shows:

> But when stone-pits and coal-pits made new hamlets that threatened to spread up to the very town, when the tape-weavers came with their news-reading inspectors and book-keepers, the Independent chapel began to be filled with eager men and women, to whom the exceptional possession of religious truth was the condition which reconciled them to a meagre existence, and made them feel in secure alliance with the

unseen but supreme rule of a world in which their own visible part was small.   (Chapter 3)

This helps to explain why Dinah's fervent sermon fails to have any great effect on the villagers of Hayslope. Her form of religion, with its emphasis on the private consciousness of the individual, on his sense of guilt and sin, is suited to conditions in industrialised towns, but it is alien to a community like Hayslope in which life is still to a large extent corporate. In the culmination of Dinah's sermon we see her forgetting about her audience as a group and appealing to separate individuals:

At last it seemed as if, in her yearning desire to reclaim the lost sheep, she could not be satisfied by addressing her hearers as a body. She appealed first to one and then to another, beseeching them with tears to turn to God while there was yet time; painting to them the desolation of their souls, lost in sin, feeding on the husks of this miserable world, far away from God their Father.   (Chapter 2)

Critics who have interpreted this scene as an illustration of the bankruptcy of religion in Hayslope have, I think, missed its point.[16]

Despite the fact that few respond to Dinah's sermon and that there is little interest in religious doctrine, religion plays an important part in the community life of Hayslope. As in Raveloe, going to church is a community ceremony in which the villagers' sense of their group identity and their sharing of certain implicit values are reinforced. Mr Irwine is a good clergyman because he encourages this social aspect of religion: 'He thought the custom of baptism more important than its doctrine' (Chapter 5). His eventual replacement by a clergyman who emphasises doctrine is regarded by the narrator as an unfortunate community development. Dinah is surely wrong to see industrialised towns such as Leeds as religiously superior to villages like Hayslope. She comments to Mr Irwine:

But I've noticed, that in these villages where the people lead a quiet life among the green pastures and the still waters, tilling the ground and tending the cattle, there's a strange deadness to the Word, as different as can be from the great towns, like

Leeds. . . . It's wonderful how rich is the harvest of souls up
those high-walled streets, where you seemed to walk as in a
prison-yard, and the ear is deafened with the sounds of worldly
toil.   (Chapter 8)

The religious quality of life in these villages is present in the image
of 'green pastures' and 'still waters' but as yet Dinah is unable to
see it. Religion being an integral part of community life in
Hayslope, sermons like the one Dinah delivers and religious
doctrine are not needed to make people respond to Christianity,
whereas in industrialised Snowfield, her form of religion is
appropriate to the different social conditions.
    General acceptance of the historically evolved social structure
is another feature of the organic nature of community life in
Hayslope. There is little sign of class struggle or the division of
society into interest groups which one would expect in an
industrialised society. Adam Bede, though a worker, feels no
resentment towards the squire:

Adam, I confess, was very susceptible to the influence of rank,
and quite ready to give an extra amount of respect to every one
who had more advantages than himself, not being a philosopher, or a proletaire with democratic ideas, but simply a
stout-limbed clever carpenter with a large fund of reverence in
his nature, which inclined him to admit all established claims
unless he saw very clear grounds for questioning them.
(Chapter 16)

In both Hayslope and Raveloe, however, it is clear that the upper
class is not as well integrated into the community as in the past.
Class and interest divisions have begun to take place.
    But though the social structure of Hayslope may be changing,
there are still several important manifestations of organic community life, most notably the rituals and ceremonies which take
place in the novel. The narrator offers no rationalist criticism of
such community beliefs as the wickedness of working on Good
Friday. It seems clear that these are seen as helping to create a
shared community consciousness. A good example of the community joining ceremonially together is the church service before
the burial of Thias Bede. This both consoles the bereaved and
helps everyone accept the fact of death. Another important

community ceremony is Arthur Donnithorne's birthday feast. It is conducted in an extremely formal manner with dinner tables arranged in such a way that everyone feels he is occupying his rightful place. Adam is at first worried that Arthur's wish that he dine upstairs will prove unacceptable to other members of the community. The dinner is followed by games and a dance. Each member has some part to play which reflects his status and reconciles him to the order of his society and its values. Later in the novel there is also the harvest supper: '*Now*, the great ceremony of the evening was to begin—the harvest-song, in which every man must join' (Chapter 53).

If one takes account of the organic community life of Hayslope, reinforced by such ceremonies, then one can argue that the greatest offence in Arthur's clandestine affair with Hetty is that it subverts the order and the values of the community. Their relationship is conducted in secret, ignoring the traditions and customs of courtship in Hayslope. The fact that Arthur could thoughtlessly involve himself in such an affair, which breaks the social conventions of Hayslope, is a sign of his detachment from the community and the growing separation of the class he represents. In Hayslope, life is corporate and shared, and all important transactions are open. A secret relationship like that between Arthur and Hetty is an offence against this shared community spirit. The community is threatened until the ritual-like casting out of the two offenders. As in *Silas Marner* the novel ends with a marriage ceremony which helps to repair the damage that has been done. The corporate identity of Hayslope is reinforced by everyone's involvement in the marriage of Adam and Dinah:

It was an event much thought of in the village. All Mr Burge's men had a holiday, and all Mr Poyser's. . . . I think there was hardly an inhabitant of Hayslope specially mentioned in this history and still resident in the parish on this November morning, who was not either in church to see Adam and Dinah married, or near the church door to greet them as they came forth.   (Chapter 55)

However there is some justification for the view of those critics who have felt that the marriage of Adam and Dinah is an artistic flaw in the novel. It has been objected that it is contrived and unconvincing, its not being part of George Eliot's original intention adding support to this view, and also that Dinah is diminished in stature by being made to give up her active religious work in industrialised towns. One important reason for one's doubts about the artistic success of the marriage is that more than love between Adam and Dinah is necessary to make Dinah's decision to marry Adam and give up her former life acceptable. Since Dinah has been part of the industrialised world of Snowfield, it is necessary that we see her becoming an integral part of the community of Hayslope, accepting its way of life and its values, in order to be convinced by the change that takes place in her life. But George Eliot fails to show that this integration has taken place, with the result that Dinah's marriage and settling in Hayslope seem willed by the author rather than a coherent artistic development. In contrast, in *Silas Marner*, the change which takes place in Silas's life is related to his integration into the community of Raveloe.

III

Though pre-industrialised organic communities could serve as an example to modern society, how could a similar shared social identity be recreated in the industrial age in which there was increasing evidence of social fragmentation and relativism of values? It is significant that the clearest picture of an alienated society in George Eliot's fiction is to be found in her most contemporary novel, *Daniel Deronda*, which is set in England during the 1860s. It was probably because of her fears of the breakdown of a sense of unified social consciousness that George Eliot was attracted to nationalism, the most powerful expression of organicist thinking in the nineteenth century. She was, however, a cultural rather than a political nationalist. It seems certain that nationalism attracted her because it was the strongest modern means of countering those forces which were undermining the traditions, values, and customs of societies. But she remained a cultural relativist who believed nationalism was compatible with the unity of humanity.

It is in *The Spanish Gypsy*, *Daniel Deronda* and her last book, *Impressions of Theophrastus Such*, a collection of essays, that this interest in nationalism is most evident. The gypsies and the Jews are examples of the people as *Volk*, races which have preserved their desire for corporate consciousness, despite being dispersed over many parts of the world, and which are seeking nationhood to stabilise their sense of racial and cultural identity. The individual in identifying fully with his race or culture possesses a sense of tribal consciousness which protects him from isolation or alienation and which shapes and directs his egotistic energies. Both *The Spanish Gypsy* and *Daniel Deronda* also celebrate cultural relativism. It is probable that in her depiction in *The Spanish Gypsy* of the Spanish, a nation which seeks to impose by force its religion on other peoples and cultures, George Eliot is attacking nineteenth-century imperialism from an organicist standpoint.

In *Daniel Deronda* the Jewish desire for a national identity symbolises a need George Eliot sees as present in all races and peoples, as the following speech by Mordecai shows: 'See, then—the nation which has been scoffed at for its separateness, has given a binding theory to the human race. Now, in complete unity a part possesses the whole as the whole possesses every part: and in this way human life is tending toward the image of the Supreme Unity' (Chapter 61). There is no particularism in Mordecai's nationalism: 'I cherish nothing for the Jewish nation, I seek nothing for them, but the good which promises good to all nations' (Chapter 42). Similar ideas can be found in Herder.[17] Deronda is drawn to Mordecai's nationalism because of its organicist nature; he has always felt the desire to be 'an organic part of social life, instead of roaming in it like a yearning disembodied spirit, stirred with a vague social passion, but without fixed local habitation to render fellowship real' (Chapter 32).

It is significant that in the chapter of *Impressions of Theophrastus Such* entitled 'The Modern Hep! Hep! Hep!', which deals at length with nationalism and the Jewish question, George Eliot sees a special affinity between the Jews and the English:

There is more likeness than contrast between the way we English got our island and the way the Israelites got Canaan. . . . Again, it has been held that we have a peculiar destiny as a Protestant people. . . . The Puritans . . . found the Hebrew history closely symbolical of their feelings and purpose. . . . We must rather refer the passionate use of the

Hebrew writings to affinities between our own race and the
Jewish.   (pp. 270–1)[18]

This suggests not only that she is interested in the Jews and the
ideal of Jewish nationhood for their own sake, but also that she is
using them as an example to the English.[19] In her last works, one
receives a strong impression that England is in danger of
becoming decadent, and even that English national identity is
under threat. In another chapter of *Impressions of Theophrastus
Such*, 'Debasing the Moral Currency', she sees the destructive
mockery of English culture and traditions as a damaging feature
of English life: 'Are we on the way to a parody which shall have no
other excuse than the reckless search after fodder for degraded
appetites' (p. 148). She calls such mockery 'the robbery of our
mental wealth', which 'turns the hard-won order of life into a
second chaos' (p. 149).

In the light of this, it seems likely that one of George Eliot's
purposes in writing of the Jews and their struggle for nationhood
is to make her English readers more aware of their own sense of
national and racial consciousness. She believes that nationalism
can reawaken the desire for spiritual harmony which is essential
to the existence of an organic society. The following passage from
'The Modern Hep! Hep! Hep!' shows particularly clearly the
connection between nationalism and the organic society, and the
relevance of this to George Eliot's feelings about England:

> The eminence, the nobleness of a people, depends on its
> capability of being stirred by memories, and of striving for
> what we call spiritual ends—ends which consist not in im-
> mediate material possession, but in the satisfaction of a great
> feeling that animates the collective body as with one
> soul. . . . It is this living force of sentiment in common which
> makes a national consciousness. . . . An individual man to be
> harmoniously great, must belong to a nation of this order, if
> not in actual existence yet existing in the past, in memory, as a
> departed, invisible, beloved ideal, once a reality, and perhaps to
> be restored. A common humanity is not yet enough to feed the
> rich blood of various activity which makes a complete
> man. . . . I am not bound to feel for a Chinaman as I feel for
> my fellow-countryman . . . Affection, intelligence, duty, radi-
> ate from a centre, and nature has decided that for us English
> folk that centre can be neither China nor Peru.   (pp. 264–6)

But no superiority is attached to being English, for she remains a cultural relativist: 'we should recognise a corresponding attachment to nationality as legitimate in every other people, and understand that its absence is a privation of the greatest good'.

For George Eliot, nationality and race are not objective realities in the sense of having a biological or genetic basis but cultural creations; they emerge from the sharing of certain feelings, traditions, and values. Her interest is in nationalism as a means of binding society by creating the common beliefs and symbols necessary to make it organic. It is the effect of nationalist feeling on consciousness which is most important. She uses such phrases as 'that sense of special belonging', 'the sense of corporate existence', 'a sense of their supreme value'. It is reasonable to suggest that she believed nationalism could form the basis of the 'new Mythus' which Carlyle thought indispensable to give new form to the essential content of religion, and which was necessary if modern society was to become organic. She repeatedly stresses the moral and spiritual benefits of nationalism: 'The pride which identifies us with a great historic body is a humanising, elevating habit of mind, inspiring sacrifices of individual comfort, gain, or other selfish ambition, for the sake of that ideal whole; and no man swayed by such a sentiment can become completely abject' (p. 280).

There is, however, one aspect of George Eliot's cultural nationalism which may cause disquiet to a modern reader, particularly in view of the development of modern British society. She sees the immigration of foreigners into England as a social danger:

> Let it be admitted that it is a great calamity to the English, as to any other great historical people, to undergo a premature fusion with immigrants of alien blood; that its distinctive national characteristics should be in danger of obliteration by the predominating quality of foreign settlers. I not only admit this, I am ready to unite in groaning over the threatened danger.   (p. 283)

She goes on to refer to the evil of 'the predominance of wealth-acquiring immigrants, whose appreciation of our political and social life must often be as approximative or fatally erroneous as their delivery of our language' (pp. 284–5). She regrets the modern tendency towards the fusion of peoples, and values nationalism because it can moderate this tendency. Again one can parallel this aspect of George Eliot's thought with that of Herder who wrote:

> Nothing . . . is more manifestly contrary to the purpose of political government than the unnatural enlargement of states, the wild mixing of various races and nationalities under one sceptre. . . . Such states are but patched-up contraptions, fragile machines, appropriately called state-*machines*, for they are wholly devoid of inner life, and their component parts are connected through mechanical contrivances instead of bonds of sentiment.[20]

But it is interesting that George Eliot still opposes any policy that would put an end to immigration. Though she fears its results, she would rather see it continued than adopt a policy of exclusiveness: 'Are we to tear the glorious flag of hospitality which has made our freedom the world-wide blessing of the oppressed? (p. 285). She even admits that the English are as much to blame as anyone else for this social development: 'for we are at least equal to the races we call obtrusive in the disposition to settle wherever money is to be made and cheaply idle living to be found'. She sees the eventual fusion of peoples as inevitable, and she believes that the most that should be done is to try to slow it down so as to moderate its effects. Given the basic tendency of her social thought, it is her lack of extremism, in contrast to many organicists,[21] which is surprising. This brings home to us one of the deepest strains in George Eliot's attitude to the world: her moderation.

It is easy to see how cultural nationalism fits in with other elements in George Eliot's thought. Her fears of the consequences of the loss of religious belief, the dangers of an individualism cut off from moral restraints, the cultural disaster that might take place if a society lost touch with its traditions—these considerations, one can infer, made her look to nationalism as a means of resisting what she saw as subversive social and cultural forces and of providing the foundation, perhaps, for an organic society in the modern industrialised world. But despite similarities between George Eliot and earlier Romantic organicists, there are important distinctions between her concept of the organic society and earlier concepts. She would not have been worried by rationalist objections that the organic society was a myth or had never existed in the past. It would not be going too far, I think, to claim that for her as a later Romantic the organic society was a useful fiction. In *Impressions of Theophrastus Such* she again asserts the value of illusions: 'the illusions that began for us when we were less acquainted with evil have not lost their value when we discern them to be illusions. They feed the ideal Better, and in loving them still, we strengthen the precious habit of loving something not visibly, tangibly existent, but a spiritual product of our visible tangible selves' (p. 42). Unlike earlier organicists, she would not have been dismayed if past societies which had been called organic had been idealised or were revealed by historical investigation to be grossly imperfect. This would not detract from the value of the organic society as an ideal which could give form to social action. Without such an ideal there would be no means of resisting the increased social fragmentation which is deplored in works like *Daniel Deronda* and *Impressions of Theophrastus Such*.

The endings of the last four novels illustrate this. Romola, Felix Holt and Esther Lyon, Dorothea and Ladislaw, and Deronda, all commit themselves in various ways to a social ideal, though their success is left in doubt. It may be argued that Deronda is a partial exception, in that his ideal of a Jewish national state, later to be called Zionism, was in fact realised. But though with hindsight one can view *Daniel Deronda* as a prophetic novel, it seems likely that George Eliot had no great confidence that such an ideal could be achieved. Deronda himself is uncertain of what the outcome of his commitment will be, as the following speech to Mordecai shows:

> Since I began to read and know, I have always longed for some ideal task, in which I might feel myself the heart and brain of a multitude. . . . You have raised the image of such a task for me—to bind our race together in spite of heresy. . . . I mean to try what can be done with that union—I mean to work in your spirit. Failure will not be ignoble, but it would be ignoble for me not to try.   (Chapter 63)

One should point out, however, that the novel played an important part in interesting Jews in this ideal and thus had a significant influence on the Zionist movement.[22]

It is also a feature of the later novels that even if the individual must live in a fragmented society with little sense of corporate consciousness, the possession of a social ideal offers protection from alienation and helps support his sense of identity. Without such an ideal it is difficult to avoid a sense of alienation, since George Eliot believes it can result from the mind adapting itself to a spiritually dead environment, as can be seen in this extract from her poem 'In a London Drawingroom':

> No figure lingering
> Pauses to feed the hunger of the eye
> Or rest a little on the lap of life.
> All hurry on & look upon the ground,
> Or glance unmarking at the passers by
> The wheels are hurrying too, cabs, carriages
> All closed, in multiplied identity.
> The world seems one huge prison-house & court
> Where men are punished at the slightest cost
> With lowest rate of colour, warmth & joy.[23]

George Eliot's positive characters in her later novels are able to avoid this state of mind by identifying with a social ideal which transcends the actual conditions of the particular societies of which they are a part. Even if the organic society as an ideal can never be fully achieved, it gives direction and purpose to their lives and leads them to devote their energies to the social good. Though they may fail to realise their ideal or even to exert any major influence on their societies, George Eliot no doubt shares the judgement of the narrator of *Middlemarch* on Dorothea and others like her: 'that things are not so ill with you and me as they might have been, is half owing to the number who lived faithfully a hidden life, and rest in unvisited tombs' (Finale).

6 Memory and *The Mill on the Floss*

Memory is another essential aspect of George Eliot's organicism. She believes that the only valid form of human identity is an organic one: there must be a sense of continuity between the formative experiences of one's past life and one's present self, and the individual should act and choose in relation to this sense of continuity. In *Impressions of Theophrastus Such* she refers to 'the divine gift of a memory which inspires the moments with a past, a present, and a future, and gives the sense of corporate existence that raises man above the otherwise more respectable and innocent brute' (pp. 261–2). Here she is referring to the general social consciousness but a similar continuity is necessary to the individual consciousness. One should note that she calls such continuity 'the sense of corporate consciousness', indicating that it is the psychological reality that is important. It is quite possible for a society or an individual to be cut off from or to reject the past. But if this occurs she believes that neither society nor the individual will possess a healthy or secure sense of identity.

Memory plays an important role in almost all of George Eliot's works. The importance of preserving continuity with one's past is particularly evident in *Silas Marner*, for example. With the loss of his religious faith, Silas feels separated from his memories: 'Minds that have been unhinged from their old faith and love, have perhaps sought this Lethean influence of exile, in which the past becomes dreamy because its symbols have all vanished, and the present too is dreamy because it is linked with no memories' (Chapter 2). He tries to forget his past and, in place of organic continuity, constructs a mechanical way of life for himself: 'Marner's face and figure shrank and bent themselves into a mechanical relation to the objects of his life.' The coming of

97

Eppie and his closer involvement with Raveloe life, which is a consequence of this, help him integrate his memories with his present life and so recover from his alienation: 'and as, with reawakening sensibilities, memory also reawakened, he had begun to ponder over the elements of his old faith, and blend them with his new impressions, till he recovered a consciousness of unity between his past and present' (Chapter 16). In living with Eppie in Raveloe he finds a form of life which can accommodate what he valued in his earlier Christianity.[1] Silas needs to feel that there is continuity between his new identity in Raveloe and his earlier life in Lantern Yard.

It is interesting that Silas has some experiences akin to involuntary memory. The first is early in his life in Raveloe and though nothing comes of it, it suggests the importance memory will have in his recovery. He promises to help a woman who is suffering from a heart complaint and he is reminded strongly of his mother: 'In this office of charity, Silas felt, for the first time since he had come to Raveloe, a sense of unity between his past and present life, which might have been the beginning of his rescue from the insect-like existence into which his nature had shrunk' (Chapter 2). Silas needs to make this momentary sense of continuity a stable factor in his life. Eppie's entry into his life leads to the creation of a sense of continuity with his past, and, significantly, her coming triggers off an involuntary memory which connects him with a valuable part of his past he has almost forgotten: 'Could this be his little sister come back to him in a dream—his little sister whom he had carried about in his arms for a year before she died, when he was a small boy without shoes and stockings?' (Chapter 12). This experience is the beginning of a new sense of connection with his past.

In Eppie's final decision to stay with Silas and to reject her natural father, memory is also important. Her relationship to Godfrey is a purely formal one. It has no roots in her past experience since she has never known him as a father. In 'organic' terms Silas is her father since they have always lived as father and daughter, as Silas points out to Godfrey: 'Your coming now and saying "I'm her father" doesn't alter the feelings inside us. It's me she's been calling her father ever since she could say the word' (Chapter 19). And it is more than life with Silas that Eppie chooses; it is life in the community of Raveloe in which she has been brought up and which she feels is inextricably a part of her.

To take her place in the class-conscious world of the Casses would cut her off from this. Eppie instinctively realises it: 'I wasn't brought up to be a lady, and I can't turn my mind to it. I like the working-folks, and their victuals, and their ways' (Chapter 19). Esther Lyon in *Felix Holt* similarly decides to reject the way of life of the Transomes partly because it would separate her from her past.

In *Silas Marner* we see alienation and lack of identity caused by the loss of formative memories. This is a recurrent experience in George Eliot's fiction. Mirah in *Daniel Deronda* feels she wants to die when she believes herself irrecoverably cut off from her memories: 'I could not hear memories any more: I could only feel what was present in me—it was all one longing to cease from my weary life, which seemed only a pain outside the great peace that I might enter into' (Chapter 20). Mordecai is able to protect himself against such feelings by the possession of the ideal of a Jewish state, which is itself closely connected with memory. It is 'the heritage of memory' and 'the inborn half of memory' (Chapter 42) which keep the idea of Israel alive.

Memory has a comparatively minor but significant role in *Middlemarch*. It is probably most important in relation to Bulstrode, who has tried to suppress his past life and create an image of himself as superior in religion and good deeds to his neighbours. George Eliot shows that this concealment of his past makes him extremely vulnerable to the judgements of others. When the role he is playing is shattered by the discovery of facts which conflict with its credibility, he has no defence against their judgements and feels compelled to accept them. By concealing his past he has tacitly admitted his guilt and shame, both to others and to himself. In refusing to acknowledge his past and incorporate it into his identity, he has denied himself a sense of unified self rooted in memory, one which can resist unfortunate circumstances and can face the judgements of others. In the crisis of exposure he realises that his past is a part of him:

It was not that he was in danger of legal punishment or of beggary: he was in danger only of seeing disclosed to the judgment of his neighbours and the mournful perception of his wife certain facts of his past life which would render him an object of scorn and opprobrium of the religion with which he had diligently associated himself. The terror of being judged sharpens the memory: it sends an inevitable glare over that long-unvisited past which has been habitually recalled only in general phases. . . . With memory set smarting like a reopened wound, a man's past is not simply a dead history, an outworn preparation of the present: it is not a repented error shaken loose from the life: it is a still quivering part of himself, bringing shudders and bitter flavours and the tinglings of a merited shame.   (Chapter 61).

This man who has dominated others by the force of his will and his assurance of superiority finds himself powerless to resist their adverse judgements of him. Dorothea and Ladislaw also have to contend with the judgements of others, some of which are prejudiced and unfair, but in acting in accordance with what they feel to be their whole selves, they are able to prevent others' judgements of them becoming a tyranny. They have sufficient assurance in their own selfhood to feel free to be true to themselves despite adverse opinions.

George Eliot's concept of memory is an essential part of her thought. Memory is crucial to what she regards as an authentic sense of identity because it allows an individual to act in accordance with his whole experience. An action which is the product of a conscious act of will or an impulse of the moment and which cannot be integrated with the sense of self as a continuity is for her inauthentic. Such actions may lead to self-alienation. Her organic view of self is implied in this quotation from 'Janet's Repentance': 'There are moments when by some strange impulse we contradict our past selves—fatal moments, when a fit of passion, like a lava stream, lays low the work of half our lives' (Chapter 14). She is aware that this continuity of self is not something given in itself; it must be chosen. Her novels contain many wilful, impulsive characters who reject such continuity. But for her the continuity of self which memory makes possible is a solution to the problem of identity in a world devoid of immanent order or meaning. Even if there is no order to which the self can relate and which can act as an external support for continuity, such continuity must be created, either through memory or through a social ideal which provides the self with a sense of stability and direction. It should be emphasised that George Eliot does not see the past as standing in a static relationship to the self, as some critics have implied in referring to the 'authority' or the 'worship' of the past and the 'doctrine of continuity' in her work.[2] Continuity does not involve passive or mechanical submission to the past; it is memory and choice that are fundamental in the creation of a sense of continuity. The psychological need to achieve a sense of whole self is what is important, not obedience to a past that stands apart from the self. This is clearly evident in *The Mill on the Floss*, in which memory receives its most complex and interesting treatment.

II

Memory is perhaps the central element in the structure of *The Mill on the Floss*. The novel itself comes into being as the result of an intense experience of memory on the part of the narrator: 'I have been pressing my elbows on the arms of my chair, and dreaming that I was standing on the bridge in front of Dorlcote Mill, as it looked one February afternoon many years ago' (Book I, Chapter 1). The influence of Wordsworth on the treatment of Maggie's early years has often been commented on, but this should not blind one to the fact that the world of *The Mill on the Floss* is very far removed from the metaphysically meaningful world presented in Wordsworth's poetry. This has important implications for George Eliot's treatment of memory and the experience of the past in the lives of the characters. The world of the novel is unstructured: it lacks an order which offers human beings a sense of meaning or definition. Chance and accident play a prominent part in the plot; events occur without having any relation to human hopes and desires; and there is no providence at work which will make everything turn out right in the end. Mr Tulliver's assertion that it is 'a puzzling world' is much emphasised, and there are numerous instances of the lack of an external order which takes account of human needs or expectations. For example, Mr Tulliver makes a disastrous mistake over Tom's schooling, one which has serious consequences for Tom's future development and which cannot be undone; Mrs Tulliver's warnings to her husband not to go to law have precisely the opposite effect, and her equally unfortunate attempt to persuade Wakem not to buy the mill puts the idea into his head; Tom's repaying of his father's debts paradoxically leads to Mr Tulliver's attack on Wakem instead of to the happy outcome Tom had anticipated.

Maggie Tulliver and the other characters are caught up in a world of disorderly and unpredictable circumstance that is indifferent to human needs and desires, and this is a significant part of the novel's meaning. Even the most dramatic event in the novel, Maggie's flight with Stephen Guest, is importantly affected by chance. It takes place only as a result of Lucy's scheming to bring about a meeting between Philip Wakem and Maggie. Philip is unable to attend and unknowingly asks Stephen to take his place and thus to encounter Maggie alone. That these chance events are the direct cause of the boating trip which leads to the elopement is part of the point. There is no fate or destiny in this novel, only chance and necessity. Though Maggie had chosen to give up Stephen, an unpredictable combination of events undermines her choice. This lack of relation between human decisions and hopes and the world beyond the human is apparent throughout the novel. An event like the flood simply happens; there is no connection between it and the human realm. Characters' lives are crucially affected by the acts of others, over which they have no control, an example being the effect of the lawsuit on Maggie and Tom, or else chance creates unexpected turns of events that no one could have anticipated. Mr Tulliver has an obsessive desire to impose his idea of the right on the world like a transcendentalist hero, in protest at what he sees as injustice and disorder, but his efforts and their results are treated ironically. The Wordsworthian element in the novel, which is present in the treatment of the childhood scenes, does not imply a Wordsworthian view of nature and the universe. There is no transcendent reality to be recaptured through the child's vision and through memory, though George Eliot believes that they can create a more limited, a more human sense of transcendence.

Memory has two important aspects in *The Mill on the Floss*: it can act as a human means of transcending the amoral, unstructured world of the novel I have already referred to, and it can act as a source of authority for feeling. The latter constitutes the dominant theme during the years after Maggie's childhood. I shall discuss first of all the former aspect of memory.

Memory as a means of limited transcendence in *The Mill on the Floss* is the experience of a sense of continuity of being, in which past and present are unified; an experience in which the individual

seems to transcend the limitations imposed on human consciousness by living in a world of time and change and being compelled
to concentrate on the present. Memory can place the individual in
contact with the felt experience of the past, or arouse feelings in
relation to objects or places because of their past associations
which would otherwise be lost to the self. If one loses contact with
these feelings, with the continuity of self they make possible, the
consequence is an unstable or fragile sense of identity or a
spiritual lack which may lead to alienation or despair. Places and
objects are particularly important in keeping one in touch with
such experience even if one remains for the most part unconscious
of it. It is often only with the departure from a place or the loss of
objects that their importance in preserving continuity becomes
apparent. Mr Tulliver, Maggie, and Tom become most aware of
how central the mill is to their lives when it is lost, and Mrs
Tulliver has a similar experience at a lower level after the loss of
her crockery and linen.[3] These losses disrupt the continuity of
being which George Eliot thinks necessary to an individual's
sense of identity. A truly human consciousness for her is one that
maintains strong connections with its past. The relation between
this and morality is that one's actions should take account of the
need for a sense of unified, continuing selfhood. It is Maggie's
feeling for the continuity of her life that makes her fear she may
commit an impulsive action in contradiction with the past self
which she feels is still present in her and which will separate her
from her past.

The way objects interact with memory and become part of the
fabric of an individual's consciousness is an important element in
the novel. When Tom comes home after his dreary time at Mr
Stelling's, he experiences again 'the warmth and the kisses of that
familiar hearth, where the pattern of the rug and the grate and the
fire-irons were "first ideas" that it was no more possible to
criticise than the solidity and extension of matter' (Book II,
Chapter 1). Though striving after something better in his
surroundings distinguishes man from the animal, 'heaven knows
where that striving might lead us, if our affections had not a trick
of twining round those old inferior things—if the loves and
sanctities of life had no deep immovable roots in memory'. In
George Eliot, as in Wordsworth, feelings become part of objects,
and in the interaction of mind with objects or places our selfhood
is built up. Memory serves to keep us in touch with these feelings

and to experience a sense of transcendence of passing time, which constantly changes our lives and compels consciousness to attend to the needs of the present. A too sudden uprooting from those objects which embody past feelings and associations can lead to a sense of spiritual impoverishment, as the experience of the Tullivers illustrates.

The early part of the novel has several scenes in which Maggie and Tom have experiences which become an integral part of their lives and which arouse such intense feelings that time can never eradicate the effects from their consciousnesses. The scene in which Tom gives Maggie a piece of cake in the attic and forgives her for letting his rabbits die is an obvious example, and another is when they go fishing together: 'They trotted along and sat down together, with no thought that life would ever change much for them: they would only get bigger and not go to school, and it would always be like the holidays; they would always live together and be fond of each other' (Book I, Chapter 5). Here the sense of timelessness that Maggie and Tom experience during the best moments of their childhood is particularly clear. Though their lives are drastically altered, these experiences always remain a part of them. Their childhood is not, however, completely idyllic, for Maggie's frustrations are as much dwelt upon as the timeless moments, and she is as often at odds with Tom as at one with him. In addition, her impulsive, passionate feelings are as much in evidence as later. But when 'the small demons' (Book I, Chapter 10) take possession of her and urge her to push Lucy in the mud and run off to the gypsies, the situation can be rectified fairly easily, unlike later events.

With the failure of Mr Tulliver's law suit, Maggie and Tom are violently cut off from their childhood. The suddenness of the change creates a breach with the past that affects all the Tullivers adversely. Mr Tulliver has lost his self-respect, Mrs Tulliver her beloved linen and crockery, and Tom must try to establish himself in an occupation and earn money quickly, equipped with an inadequate education. They become obsessed with the necessities of the present and in consequence ignore the past. This also has a serious effect on Maggie, since she feels cut off from the two most important people in her life, her father and Tom. She suffers a 'sense of loneliness, and utter privation of joy' (Book IV, Chapter 3).

Critics are often antagonistic to Tom but it is important to notice that, like Maggie, he is harmed by the loss of continuity with his early life. He is the victim of unfortunate circumstances which distort his development and play an important part in turning him into the inflexible, rigid person of the later part of the novel. He would have been quite happy to inherit the mill and carry on his father's work, but Mr Tulliver is determined, because of his obsession with the law, to impose a different pattern on his life. His education has an adverse effect on his personality. George Eliot subtly shows how he is made to distrust his right to be himself. His experience with the Stellings gave him 'a general sense that his theory of life was undermined', and 'for the first time in his life he had a painful sense that he was all wrong somehow' (Book II, Chapter 1). His pride meeting 'with nothing but bruisings and crushings', he becomes distrustful of himself and subject to self-consciousness. He is then suddenly forced to make his way in the world after the bankruptcy and loss of the mill, which comes as a crushing blow to the expectation of inheriting it which he had entertained since childhood, and he must face this crisis with all the disadvantages of an unsuitable education. It is no surprise that the most rigid side of his personality becomes dominant and that he devotes himself entirely to the present, dismissing the past from his mind. He is not the only victim, for this alienates him from Maggie, who suffers from the loss of their former contact. He is compared with men so devoted to action that they are forced into 'quenching memory in the stronger light of purpose' (Book V, Chapter 2). Feeling and memory are suppressed in favour of the duties of the present. This enables him to act single-mindedly and purposefully and to be a success in business, but only at the cost of an empty inner life.

Both Maggie and Tom are vulnerable to opposite tendencies. The danger for Maggie is that she will lose control over her strong feelings, while for Tom it is the suppression of feeling that is the danger. The events which create a sharp break with their childhood experience threaten to bring this about. Tom's personality suffers badly as a result. He lives an isolated life and is morose. He confesses to his uncle that all he cares about is work, which, the narrator comments, is 'rather sad' in a young man of twenty-three. It could be argued that Tom suffers as great a spiritual loss as Maggie in being cut off from his past memories and experiences.

It is the mill itself which epitomises the importance of memory and the past in the lives of all the Tullivers. It is the centre of Mr Tulliver's life:

> The Tullivers had lived in this spot for generations. . . . It was when he got able to walk about and look at all the old objects, that he felt the strain of this clinging affection for the old home as part of his life, part of himself. . . . Our instructed vagrancy . . . can hardly get a dim notion of what an old-fashioned man like Tulliver felt for this spot, where all his memories centred.   (Book III, Chapter 9)

The mill is likewise a central part of Maggie's and Tom's lives. For all of them it expresses their need for continuity with the past and a sense of transcendence of passing time.

The ending of the novel has been much criticised, mainly on the grounds that it is an escape from the problems raised by the work or that it is a emotional indulgence on George Eliot's part. In my view these criticisms arise out of a failure to grasp the structure of the novel. The ending can be defended in several ways. For example, it can be argued that it successfully brings together in a single scene two of the novel's most important concerns: its interest in memory as a means of limited transcendence and its awareness of the recalcitrance of the external world. The deaths of Maggie and Tom in the flood are, like so many other events in the novel, accidental. Such a flood has always been a potential threat in this part of the country, but when it comes there is no reward or punishment, since it remains quite indifferent to the affairs of men. Hardy communicates in his novels a strong sense of protest about the lack of an order in the world that takes account of humanity, but George Eliot seems to accept more easily that this is how things are. This recognition is basic to her humanist philosophy. It creates the motive in men to strive to build a human order which will bind men together and protect them against the amoral otherness of the world.

Though Maggie and Tom are destroyed by the flood, they have a human vision which affirms the value of their existence even in the midst of destruction. Maggie's earliest memory of standing with Tom at the side of the Floss is basic to her being: 'the first thing I ever remember in my life is standing with Tom by the side of the Floss, while he held my hand: everything before that is dark to me' (Book V, Chapter 1). This memory is the most important symbol of value in her life and one to which she feels she cannot be false without betraying her deepest self. Thus Tom 'had his terrible clutch on her conscience and her deepest dread' (Book V, Chapter 5), and the division that develops between them is one that seems to rend her in two: 'To have no cloud between herself and Tom was still a perpetual yearning in her, that had its root deeper than all change' (Book VI, Chapter 12). During the flood, when she becomes aware of the dangers to Tom and the mill, past resentment against him and fears for herself fall away and leave 'only the deep, underlying memories of early union' (Book VII, Chapter 5). Her action in rescuing him despite all the dangers to herself is a revelation which at last breaks down the barriers between them, and they again experience their childhood sense of unity. The word 'Magsie' immediately links them both in memory with their best childhood experiences. Past and present become one in their transcendence of their time-bound situation. They affirm the continuity of being which only their union can fully achieve, despite all the circumstances which have previously divided them. It is a return to that earliest memory of standing together by the side of the Floss. This sense of transcendence is possible even in an unstructured world, though it possesses only a human significance. The experience cannot prevent their being crushed by the forces of amoral otherness 'hurrying on in hideous triumph'. But though Maggie and Tom are destroyed, by re-affirming 'in one supreme moment' the deepest memories of their lives, they experience a sense of human value which, George Eliot suggests, transcends the indifference of external reality and makes their deaths tragic. The highest form of tragedy, for her, is produced by being true to human values or ideals even in the face of a resistant world that must inevitably triumph, causing human destruction or defeat.

It may be argued, however, that the 'Conclusion' weakens the tragic ending by introducing a consoling element which suggests that life continues, and that for both nature and man there is eventual recovery from the effects of the flood. But if read carefully, the 'Conclusion' is quite opposed to the underlying philosophy embodied in the endings of the vast majority of nineteenth-century novels: that everything finally turns out for the best, or that if the world is seen in proper perspective a moral order is discernible. The narrator chooses to emphasise the fact that though nature appears to have renewed itself, this is not the case, at least from a human point of view: 'The uptorn trees are not rooted again; the parted hills are left scarred. . . . To the eyes that have dwelt on the past, there is no thorough repair.' Though nature itself is indifferent to past destruction, human consciousness remains aware of what has been destroyed and cannot identify nature's renewal with order. In the human realm the destruction of the past is even less capable of being accepted as part of a restored order in the world. Though it is implied that Stephen eventually marries Lucy, Philip remains unconsoled, and both men 'felt that their keenest joy and keenest sorrow were for ever buried there'.

The 'Conclusion' reiterates what the rest of the novel has communicated: that time moves on relentlessly and stops neither for human happiness nor for human tragedy. But human beings can in a limited way resist the indifference of time. They remain conscious of the past through the power of memory and that past can influence and shape their lives in the future, though this may involve living with a tragic sense of loss. Time stops for Maggie and Tom, but they achieve limited transcendence even after their deaths in that they continue to be remembered by those who live after them and to affect their lives.

III

There is, of course, another side to the novel: Maggie's life after her childhood and her problems and struggles. Though there may seem to be only a marginal relation between the aspect of the novel I have already discussed and the moral dilemma created by Maggie's love for and elopement with Stephen Guest, memory and the past are equally crucial to the latter aspect, and an awareness of this helps one to appreciate the novel as a single structure. Memory can not only achieve a sense of human transcendence, but also gives the individual a basis for responding morally to experience even if there is no external moral authority.

Maggie's development in the later part of the novel shows strong similarities to that of Romola, which I have already discussed. Like Romola, she is a girl who possesses great strength of feeling, and her problem is how her impulsive feelings are to be controlled and directed, especially as her egotistic tendencies are strong and interact with feeling. As in *Romola* the difficulty is that if there is no unquestionable moral authority apart from moral feelings, how is the individual to lead an ordered moral life? Though George Eliot denied that Christianity as a system was necessary to act as a guarantee for morality and argued that we have feelings of love, of pity, of justice and similar 'moral' feelings, she was also well aware that we have feelings of a very different sort, which create hate, lust, resentment, and violence. How are we to control feelings or choose between them if there is no moral authority external to feeling? This is one of the major philosophical problems in *Romola*, and in *The Mill on the Floss* it is considered from a different point of view and in a different context.

When Maggie is a child the problem of controlling her feelings is not a serious one. Though they are subject to violent changes, from intense affection towards Tom to acts of wilful egotism like cutting her hair or pushing Lucy in the mud, the stability of family life, the love and protection of her father, her good times with Tom, all of these provide a stable, secure existence that keeps her more violent outbursts of 'overmastering impulse' (Book I, Chapter 11) in check. She is part of a family with strong roots, and though her childhood has as at least as many frustrations as idyllic moments, she can always be reconciled with her parents or Tom without the need to exert any formal control over feeling. The structure of family life serves as sufficient control.

When she grows up, things are very different. The disastrous outcome of the law suit breaks up this valuable family life. Tom and her father are so concerned to pay off their debts that they have little time to devote to her. Though she draws closer to her mother, this is not sufficient compensation for the loss of connection with a family unit which took a loving, compassionate interest in her. Feeling is as dominant a part of her personality as before, but there seems little outlet for it other than in rebellion. Emotionally isolated and with little scope for expressing her most powerful feelings, she leads a joyless life. She needs to understand what has happened to her family rather than to escape into a dream world, for without this she knows there is a danger that impulsive feeling will urge her to rebel. She feels fits of anger and hatred towards her parents and Tom which 'would flow out over her affections and conscience like a lava stream, and frighten her with a sense that it was not difficult for her to become a demon'

(Book IV, Chapter 3). Maggie clearly has a Romantic sensibility, one in which the egotistic drive is particularly strong, and this tempts her to give way to strong impulse and to demonic forces in her nature.

She is aware of a serious need to find an authority outside her own feelings which can exercise control over her more impulsive tendencies. Without this she will be vulnerable to the wilful acts of egotism and rebellious impulses which affected her so often in childhood, and which might have irreversible consequences now that she is an adult. Out of her great need for direction and self-control, she constructs from the writings of Thomas à Kempis a philosophy of resignation and renunciation.

Maggie's period under the influence of à Kempis corresponds somewhat to Romola's period under the influence of Savonarola and Catholicism. Both are unsatisfactory because they are adopted as rigid moral frames to suppress all strong feeling in the interest of moral action, and also to escape the inner turmoil created by conflicting feelings. But this can be no lasting solution for girls so passionate by nature. Not that there is anything wrong with à Kempis's philosophy or with the human essence of Savonarola's religion, but accepting them as controlling systems to be mechanically obeyed, instead of experiencing their truth through feeling itself, has a divisive effect on the consciousnesses of both Romola and Maggie. Though Maggie is now reconciled to the limitations of her lot, she still experiences 'some volcanic upheavings of imprisoned passions' (Book IV, Chapter 3). Philip Wakem's later criticism that this form of renunciation is repressive and can only inflict psychological harm on her mind and feelings is self-interested but nevertheless true: 'You want to find out a mode of renunciation that will be an escape from pain. I tell you again, there is no such escape possible except by perverting or mutilating one's nature' (Book VI, Chapter 7).

Repression of the passions is no solution for Maggie and may even be more dangerous, since the bottling-up of feeling may lead to its breaking out all the more powerfully, overcoming her conscious resistance, as the narrator suggests: 'Yet one has a sense of uneasiness in looking at her—a sense of opposing elements, of which a fierce collision is imminent' (Book V, Chapter 1). Since she lacks a sense of control built into feeling itself, blind obedience to her rigid doctrine of resignation could eventually make her more vulnerable to strong impulse. The impending conflict becomes inevitable with the development of her sexual nature, which puts the greatest strain on her. All her most impulsive feelings urge a passionate relationship with Stephen Guest, and à Kempis's philosophy, already undermined, is quite inadequate in this situation.

Meeting Philip Wakem again after the bankruptcy is the first occasion on which her doctrine is seriously tested. He urges on her complete emancipation of feeling and awakens discontent in her. He sets off a conflict between resignation, which demands that she reconcile herself to her present life and the denial of feeling it involves, and her latent yearnings to give herself up to immediate feeling. But this is really a pseudo-conflict. For renunciation in the form in which she adheres to it at this time is an escape from feeling for the purpose of reconciling her to her lot; it frees her from the pain of frustration and from self-conflict. It is thus largely an inverted form of gratification: 'renunciation seemed to her the entrance into that satisfaction which she had so long been craving in vain. She had not perceived . . . the inmost truth of the old monk's outpourings, that renunciation remains sorrow, though a sorrow borne willingly. Maggie was still panting for happiness, and was in ecstasy because she had found the key to it' (Book IV, Chapter 3). There is then a serious danger when she is tempted by a more effective gratification.

But this temptation leads to the discovery of what for her is a true moral authority, though she cannot yet recognise it for what it is. This authority has its basis in feeling, the feelings created in her by her past which remain an integral part of her life, preserved by memory. Philip urges her to have secret meetings with him but she feels 'the warning that such interviews implied secrecy—implied doing something she would dread to be discovered in—something that, if discovered, must cause anger and pain; and that the admission of anything so near doubleness would act as a spiritual blight' (Book V, Chapter 1). To meet Philip secretly would contradict claims and duties created by the past, present in her as feelings through the power of memory. To act against these promptings would bring her sense of identity under stress since she would 'dread' discovery. She knows that having a relationship with Philip would inflict pain on her family. It is this consideration which restrains her, not mechanical resignation. Her choice is not to agree to Philip's proposal and even though she lets herself drift into meeting him she never feels she has made a conscious decision to do so. She is confused because she thinks the conflict is between 'resigned imprisonment' (Book V, Chapter 3) and the feelings meeting Philip arouses in her. Matters are further complicated by the fact that childhood memories connect her with Philip, and she knows it would cause him pain to be rejected. His argument that 'It is mere cowardice to seek safety in negations' (Book V, Chapter 3) is a true attack on her doctrine of resignation, but it merely clouds the more important consider- ations that such meetings could take place only secretly, since they would be unacceptable to both families, and that Maggie could never consciously choose to break with her family. She also fears that, 'by forsaking the simple rule of renunciation, she was throwing herself under the seductive guidance of illimitable wants'. If she responds to the impulse to meet Philip, which conflicts with other claims on her, and rejects à Kempis's philosophy, then she is faced again with the problem of how to control strong feeling if she has no authority beyond feeling.

Maggie does not make a conscious decision to offend her family by meeting Philip. She allows her feelings to have it seemingly both ways when Philip says they may meet by chance. The narrator comments: 'And it was in this way that Philip justified his subtle efforts to overcome Maggie's true prompting against a concealment that would introduce doubleness into her own mind, and might cause new misery to those who had the primary natural claim on her' (Book V, Chapter 3). This situation is the first clear indication that the means of moral control over the instability of feeling and impulse lies in feeling itself, in those memories and claims created in her life by the past and which she feels are a fundamental part of her. Though she profits from her meetings with Philip, she confesses to him that they have made her restless and weary of her home and her parents. She never rids herself of the feeling that she made a mistake not to hold fast to her original choice, and when the meetings are ended she feels great relief at this 'deliverance from concealment' (Book V, Chapter 5).

Maggie's failure to be true to her choice of those feelings and memories which are central to her past, and to resist an impulse which conflicts with past claims, has important consequences. It has the unfortunate result of involving her in a personal relationship with Philip. His primary aim is to make her respond to his love for her by encouraging her to give free rein to her natural feelings. But the novel's treatment of Philip's love for Maggie is both complex and ironic. His belief in the liberation of feeling, to a large extent the product of his longing for passionate love, can lead only to frustration in his own life since his bodily appearance does not make him physically attractive to women, or at least to Maggie. He cannot sublimate his desires in his painting or, at first, reconcile himself to renunciation, the conscious acceptance of pain and limitation. His love for Maggie is clearly physical and it is equally clear that she cannot return it. But with her inexperience and her feelings of pity for him because of his deformity, she allows herself to believe she loves him, though her love has no sexual content: 'Even to Maggie he was an exception: it was clear that the thought of his being her lover had never entered her mind' (Book V, Chapter 3). It is ironic that Philip repeatedly urges her to give herself up to her spontaneous feelings in an effort to make her respond to his love, but if she did so she would reject him as a lover. It is only her pity and a lingering attachment to resignation, the philosophy he is so critical of, that make her accept his love. This is shown in the form of her happiness after she first lets him kiss her: 'She had a moment of real happiness then—a moment of belief that, if there were sacrifice in this love, it was all the richer and more satisfying' (Book V, Chapter 4). This is certainly not what Philip wants, and he himself fears she loves him out of pity. It is also ironic that his attack on her resignation and renunciation, which makes him predict that 'You will be thrown into the world some day, and then every rational satisfaction of your nature that you deny now, will assault you like a savage appetite' (Book V, Chapter 3), should rebound on his own hopes of marrying her. The relationship between Philip and Maggie is, I think, more subtly treated by George Eliot than most critics have realised.

In this relationship, Maggie felt that the claims of the past, preserved by memory, constituted a body of feelings she could choose to obey and so control the more impulsive feelings which were also part of her nature. But by confusing these claims with her doctrine of resignation and allowing herself to be taken in by Philip's casuistry, her choice is negated. This creates a sense of confusion, since she enjoys the meetings but still feels she is acting wrongly. When she is discovered by Tom, this confusion is increased, for though she feels in the wrong, the absoluteness of Tom's condemnation and the manner of his attack on Philip make her rebel against his judgement and feel the more attached to Philip: 'So I *will* submit to what I acknowledge and feel to be right' (Book V, Chapter 5; George Eliot's italics). She is thus further away than ever from being fully conscious that her memory of the claims of the past constitutes the authority she has been seeking to provide the basis for exercising control over the diversity of her feelings. This leaves her vulnerable to a powerful impulse.

When she encounters Stephen Guest her situation has become especially dangerous: 'her future, she thought, was likely to be worse than her past, for after years of contented renunciation, she had slipped back into desire and longing . . . she found the image of the intense and varied life she yearned for, and despaired of, becoming more and more importunate' (Book VI, Chapter 2). Her doctrine of resignation has broken down; she has claimed the right to go her own way, breaking with Tom who is inseparably a part of her feelings for the past; and she feels herself committed to Philip without being able to love him in the fullest sense. This confusion in her mind and feelings makes her extremely vulnerable in her relationship with Stephen Guest, the first physically attractive man she has met, who arouses the sexual desires which George Eliot has taken care to show are a strong feature of her nature. In making Maggie's conflict a sexual one, George Eliot is setting the strongest natural feelings against another set of feelings which call on her to resist. For those egotistic Romantics who believed in the liberation of impulse, one discovered one's truest sense of self by obeying the promptings of one's strongest natural feelings, but George Eliot rejected this philosophy on human and social grounds. For her, the individual should resist impulsive and natural feelings if they could not be reconciled with his sense of whole self.

It may be objected that this conflict is weakened in artistic terms by George Eliot's presentation of Stephen Guest. His characterisation has been attacked from various points of view, from the Victorian attitude that he is not worthy of Maggie to a modern view that George Eliot over-emphasises his negative qualities in order for the reader to feel that the other claims on Maggie are stronger. But one should appreciate that it is artistically necessary for George Eliot to preserve a careful balance in her characterisation of Stephen. Maggie must feel genuine love for him, otherwise there would be no real sense of conflict, but Stephen must also possess the egotistic qualities that tempt him to elope with Maggie without obtaining her consent and which lead him to argue that strong feeling must triumph under any circumstances. It seems to me that George Eliot achieves the right balance. The reader retains sufficient sympathy for Stephen to understand Maggie's love for him and also to feel that they could have had a successful marriage if there had been no obstacles in the way, but we are also aware from his first appearance of his egotistic tendencies, in which there are traces of the Byronic, though these do not express themselves negatively. They are sufficient, however, to tempt him into the elopement and to make him advocate the primacy of natural feeling. It is significant also that though George Eliot disapproves of his views, her moral objection to his arguments is combined with a sympathetic presentation of his character throughout his relationship with Maggie. He is motivated not by narrow selfishness but by real love for her.

Stephen's attempt to persuade Maggie to marry him is another serious 'temptation' for her. It is a fairly common view that George Eliot is able to resolve the difficulties raised by this part of the novel only by the escapist means of bringing about Maggie's death. However I shall argue that George Eliot is firmly in control of the novel's structure, which is based on the conflict between feelings that are the product of natural impulses and feelings that are an integral part of one's sense of one's past. This conflict had been present earlier in Maggie's relationship with Philip, who exhorted her to give way to her natural feelings: 'no one has strength given to do what is unnatural' (Book V, Chapter 3), but Stephen asserts this much more strongly. He repeatedly tells ⸗ Maggie that her resistance to their love is 'unnatural': 'It is unnatural—it is horrible'; 'It is come upon as without our seeking: it is natural' (Book VI, Chapter 11); 'See how the tide is carrying us out—away from all those unnatural bonds that we have been trying to make faster round us, and trying in vain' (Book VI, Chapter 13); and most powerfully: 'We have proved that the feeling which draws us towards each other is too strong to be overcome: that natural law surmounts every other; we can't help what it clashes with' (Book VI, Chapter 14). Like Philip, but with much greater force, Stephen is calling on Maggie to follow her natural impulses, since any restraint on natural feeling is a denial of one's real self. But for Maggie there are other feelings, which are also part of her self. It is the conflict between the natural side of feeling, her sexual impulses, and those other feelings with their roots in her 'long deep memories of early discipline and effort, of early claims on her love and pity' (Book VI, Chapter 9) which dominates her relationship with Stephen, and she feels that to submit to Stephen's argument from nature would entail a rejection of her sense of her past. But because of the confusion in her mind and feelings she is not at first able to exert a firm control over herself and resolve the conflict. The desire to give way to natural impulse and the feelings of the moment is almost irresistible when she is dancing with Stephen: 'for life at this moment seemed a keen vibrating consciousness poised above pleasure or pain. This one, this last night, she might expand unrestrainedly in the warmth of the present, without those chill eating thoughts of the past and the future' (Book VI, Chapter 10).

But she succeeds in resisting him, for she is intuitively aware that to give way would cut her off from the continuity she needs to feel with her past and the claims it has created in her life. She is able later to articulate the nature of the conflict she feels:

> It seems right to me sometimes that we should follow our strongest feeling;—but then, such feelings continually come across the ties that all our former life has made for us—the ties that have made others dependent on us—and would cut them in two. . . . I must not, cannot seek my own happiness by sacrificing others. Love is natural; but surely pity and faithfulness and memory are natural too. And they would live in me still, and punish me if I did not obey them. . . . Our love would be poisoned.   (Book VI, Chapter 11)

In this conflict between feelings, Stephen's temptation creates in her 'a feeling that clashed with her truth, affection, and gratitude' (Book VI, Chapter 13). In the lower animals, the strongest feeling of the moment would triumph, but George Eliot believes human consciousness is quite different and rejects Stephen's argument from nature. Human consciousness is only partially animal; it has also been conditioned by social and cultural factors which enable it to know itself as a continuity. The need for human identity requires that certain strong impulses be resisted if they conflict with this sense of continuity. After the elopement Maggie experiences an identity crisis because her sense of continuity of self is threatened: 'she had rent the ties that had given meaning to duty, and had made herself an outlawed soul, with no guide but the wayward choice of her own passion . . . she must for ever sink and wander vaguely, driven by uncertain impulse (Book VI, Chapter 14).

She never deliberately consented to this; it was the product of circumstances. In her decision to reject Stephen at her Aunt Moss's, she had called on memory to find an authority in feeling itself to resist his view that natural love should have precedence over everything else. She repeats the same argument to him in Mudport when she decides to leave him: 'it would rend me away from all that my past life has made dear and holy to me. . . . I must go back to it, and cling to it, else I shall feel as if there were nothing firm beneath my feet' (Book VI, Chapter 14). Her decision is to be true to her sense of whole self, which is not merely the person she is at the moment, but the continuing self that has developed since childhood and with which memory keeps her in contact.

Nevertheless, an unpredictable turn of events and the strain of the conflict had led her to acquiesce passively in Stephen's plan. She feels guilty later because her resistance was not strong enough. This was because her sense of the past temporarily left her. In her dream-like drift down the river, 'Memory was excluded' (Book VI, Chapter 13). It is only memory which can keep her in touch with those other feelings which urge her to resist her natural passion. But it cannot be denied for long: she feels 'the terrible shadow of past thoughts' and when she recovers herself next day 'she was alone with her own memory and her own dread' (Book VI, Chapter 14). Her whole self could never have assented to this action.

Stephen's great offence has been to deprive her of a conscious choice, something she repeatedly accuses him of. Though he argues that 'We must accept our own actions and start afresh from them' (Book VI, Chapter 14), Maggie does not feel she has chosen to perform an action: 'I have caused sorrow already—I know—I feel it; but I have never deliberately consented to it. . . . It has never been my will to marry you: if you were to win consent from the momentary triumph of my feeling for you, you would not have my whole soul.' This emphasis on choice is important, for in George Eliot's view, a human being differs from the lower animals in being able to choose between his feelings. Stephen in urging the natural is not allowing a choice of the 'unnatural';

namely, a rejection of the most powerful impulses in favour of other considerations.[4] His view that one should obey the promptings of one's strongest natural feelings would offer the self no sense of continuity on the basis of which one could choose: 'We should have no law but the inclination of the moment.' Stephen's position is an egotistic Romantic one and would be shared by Mrs Transome, Don Silva, Deronda's mother, and Gwendolen Harlèth, but for George Eliot it reduces the human to the level of the animal. If memory and one's sense of the past do not act as an authority for feeling by which one can choose to be 'unnatural', to resist one's strongest impulses, then man is no more than an animal. But memory will not let Maggie forget that her past is in conflict with her impulses, and the need for continuity of being proves to be the stronger: 'There are memories, and affections, and longings after perfect goodness, that have such a strong hold on me; they would never quit me for long.' Maggie has not chosen to reject love for a mechanical form of duty or a passive obedience to past claims; she has chosen to be true to what she regards as her whole self.[5]

She is now most fully aware that memory can provide the basis of a moral authority which is built into feeling itself. It is not a rigid moral framework which demands the denial of feeling, like her previous renunciation. It embodies powerful feelings which are an integral part of her past life and which she can choose to be faithful to, and so exercise control over her strongest impulses and her rebellious tendencies. Memory puts her in touch with feelings which she regards as fundamental to her whole life. If she committed an act that contradicted these feelings she would experience a loss of personal identity, since she would be acting contrary to her deepest sense of self. To respond to Stephen's physical attraction would not only betray Lucy and Philip, it would be treachery 'to her own better soul' (Book VI, Chapter 10).

Like Romola, Maggie finds a moral orientation which does not require that she suppress feeling. By recognising that she must act in accordance with her whole self as experienced through her memory of past feelings and claims, she is able to exercise control over purely impulsive or passionate feelings. When a conflict of feeling arises, she has a basis in feeling itself for knowing how to choose. No authority external to the self is necessary. But this requires that she is able to renounce those feelings which may be the most powerful. Renunciation is a central theme in the novel and an idea basic to George Eliot's moral thought. It is her answer to Romantic extremists who advocated the free expression of strong feeling, which she thought would leave men at the mercy of impulse and offer no security of identity. A discipline on feeling is needed which does not result in its repression and so lead to dangerous psychological consequences, and this is provided by renunciation. For Maggie renunciation is especially important, for unlike Romola, Esther, or Dorothea, she has no ideal social vision available to her which she can serve and which can direct her energies.

In her early a Kempis period, renunciation was a form of indirect gratification in that she escaped from pain, frustration, and self-conflict. But she realises later that it 'remains sorrow, though a sorrow borne willingly' (Book IV, Chapter 3). Since the pain of renouncing her strongest impulses is fully accepted, repression is avoided. It is when she experiences her greatest temptation in receiving Stephen's letter that she accepts the full implications of renunciation. Reading it 'she felt as if her real temptation had only just begun' (Book VII, Chapter 5). In her situation at St Ogg's, condemned by almost everyone, urged by Dr Kenn to leave and so become 'like a lonely wanderer—cut off from the past' (Book VII, Chapter 2), and feeling 'unspeakably, sickeningly weary!' (Book VII, Chapter 5), the pressure on her is greater than ever. In addition to this, she has strong feelings of pity for Stephen and fears that her choice may have been a selfish one. It was the thought of causing him pain that had been an important factor in undermining her resistance to him when they were on the boat: 'This yielding to the idea of Stephen's suffering was more fatal than the other yielding, because it was less distinguishable from that sense of others' claims which was the moral basis of her resistance' (Book VI, Chapter 13). But Stephen's letter forces her to face this problem again.

One of the reasons she had given for leaving him was that she could not accept personal happiness if it meant 'sacrificing' others. Since she now seems to be sacrificing Stephen, she feels confused. His letter is her most serious temptation since it seems to show up a contradiction in her position. But she had earlier realised that this problem could be solved only by making a choice which took into account her sense of whole self, 'being true to all the motives that sanctify our lives' (Book VI, Chapter 14). In her present situation she must inflict suffering on someone, no matter what she does. It is no solution to let the needs of others shape her action, and these can never be fully known in any case. But equally, to submit to 'the wayward choice of her own passion' would leave her at the mercy of 'uncertain impulse'. Her only course of action must be to make a choice which is true to her sense of self as continuity. The role of memory in her decision illustrates this. When she is tempted to give way to Stephen, 'the sense of contradiction with her past life in her moments of strength and clearness, came upon her like a pang of conscious degradation' (Book VII, Chapter 5). She waits for guidance from her feelings to help her decide, and again memory is primary: 'It came with the memories that no passion could long quench; the long past came back to her, and with it the fountains of self-renouncing pity and affection, of faithfulness and resolve.' She remembers the words of *The Imitation of Christ*, but this time she fully appreciates what renunciation involves.

This part of the novel has, however, been widely criticised, and two objections in particular need to be answered. One is that Maggie's rejection of Stephen leads to no positive solution to the problem she is faced with, since not only does she lose the man she loves but her renunciation does nothing to benefit Philip or Lucy, for marriage to them without love is now surely out of the question for both her and Stephen. It is only Maggie's death that offers any possibility of a way out, and if she had not been killed in the flood what kind of life could she have led? The other objection is that her death is not a tragic one, since it is the result of mere chance and is essentially unconnected with her flight with Stephen.[6] For such reasons many have seen Maggie's death as an inadequate solution to problems George Eliot found intractable. But in my view these objections can be overcome if one realises that the tragic nature of Maggie's life is revealed both by the decision she takes to renounce Stephen and by her death in attempting to rescue Tom. These are related events.

She says to Stephen in Mudport: 'If I could wake back again into the time before yesterday, I would choose to be true to my calmer affections, and live without the joy of love' (Book VI, Chapter 14). To make the decision to renounce her love, even when the pressure of circumstances urges her to marry Stephen since it now seems the only practical solution, gives further emphasis to the tragic choice she is prepared to make. That

George Eliot saw Maggie's choice as a tragic one is suggested by her 'Notes on the Spanish Gypsy and Tragedy in General', in which she makes the following comment on the renunciation of love:

> With regard to the supremacy of Love; if it were a fact without exception that man or woman never did renounce the joys of love, there could never have sprung up a notion that such renunciation could present itself as a duty. . . . Will any one say that faithfulness to the marriage tie has never been regarded as a duty, in spite of the presence of the profoundest passion experienced after marriage? Is Guinevere's conduct the type of duty?[7]

Maggie's life is deeply tragic, and this involves more than just her death during the flood. She has been presented throughout as a girl of the strongest passions with a profound need for love, but when she experiences the greatest intensity of love it conflicts with other claims and duties which she also feels strongly are part of her self. She therefore makes the tragic choice to renounce love and to face a life that seems to offer her no hope of happiness, in order to be true to the values she identifies with her sense of whole self.

The connection between Maggie's renunciation of Stephen and her death attempting to rescue Tom is that both present a conflict between a human value or ideal and forces resistant to it. In renouncing her love for Stephen, Maggie resisted the strongest natural passion in favour of feelings and duties she regarded as intrinsic to her whole self. Similarly, in her attempted rescue, her love for Tom is in conflict with the resistant otherness of nature, external nature this time. Her love for Tom is, of course, an integral part of her sense of whole self. George Eliot intends, I think, a parallel to be drawn between Maggie's impulsive natural feelings, compared at one point to a lava stream, and the violence of the overflowing river. Both aspects of nature, the inner and the outer, represent a threat to the human world. In each case Maggie chooses to resist nature, sacrificing the joy of love in the first instance and her life in the second.[8] On both occasions she proves herself worthy to be a tragic heroine.

Though Maggie is killed in her attempted rescue, her action and the sense of transcendence she achieves in the process of undertaking it make her comparable to the patron saint of St Ogg's, as the religious language used to describe her suggests: 'In the first moments Maggie felt nothing, thought of nothing, but that she had suddenly passed away from that life which she had been dreading: it was the transition of death, without its agony—and she was alone in the darkness with God' (Book VII, Chapter 5). She has attained a sense of spiritual presence which raises her above the fears of ordinary mortals, and she performs an act which resembles that of the legendary St Ogg. It is significant that her strong impulse to try to rescue her mother and Tom stems from her sense of whole self: 'Her whole soul was strained now on that thought; and she saw the long-loved faces looking for help into the darkness, and finding none.' In contrast also to her previous drift down river, this time she is rowing against the current. Though Maggie is destroyed by a world without moral order, her action possesses a human meaning which lives on, recreating the meaning of the town's central myth, and showing that though the legend had no outward truth, it contained an inner human truth to which Maggie gives new expression.

7 *Middlemarch* I

I

In this chapter and the next I shall try to show the relation of *Middlemarch*, generally considered George Eliot's greatest work, to the central problems and issues I have discussed in previous chapters. *Middlemarch* shows, I believe, George Eliot as a later Romantic thinking about these problems and issues in a particularly subtle and interesting way. There is no change in point of view: the egotism and social alienation associated with the Romantics are again attacked, and the need for Romantic energies to be socially directed is asserted, but her treatment is generally more complex than in her previous fiction, and weaknesses in dramatic presentation which were apparent in *Romola* and *Felix Holt* are to a considerable degree overcome.

Middlemarch is also a much more ambitious work than anything George Eliot had attempted previously. It reflects to a greater extent than any of her other novels the wide range of her intellectual interests, in sociology, psychology, philosophy, science, religion and art, to name only the most obvious, and it is arguable that no other nineteenth-century novel can compete with it in terms of the breadth and complexity of the intellectual issues with which it deals. Some of these issues require a more abstract treatment and for this reason I am devoting two chapters to *Middlemarch*. In the next chapter I shall discuss some of the philosophical problems the novel is concerned with in a more direct way, especially as they relate to perceptual and epistemological matters. But it is one of the great artistic merits of *Middlemarch* that its interest in a wide range of intellectual issues does not diminish the quality of its human and social presentation, since George Eliot is largely successful in integrating the intellectual and philosophical aspects of the novel with the human and social. In this first chapter I shall try to show this by concentrating on the role of the main characters in the structure of the novel.

In *Middlemarch*, George Eliot is concerned with the same fundamental problems in her study of character, as regards both individual psychology and human and social relationships, as she is in her other novels, but her characters are placed in a much more intricate and dominant environment and involved in a more complex social life than the characters in her other fiction. This leads to important changes in her treatment of character with regard to some of the concerns I have discussed in earlier chapters, such as egotism, feeling, and sublimation. With society being more at the centre of the novel and dominating character, such problems as the moral dangers of Romantic egotism or the conflict between strong impulse and the need for a sense of continuity of self, are treated more in a social context with less detailed concentration on individual psychology.

Despite the greater prominence of society in *Middlemarch*, which results in less emphasis being given to the individual problems of the main characters, at least in comparison with earlier novels such as *The Mill on the Floss* or *Romola* and her later novel, *Daniel Deronda*, there are important continuities between the characters in *Middlemarch* and those in her other novels, and their Romantic connections are equally clear. The most obvious similarity is between Dorothea Brooke and George Eliot's previous heroines. Dorothea possesses the same strength of feeling and potentially dangerous egotistic energies as Maggie Tulliver, Romola and Esther Lyon. Her Romantic affinities are suggested by the frequent use of the word 'ardour' in connection with her. This suggests the kind of idealistic enthusiasm associated with a figure like Shelley. She is seen in a Romantic light by Ladislaw, who thinks of the Aeolean harp, a key Romantic image,[1] when he first meets her and again in Rome, and Naumann, a Romantic painter, sees her as 'a sort of Christian Antigone—sensuous force controlled by spiritual passion' (Chapter 19), a juxtaposition which again calls to mind Shelley. It seems clear that George Eliot intends Dorothea's ardent nature to be seen as Romantic.

The prime characteristic of Romantic feeling is that it operates as a means of spontaneous knowledge, prior to rational thought, and I quoted earlier the important passage in which she tells Ladislaw that, for her, knowledge passes directly into feeling. Feeling and thought are inseparable for her, and it is natural for her to respond to experience with a unified consciousness: 'But in

Dorothea's mind there was a current into which all thought and feeling were apt sooner or later to flow—the reaching forward of the whole consciousness towards the fullest truth, the least partial good' (Chapter 20). The word 'current', which is used several times in connection with her, suggests, like 'ardour', a Romantic sensibility.

But while the main problem for Maggie and Romola is that their strong feelings make them vulnerable to impulsive acts which contradict their past lives and past selves, Dorothea is at first faced with a different danger. Her most serious temptation is that form of idealism which longs for belief in an external order and meaning which one can serve with complete devotion because one believes utterly in its truth and value. Though Dorothea possesses such strong feelings, she at first distrusts what they tell her. She desires a form of knowledge and sense of truth which will be superior to subjective feeling. This is why she is so upset when Casaubon regards her only as a creature of feeling: 'She was humiliated to find herself a mere victim of feeling, as if she could know nothing except through that medium' (Chapter 20). She fears that what her feelings communicate to her may be wrong, and believes she needs a standpoint based on objective knowledge:

> Those provinces of masculine knowledge seemed to her a standing-ground from which all truth could be seen more truly. As it was, she constantly doubted her own conclusions, because she felt her own ignorance: how could she be confident that one-roomed cottages were not for the glory of God, when men who knew the classics appeared to conciliate indifference to the cottages with zeal for the glory?   (Chapter 7)

Though this passage satirises her belief that knowledge is required to support feeling over the cottages, this does not solve the problem created by the over-subjective and unstable nature of feeling on its own. As I have previously argued, one of George Eliot's main concerns in her studies of Maggie Tulliver and Romola was how impulsive and egotistic feelings could be controlled without accepting some moral frame external to feeling. Dorothea believes religion combined with knowledge will provide a sense of moral direction for the self which will be independent of subjective feeling.

Her desire to devote herself utterly to the service of a religious ideal is repeatedly stressed: 'Her mind was theoretic, and yearned by its nature after some lofty conception of the world which might frankly include the parish of Tipton and her own rule of conduct there' (Chapter 1). The use of the word 'theoretic' to characterise her idealism suggests a link with Savonarola in *Romola* who views the world with 'the eyes of theoretic conviction' (Chapter 61). Both passionately yearn for a total religious explanation of reality. Dorothea longs 'for a binding theory which could bring her own life and doctrine into strict connection with that amazing past, and give the remotest sources of knowledge some bearing on her actions' (Chapter 10). This longing is not wrong in itself, but the form in which she hopes for its realisation is untenable. Guildenstern in 'A College Breakfast-Party' believed in the possibility of creating a 'binding law' on purely human grounds, and Mordecai in *Daniel Deronda* thinks the idea of national identity can provide 'a binding theory' for mankind. But Dorothea in her early idealistic stage desires a theory which will prove that there is a religious meaning in reality itself, and that knowledge will reveal this.

It is this religious longing that lies at the root of her attraction to Casaubon. It is his intellectual aim to provide the 'lofty conception of the world' and 'binding theory' which would create the basis for a unified Christian world-view similar to that which existed in the time of St Theresa, and which Dorothea could serve with certainty because knowledge had been used to establish in unquestionable terms the truth of Christianity. He says of himself: 'My mind is something like the ghost of an ancient, wandering about the world and trying mentally to construct it as it used to be, in spite of ruin and confusing changes' (Chapter 2). This grandiose aim immediately appeals to Dorothea's Christian idealism: 'To reconstruct a past world, doubtless with a view to the highest purposes of truth—what a work to be in any way present at, to assist in, though only as a lamp-holder!' The theoretic side of her nature seeks an explanation of the world which will reveal the existence of a religious meaning and order external to the mind, and which would in consequence provide an absolutely firm basis for moral and social values. In other words, she sets her hopes on the establishment of a pre-Romantic world-view, as her Enlightenment faith in knowledge indicates: 'something she yearned for by which her life might be filled with action at once rational and ardent; and since the time was gone by for guiding visions and spiritual directors, since prayer heightened yearning but not instruction, what lamp was there but knowledge?' (Chapter 10).

It is natural then that she should be attracted to Casaubon. The aim of his 'Key to All Mythologies' is to counteract the fragmentation of man's knowledge and to provide the foundation for 'the coherent social faith and order' which a new St Theresa would require to give direction and purpose to her life. He will accomplish this by revealing that all mythologies are really only transformations or corruptions of the events in the Bible, which embodied religious truth: 'all the mythical systems or erratic mythical fragments in the world were corruptions of a tradition originally revealed. Having once mastered the true position and taken a firm footing there, the vast field of mythical constructions became intelligible, nay, luminous with the reflected light of correspondences' (Chapter 3). It is not, I think, over-ingenious to see a parallel between the image of light arranging mythologies in a meaningful pattern and the image, at the beginning of Chapter 27, of the candle giving the appearance of pattern to scratches on a pier-glass which are in reality unpatterned. Casaubon's aim makes him for Dorothea 'a living Bossuet, whose work would reconcile complete knowledge with devoted piety; here was a modern Augustine who united the glories of doctor and saint' (Chapter 3). Here again we see Dorothea interpreting Casaubon in pre-Romantic terms as someone who could use knowledge to establish the existence of a spiritual order in the world which could be the beginning of a new age of faith.

In the above account of Dorothea's relationship with Casaubon I have concentrated on the role of these characters in the philosophical structure of the novel. But one of the artistic achievements of *Middlemarch* is that to a very great extent the philosophical and human aspects are integrated. One does not feel, as one does with *Romola*, for example, that the human side of the novel is only a vehicle for the ideas and problems with which George Eliot is mainly concerned. There are many factors that must be taken into account in understanding why Dorothea chooses to marry Casaubon. She is an orphan who has never known a father's influence and therefore is drawn to Casaubon as a kind of father figure. She also wishes to play a more active role in the world than a conventional marriage would normally offer a woman. Marriage to Casaubon, she thinks, would give her the opportunity to do something significant by helping him with his work, and thus it could provide a partial escape from the social limitations placed on women. A conventional marriage to someone like Sir James Chettam has no attraction for her, and it is implied that she is afraid of her own sexuality. Casaubon proposes on a day during which she has suffered several minor frustrations, and this also has some influence on her decision to accept him. But these motivations are not sufficient in themselves to account for her attraction to Casaubon and her determination to marry him. They must be seen together with her idealistic longing for a complete religious explanation of the world and with the fact that it is Casaubon's aim to create the foundation for this. If Casaubon's work had no relation to her idealism, it would be hard to accept her determined resolution to marry him. To understand more fully her relationship with him and the consequences of her disillusionment, it will be useful to look in more detail at the nature of his work.

The title of Casaubon's great work of reconstruction, 'Key to All Mythologies', is very suggestive. In the nineteenth century, there was an unprecedented increase in knowledge which led to its becoming more and more fragmented. There were numerous attempts to create systems which endeavoured to discover a meaningful order underlying the apparent diversity and fragmentation which had resulted from this expansion of knowledge. Without any such synthesis, established moral and social values seemed threatened. The attempt by George Eliot's friend, Herbert Spencer, to construct a synthesis was probably the most ambitious of these nineteenth-century systems, and he saw his most important concern as providing the fundamentals of a world-view which could perform a function similar to that of religion in the past. Casaubon is compared to numerous past figures who had been able to construct systems which seemed to reconcile knowledge and faith. The most important comparison is with the greatest creator of a synthesis, Thomas Aquinas. He poses as Aquinas for the painter Naumann, he defends him when Brooke says nobody reads him any more, and Mrs Cadwallader refers to him openly as Thomas Aquinas.

It was virtually impossible however, in the nineteenth century to create a synthesis of faith and knowledge on a similar scale to that of Aquinas,[2] because of the scale and diversity of knowledge.

Casaubon can only attempt to show that in one particular field, the study of myth, there is a unity underlying the apparent diversity. All mythologies are structurally related by reason of being descended from the historically true events in the Bible.[3] He thus regards all mythic systems as codes which can be interpreted by one universal key, and since this key is supplied by Christianity, he will effect a reconciliation between knowledge and faith if he can prove his theory. The fragmentation of our knowledge of the world is only apparent; there is a deeper order underlying it, a Christian order. This is the belief on which his work is founded. It is tempting to believe that the word 'Mythologies' has symbolic connotations in the novel; that it refers not merely to myths in the ordinary meaning of the word, but to any field of knowledge which tries to order, in a systematic way, our understanding of reality, in the sense that religions, philosophical systems, psychoanalysis, even science, have been said to be mythologies.

I have already argued that George Eliot should be seen as an advanced Romantic who rejects the pre-Romantic view that reality possesses a meaningful order and structure which exists independently of the mind, the view that, as Sir Isaiah Berlin puts it, 'there existed a reality, a structure of things, a *rerum natura*, which the qualified inquirer could see, study and, in principle, get right'.[4] For her, it was no longer possible to believe that there was an immanent order in the world identical in structure with human thought. Probably she believed that the key to all mythologies, if it existed, was to be found not by trying to find a coherent structure underlying the diversity of knowledge but by investigating the mind itself. The key that would unlock all mythologies and systems was to be discovered in psychology. This is implicit in the philosophies of Feuerbach and Lewes. Even if Casaubon had succeeded in finishing his 'Key to All Mythologies', he would only have created a closed system, incapable of being either proved or disproved, and so able to appeal only to the converted. This seems to be the point of the narrator's comment that his theory was based on 'a method of interpretation which was not tested by the necessity of forming anything which had sharper collisions than an elaborate notion of Gog and Magog: it was as free from interruption as a plan for threading the stars together' (Chapter 48).[5] George Eliot is perhaps suggesting that such a theory could never establish the objective truth of Christianity, and indeed that religion cannot be proved in scientific terms. Dorothea's hope that knowledge could reveal the existence of a religious order in the world, which everyone would have to recognise and accept, is misconceived, and she eventually realises this.

Her disillusionment with Casaubon and his work leads to a reluctant acceptance that the world lacks an immanent order which knowledge would discover and which would support Christian values. Her religious idealism seemed to her to justify moral action in the world, to create the foundation for a larger social faith, and to give her own life direction and purpose. Its breakdown, then, is a crisis in her life. She must come to terms with the failure of her pre-Romantic belief in a coherent order in the world, which revealed the existence of divine purpose. It is her experience in Rome which does most to make her aware of a disorder in the world that cannot be reconciled with her narrow religious principles. There she discovers a complexity and sense of the contradictory in her experience which shatters the excess of order in her religious theories about the world, and causes severe disorientation:

> the gigantic broken revelations of that Imperial and Papal city thrust abruptly on the notions of a girl who had been brought up in English and Swiss Puritanism, fed on meagre Protestant histories and on art chiefly of the hand-screen sort; a girl whose ardent nature turned all her small allowance of knowledge into principles, fusing her actions into their mould, and whose quick emotions gave the most abstract things the quality of a pleasure or a pain.   (Chapter 20)

The ideas with which she has been used to order experience cannot cope with 'The weight of unintelligible Rome' in which grandeur and squalor, religion and superstition, seem inextricably mixed: 'all this vast wreck of ambitious ideals, sensuous and spiritual, mixed confusedly with the signs of breathing forgetfulness and degradation, at first jarred her as with an electric shock, and then urged themselves on her with that ache belonging to a glut of confused ideas which check the flow of emotion'. The narrow principles that had supported her identity 'are tumbled out among incongruities' and she is faced with a disorder in her experience of the world that conflicts with her religious ideals.

It is implied that personal disenchantment with Casaubon is in part responsible for creating the frame of mind which makes her respond to Rome in this way, for George Eliot again brings together the philosophical and the human significance of Dorothea's experience. After discovering that the reality of marriage bears little resemblance to what she had expected, she 'found herself plunged into tumultuous preoccupation with her personal lot'. It is tempting to believe that George Eliot intends to suggest that Dorothea's experience of his physical impotence leads to an awareness of his intellectual impotence, though strictly speaking such an interpretation has to be read into the text. However, the crisis she suffers in Rome produces a state of mind in which she can see Casaubon's work critically instead of, as formerly, in the light of her religious hopes. Her loss of faith in him and his work undermines further her religious world-view; if her belief in him could have been sustained and he had been one of the wisest of men, 'In that case her tottering faith would have become firm again' (Chapter 22). But she eventually realises that the fragments he is trying to put together disintegrate again in his hands and can only support 'a theory which was already withered in the bud like an elfin child' (Chapter 48). She finally accepts that he will never be able to create a synthesis which will reconcile faith and knowledge, and it is implied that she believes it is impossible; after his death his notebooks resemble 'the mute memorial of a forgotten faith', and she must reject his request that she carry on his work: it would be 'working hopelessly at what I have no belief in' (Chapter 54).

Though it is not stated openly that she has lost her religious faith, these passages suggest that her belief that knowledge would reveal the presence of a Christian order in the world has gone. She does, however, preserve a religious world-view, even though she says she hardly ever prays. The following declaration she makes to Ladislaw suggests that she becomes a transcendentalist: 'That by desiring what is perfectly good, even when we don't quite know what it is and cannot do what we would; we are part of the divine power against evil—widening the skirts of light and making the struggle with darkness narrower' (Chapter 39). But her main problem now is how to confront life without the 'binding theory' she had hoped for. This creates for her the difficulty, faced also by George Eliot's previous heroines, of supporting her sense of identity solely from her inner resources, without succumbing to

negative egotistic forces in herself or to impulsive feeling. There
are two important occasions in which the strongly egotistic side of
her nature threatens to gain control: when she is nearly overcome
by an impulse of the moment and when she almost lapses into
selfish despair.

The first of these occurs after Casaubon has snubbed her,
having learned from Lydgate that he might not live long. All
through her married life with Casaubon, Dorothea has restrained
the strong feeling which is natural to her, and such feeling
becomes transformed into egotistic revolt against her lot: 'She
was in the reaction of a rebellious anger stronger than any she had
felt since her marriage' (Chapter 42). Impulsive, resentful feeling
threatens to overcome her more stable, sympathetic emotions.
She wants to tell Casaubon 'the truth about her feeling' and to
hurt him. But gradually she becomes aware of the danger of
allowing 'her resentment to govern her', and that such feeling is
false to her more persistent sense of self. She has to struggle hard
to find an alternative feeling which is truer to her sense of whole
self and not the expression of pent-up resentment: 'But the
struggle changed continually, as that of a man who begins with a
movement towards striking and ends with conquering his desire
to strike. The energy that would animate a crime is not more than
is wanted to inspire a resolved submission, when the noble habit
of the soul reasserts itself.' Despite the loss of her religious
idealism, in a moment of crisis in which she can rely only on her
own resources, she is able to overcome a strong impulse. Her
sympathy with how Casaubon must feel on learning that he might
not have long to live and her own sense of continuity of self allow
her to overcome a crisis, even though she is no longer supported
by an external framework of Christian belief.

Her second serious crisis takes place when she sees Rosamond
and Ladislaw together, believes that they are lovers, and that she
has lost all hope of personal happiness through love. Like
Romola when she has been forced to give up all affectionate
feeling for Tito and lost her faith in Savonarola, Dorothea feels a
sense of despair. While for Romola it had been Savonarola and
religion which had provided her with greatest support after her
original disillusionment with Tito, with Dorothea this process is
reversed; it is her relationship with Ladislaw, which has developed
into love, that has sustained her after the breakdown of her
Christian idealism. In each case disappointment leads to despair,

but as with Romola, Dorothea overcomes this and finds through feeling the means of reconstituting her life. She must come to terms with the fact that the world is indifferent to her own hopes and desires, just as she has had to accept already that reality does not conform to the structure of her Christian ideals. But the underlying feelings which were the real basis of her former Christian idealism are still valid, though she must not expect the world to conform with human ideals or take account of human hopes and desires. Her idealistic feelings remain valuable even if they must be projected onto an indifferent, unstructured world. This realisation comes to her when she recovers, after a night of conflict, the original sympathetic feelings which motivated her in the first place to visit Rosamond. These have not been shown to be false, despite what she thought she saw at Lydgate's house, and in her new self-knowledge she can use them to overcome the egotistic feelings of anger, resentment, and despair aroused by the disappointment of her hopes and expectations:

> But that base prompting which makes a woman more cruel to a rival than to a faithless lover, could have no strength of recurrence in Dorothea when the dominant spirit of justice within her had once overcome the tumult and had once shown her the truer measure of things. All the active·thought with which she had before been representing to herself the trials of Lydgate's lot, and this young marriage union which, like her own, seemed to have its hidden as well as evident troubles—all this vivid sympathetic experience returned to her now as a power: it asserted itself as acquired knowledge asserts itself and will not let us see as we saw in the day of our ignorance.
>
> (Chapter 80)

Sympathetic feeling, with its basis in the human and social aspect of the self, triumphs over animal egotism and becomes her source of knowledge.

Even though she can no longer accept that there is religious meaning immanent in the world, and believes, mistakenly as it turns out, that events have frustrated her own hopes of happiness, this sympathetic feeling remains to give her life moral direction and to discipline egotistic impulse. It can be the foundation of an ideal value which can 'rule her errant will' and shape human action in the world. Dorothea also resembles Romola in that this inner moral feeling leads to a larger, more social vision when she opens the curtains of her room and looks out at the world beyond her own ego: 'Far off in the bending sky was the pearly light; and she felt the largeness of the world and the manifold wakings of men to labour and endurance.' During her Christian phase she had hoped that knowledge would reveal religious meaning in external reality, but now she discovers that though there may be no such meaning objectively in the world, it is present in her intense human feeling and vision. Her earlier Christian beliefs and idealism were the projection into objective form of this feeling, and despite the breakdown of her projection, the underlying feeling remains valid. She can go on to create a new orientation which supports her sense of identity and directs her life.

However, in the social world of *Middlemarch*, there is little that Dorothea can do to exert any great influence on her society. Despite her strength of feeling and idealistic temperament, she is restricted to the role of wife and mother and giving 'wifely help' (Finale) to her husband. And though the people who know her realise that this does not fulfil her potential, 'no one stated exactly what else that was in her power she ought rather to have done'. George Eliot's previous heroines also have to accept a restricted life that offers only a limited scope for their energies, but the domination of the individual by society is much more powerfully presented in *Middlemarch*. A tragic note is also present in the 'Finale' which repeats the comparison between Dorothea and St Theresa. This stresses the heroic potential of Dorothea which is unable to be realised because she is unfortunate enough to live 'amidst the conditions of an imperfect social state'. She has to be content with having an 'incalculably diffusive' influence on those closest to her.

II

The relationship between Dorothea and Ladislaw has been generally regarded as one of the artistic weaknesses of *Middlemarch*, primarily on the grounds that Ladislaw is too idealised or too lightweight to be worthy of Dorothea. It is probable that Ladislaw had to perform too many functions in the plot for George Eliot to succeed fully in creating both a complex psychological portrait and a character who plays an important part in the novel's philosophical structure. But he seems to me to be much more central to the novel and more successfully characterised than most previous critics have tended to think. His importance is closely connected with the novel's Romantic concerns. He is the character most obviously associated with the Romantics. For example, he has been educated at Heidelberg, one of the most important centres of German Romanticism; he is twice compared to Shelley by Mr Brooke: 'he has the same sort of enthusiasm for liberty, freedom, emancipation' (Chapter 37); and he is described by Mrs Cadwallader as 'A sort of Byronic hero' (Chapter 38). His flamboyant appearance, his experiments with opium and his general attitudes all contribute to building up a picture of a Romantic, and this seems clearly to be George Eliot's intention.

But it is the development of Ladislaw as a Romantic that is important. At the beginning of the novel he is attracted towards the egotistic side of Romanticism. He sees himself as 'Pegasus' and he regards 'every form of prescribed work' as 'harness' (Chapter 9). The words 'pride', 'defiance', and 'rebellion', all of which have a Byronic connotation, are frequently associated with him. He tells Dorothea proudly that he comes 'of rebellious blood on both sides' (Chapter 37). Casaubon's opinion of him is 'that he was capable of any design which could fascinate a rebellious temper and an undisciplined impulsiveness' (Chapter 42). He is also Byronic in being an outsider and an alien, a role he takes some pleasure in: 'he was a sort of gypsy, rather enjoying the sense of belonging to no class; he had a feeling of romance in his position, and a pleasant consciousness of creating a little surprise wherever he went' (Chapter 46). He feels little connection with any country or social group, nor at the beginning of the novel does he wish to have any. He is a rootless wanderer, associated with gypsies and Jews.

In the dominating social world of *Middlemarch*, however, Ladislaw's rebellious and egotistic tendencies present little threat to society. The common criticism that Ladislaw is an insubstantial character perhaps does not take sufficient account of the fact that in the world of the novel the Romantic rebel is inevitably a lightweight figure. His egotistic rebellion expresses itself only in aestheticism and dilettantism. When Dorothea asks him what his religion is, he replies: 'To love what is good and beautiful when I see it. . . . But I am a rebel: I don't feel bound, as you do, to submit to what I don't like' (Chapter 39). Naumann believes he is incapable of devoting his attention to any one subject: 'His walk must be *belles-lettres*. That is wi–ide' (Chapter 22), and Casaubon considers him to be 'a man with no other principle than transient caprice' (Chapter 42). But his aestheticism and dilettantism are sufficient to alienate him from society or from any chosen vocation. Without the influence of Dorothea on his life, it seems certain that he would have remained a rootless aesthete.

The change that takes place in Ladislaw is an important element in the novel's structure. Dorothea's influence encourages him to direct his Romantic energies into social channels. He had previously believed that genius was 'intolerant of fetters' (Chapter 10), but his feeling for Dorothea makes him accept the 'harness' he had formerly rejected, 'having settled in Middlemarch and harnessed himself with Mr Brooke' (Chapter 47). The same image is present in the following passage: 'Ladislaw had now accepted his bit of work, though it was not that indeterminate loftiest thing which he had once dreamed of as alone worthy of continuous effort. His nature warmed easily in the presence of subjects which were visibly mixed with life and action, and the easily stirred rebellion in him helped the glow of public spirit' (Chapter 46). The last part of this passage shows how his former rebellious energy is being socially directed. He no longer cuts himself off from society but devotes energies, once taken up by the study of art as a form of escape from society, to working for the social good: 'he studied the political situation with as ardent an interest as he had ever given to poetic metres or mediaevalism'. Dorothea has made him feel that Romantic ardour must be given a social expression. His transformation is shown in Dorothea's conversation with him when he is on the point of leaving Middlemarch: 'And you care that justice should be done to every one. I am so glad. When we were in Rome, I thought you only cared for poetry and art, and the things that adorn life for us who are well off. But now I know you think about the rest of the world' (Chapter 54). Significantly by the end of the novel this former Romantic rebel has become 'an ardent public man' (Finale).

Dorothea's ardent desire to do some good in the world and her implied criticism of Ladislaw's attitudes are the most important factors in making him give up his rootless existence and involve himself in society. Her idealistic conception of him becomes part of his sense of self, and the need to earn her respect brings out tendencies in himself that might otherwise have been overwhelmed by his attraction to egotistic Romantic attitudes: 'that simplicity of hers, holding up an ideal for others in her believing conception of them, was one of the great powers of her womanhood. And it had from the first acted strongly on Will Ladislaw . . . he felt that in her mind he had found his highest estimate' (Chapter 77).

Though Ladislaw has a rebellious and impulsive temperament, he is similar to Dorothea in his ardent feeling. The words 'ardent' and 'ardour' are used several times in connection with him, suggesting his kinship with her. It is this quality that makes him able to respond to her idealistic nature. Even when he gives way to rebellious impulse, egotistic energy and moral feeling are combined, since he is conscious of his whole self. This is seen in his response to Bulstrode's offer of money: 'He was too strongly possessed with passionate rebellion against this inherited blot which had been thrust on his knowledge to reflect at present whether he had not been too hard on Bulstrode' (Chapter 61). His feeling immediately rebels against forming any connection that could taint his character, both in his own eyes and in those of Dorothea. The fact that he is poor and she a rich widow makes any relationship between them difficult, which could make the prospect of a share in Bulstrode's wealth tempting, but he has no hesitation in rejecting money from such a source. This parallels Mary Garth's refusal to take money from Featherstone to burn his will, and contrasts with Lydgate's eager acceptance of Bulstrode's money without thinking of anything but his own financial difficulties. For Ladislaw, Dorothea's good opinion of him has become a central part of his idea of himself, as the Bulstrode incident shows: 'And in the rush of impulses by which he flung back that offer of Bulstrode's, there was mingled the sense that it would have been impossible for him ever to tell Dorothea that he had accepted it.'

The influence of women on men is a significant theme in several of George Eliot's novels. Its importance is emphasised in *Middlemarch* by its restatement in the relationship between Mary Garth and Fred Vincy. Like Ladislaw, Fred is at first drawn to socially irresponsible attitudes and actions, but the influence Mary exerts on his consciousness prevents him from giving way to the drive for self-gratification. With her encouragement he eventually, like Ladislaw, involves himself responsibly in society and gives up most of his vices. Both Ladislaw and Fred Vincy possess some good qualities, but George Eliot is perhaps suggesting that without the support of the women in their lives, their negative egotistic tendencies would have been predominant. Thus even if women are considerably restricted in the active roles they can play in their society, it is possible for them to use their power of idealistic feeling to influence men to devote their energies to the social good.

But though Ladislaw is able to play an active role in society and directs his energies in a socially responsible way, society is as little affected by this as it was by his period of rebellion and social alienation. The 'Finale' suggests that, like Dorothea, he is subject to the limitations that result from living in 'an imperfect social state'. Though he devotes himself energetically to trying to reform his society, this seems to lead to no obvious benefit: 'working well in those times when reforms were begun with a young hopefulness of immediate good which has been much checked in our days'.

It might be objected that despite Ladislaw's importance in the novel's philosophical structure, he is still an artistic failure. But in my view those who have criticised Ladislaw's characterisation have not sufficiently recognised that in *Middlemarch* George Eliot has made considerable progress in the dramatic presentation of what I have called sublimated egotism. In her previous novels, her positive characters often appeared to be idealised and one-dimensional in comparison with her negative egotists. In *Middlemarch* this artistic weakness is to a great extent overcome, particularly in the characterisation of Dorothea and Mary Garth. But even Ladislaw, though less convincing than Dorothea or Mary, is not the idealised figure many critics have seen him as being. Even after Dorothea's reforming influence on him, he remains strongly egotistic, and this is not merely stated but presented in dramatic terms. We see, for example, in a convincing and psychologically credible scene, how he succumbs to the egotistic temptation of going to church in Lowick to see Dorothea, realises his 'wretched blunder' when Casaubon and Dorothea enter, and feels 'utterly ridiculous, out of temper, and miserable' in the 'cage' he has created for himself (Chapter 47). We also see how his egotism shapes his interpretation of his relationship with Dorothea in their difficult meetings after

Casaubon's death, and his vulnerability to a strong impulse of the moment in his cruel treatment of Rosamond when Dorothea surprises them together, an experience which makes him realise later that he is in danger of drifting into an affair with Rosamond and that he might not be capable of resisting this. To see Ladislaw as merely an idealisation of the Romantic, as 'sentimental because he lacks the adult energies that would make his freedom problematic',[6] is to overlook George Eliot's dramatic presentation of the tension between the egotistic and the idealistic sides of his character, even if this tension is not consistently maintained.

Lydgate's Romantic connections are less obvious than those of Dorothea and Ladislaw. This is partly because he is more integrated into society than they are, as he is a doctor who is economically dependent on it, and partly because he seems to have committed himself to work for social improvement. Yet there are, I think, clear links between him and the Romantic egotist; at times, indeed, these links are too apparent and jar a little with his presentation in social terms. Though Lydgate appears to have chosen a profession dedicated to serving the needs of society, the egotistic force of his character is nevertheless predominant. His real motive is to achieve a position of power in society by overcoming resistant forces through the strength of his own will. He bears some resemblances to Harold Transome in *Felix Holt*, who also appears to be working for the good of society while in reality desiring to play a masterful role which would gratify ego and will. In the scientific research which he regards as the most important aspect of his work, his quest for 'the primitive tissue' (Chapter 15) is motivated by his desire for heroic self-realisation rather than by social idealism. This distinguishes him from Dorothea and, ultimately, Ladislaw.

Lydgate's connection with Romantic egotism is also shown by the Byronic quality of the language used to describe him: 'About his ordinary bearing there was a certain fling, a fearless expectation of success, a confidence in his own powers and integrity much fortified by contempt for petty obstacles or seductions of which he had had no experience' (Chapter 13). His pride is repeatedly emphasised, and his conceit is 'massive in its claims and benevolently contemptuous. He would do a great deal for noodles, being sorry for them, and feeling quite sure they could have no power over him' (Chapter 15). Rebellion and defiance are

important aspects of his personality. He reacts to the circumstances that are gradually overcoming his will 'with a renewed
outburst of rebellion against the oppression of his lot' (Chapter
73), and he refuses to desert Bulstrode though he risks being
implicated in his disgrace: 'It belonged to the generosity as well as
defiant force of his nature that he resolved not to shrink from
showing to the full his sense of obligation to Bulstrode . . . (for,
remember, he was one of the proudest among the sons of men).'
When he is slowly being crushed, imagery of being yoked, galled
and fettered is often used, calling to mind a Promethean figure in
chains.

As well as possessing several characteristics associated with
Romantic egotism, Lydgate significantly lacks one quality which
Ladislaw and especially Dorothea have as part of their natures:
ardent feeling. He does possess 'intellectual ardour' but this is
accompanied by 'vulgarity of feeling' (Chapter 15). It is this which
is mainly responsible for his total failure. Though in a sense
Dorothea also fails, in that her earlier aspirations have to be
greatly reduced in scale, she does play some part in the effort to
achieve social progress, in sharp contrast to Lydgate. It is
Lydgate's low quality of feeling which is responsible for his
alienating people by pride and arrogance, for allowing him to
think he can use Bulstrode for his own purposes, and, most
important, for leading him into his fatal marriage with
Rosamond, all of which contribute to his defeat.

Lydgate and Ladislaw have a debate over personal independence which reveals important differences between them.
Ladislaw hates the thought of having expectations from Brooke
or Casaubon or being dependent on them. Not to stand on his
own feet would, he feels, taint his better self. When Bulstrode
offers him money, his immediate response is to refuse it: 'The
impulse within him was to reject the disclosed connection'
(Chapter 61). The concept he has of his better self, which owes a
good deal to Dorothea's opinion of him, leads him to reject forms
of dependence which compromise it. But Lydgate's reasons for
personal independence are somewhat different. His determination to remain free from obligations to Bulstrode, and the pride
that makes him hate asking for help when in financial difficulties,
derive rather from a fear that he will no longer be his own master.
To incur obligations to others will restrict his own power of will.
His original decision not to marry is based on similar consider-

ations, for to become involved with women would, he thinks, impose too many limitations on him. He has little appreciation of the special qualities of women, as his initial dismissal of Dorothea indicates. He thinks marriage to Rosamond will make little alteration to his life; she will only provide some pleasant relaxation after the serious labours of the day. The influence of women is important in redirecting the lives of Ladislaw and Fred, but Lydgate considers them extraneous to his life, and his 'vulgarity of feeling' entangles him with a woman who destroys him.

Harness imagery is often used in connection with both Ladislaw and Lydgate. Lydgate is determined to avoid having to 'wear the harness and draw a good deal where your yoke-fellows pull you' (Chapter 17). But he becomes 'a man galled with his harness' (Chapter 58), and he 'writhed under the idea of getting his neck beneath this vile yoke' (Chapter 64). This kind of imagery is used repeatedly as he becomes mastered by debt and by Rosamond's stronger will. Ladislaw is also 'harnessed' and forced to accept 'his bit of work'. But while Lydgate is yoked against his will, Ladislaw himself chooses to be harnessed and to give up his former Pegasus-like freedom. He does this in order to devote his energies to social action. His harnessing is positive, the outcome of an authentic social commitment; while Lydgate's is negative, the consequence of his belief that the will can triumph over all external obstacles. He is inevitably crushed.

Lydgate's devotion to his personal will and his low quality of feeling are also responsible for creating self-division in him. Unlike Ladislaw or Dorothea he lacks a sufficiently strong sense of continuity of self to resist impulses of the moment which conflict with his more stable feelings. The experience of such impulses and of a sense of self-division are additional Romantic features of his character. His passion for the French actress Madame Laure is the obvious example:

He knew that this was like the sudden impulse of a madman—incongruous even with his habitual foibles. No matter! It was the one thing which he was resolved to do. He had two selves within him apparently, and they must learn to accommodate each other and bear reciprocal impediments. Strange, that some of us, with quick alternate vision, see beyond our infatuations, and even while we rave on the heights, behold the wide plain where our persistent self pauses and awaits us. (Chapter 15)

The Laure episode presents Lydgate's egotism in too obviously Romantic terms to be quite appropriate in *Middlemarch*. George Eliot's expression of the philosophical point that Lydgate's devotion to the will has deprived him of a strong enough sense of 'persistent self' to control such impulses, a common criticism she makes of her Byronic characters in other works, leads to a temporary breakdown of the integration she has created between her Romantic concerns and the presentation of a dominating social world. The episode seems to belong in a different kind of novelistic world from that of *Middlemarch*. A similar point is made more satisfactorily when Lydgate is overcome by impulsive feelings which lead him into proposing to Rosamond, despite his earlier decision to avoid marriage: 'Lydgate, forgetting everything else, completely mastered by the outrush of tenderness at the sudden belief that this sweet young creature depended on him for her joy . . . poured out words of gratitude and tenderness with impulsive lavishment' (Chapter 31). Being accustomed to exerting his power of will, and caring little for the notion of continuity of self, his strongest impulse inevitably triumphs.

Lydgate possesses, then, several of the characteristics associated with the Romantic egotist. Though his energies seem to be directed towards working for the social good, his real desire is to redeem society by the power of his own mind and will. He also lacks the ardent quality of feeling which Dorothea and Ladislaw possess, and is vulnerable to strong impulses of the moment that have a divisive effect on his consciousness. Dorothea and Ladislaw, in contrast, become what I have called organicist Romantics. For them, feeling and knowledge are inseparable, they have a strong sense of continuity of self which allows them to exercise some control over and to direct their most impulsive feelings, and they are eager to work towards the achievement of a larger social ideal which will help create a unified society.

In this chapter I have tried to show that though *Middlemarch*, as the title suggests, is more centrally concerned with society than any of George Eliot's other novels, her interest in Romantic problems and issues has not diminished. Her other novels also show how the individual is shaped by society, but in no other novel does she present this idea in such powerful dramatic terms;

as she puts it in the 'Finale': 'there is no creature whose inward being is so strong that it is not greatly determined by what lies outside it'. But though this leads to less concentration on character and the psychological aspect of the Romantic issues which she had been concerned with in her previous fiction and which she would return to in *Daniel Deronda*, Romantic interests are clearly present in *Middlemarch*. Dorothea, Ladislaw, and Lydgate are not only characterised very much in Romantic terms, but they are also contrasted with two obviously pre-Romantic figures: Casaubon, with his aim of using knowledge to discover an immanent order in the world which will provide the foundation for a reconstituted Christian world-view; and Bulstrode, who tries to base his life on the belief that reality is governed by a divine, providential order. Both of their orientations fail to survive confrontation with the world. Only Dorothea's and Ladislaw's organicist Romantic position proves capable of surviving this confrontation, though their influence on their social world is slight.

8 *Middlemarch* II

It is one of the great achievements of *Middlemarch* that it operates successfully on a number of levels. It can be read on an ordinary human level as a study of character and society, or for its concern with a variety of intellectual subjects, or as a work of considerable interest on account of its style and use of language. In the previous chapter I approached the structure of the novel through an analysis of the role of the major characters. In this chapter I shall discuss in a more abstract way the novel's concern with some philosophical issues, but at the same time I shall try to show how they are integrated into the structure of the novel by relating them to its language, the lives of its characters, and the narrative form.

Middlemarch is, I believe, written from an advanced Romantic standpoint. Previous writers on the novel have shown little awareness of the deep intellectual scepticism that underlies it. It implies, for example, that there are no facts or truths which are independent of human perception or thought and which therefore are not interpretations; that all interpretations are determined by explicit or implicit human interests; and that all points of view, including the author's own, are partial and relative. Such scepticism could, of course, encourage subversive and anti-humanist ideas, and one of the most interesting things about *Middlemarch* is how George Eliot nevertheless attempts to justify a complex and subtle humanist philosophy. In order to discuss this aspect of the novel, I shall examine the philosophical and psychological implications of three recurrent or key words: 'sign', 'interpretation' and 'expectation'.[1]

One of Nietzsche's best-known statements is that 'There are no facts, only interpretations.' George Eliot's narrator in *Felix Holt* expresses a similar view: 'Even the bare discernment of facts, much more their arrangement with a view to inferences, must carry a bias: human impartiality, whether judicial or not, can hardly escape being more or less loaded' (Chapter 46). George Eliot had probably been influenced by Lewes's view on this question:

> Man is *interpres Naturae*. Whether he be a metaphysician or man of science, his starting-point is the same; and they are in error who say that the metaphysician differs from the man of science in drawing his explanation from the recesses of his own mind in lieu of drawing it from the observation of facts. Both observe facts, and both draw their interpretations from their own minds. Nay, as we have seen, there is necessarily, even in the most familiar fact, the annexation of mental inference—some formal element added by the mind, suggested by, but not given in, the immediate observation. Facts are the registration of direct observation and direct inference, congeries of particulars partly sensational, partly ideal.[2]

If interpretation by the mind is present even in the discernment of facts, then a fact may be defined as an interpretation of certain signs which it seems impossible for the human mind to interpret otherwise. For this reason it is possible for 'facts' to cease to be 'facts'. For example, to take an obvious instance, at one time it was regarded as a certain fact that the sun circled the earth. All the signs seemed to confirm that this was true. This 'fact' was reversed though the signs remained unchanged: it was only their interpretation which altered. The taking into account of additional signs created a new interpretation of the original signs and a new 'fact'. In relation to consciousness and perception, then, the world may be regarded as a vast accumulation of signs which the human mind must try to interpret. It is this problem and its implications which interest George Eliot in *Middlemarch*.

There are numerous references in the novel to 'signs' and 'interpretation'. One of the most interesting of the passages in which these words occur together refers to Dorothea and illustrates well the problem George Eliot is concerned with: 'Signs are small measurable things, but interpretations are illimitable, and in girls of sweet, ardent nature, every sign is apt to conjure up wonder, hope, belief, vast as a sky, and coloured by a diffused thimbleful of matter in the shape of knowledge' (Chapter 3). Not only can signs be interpreted in a variety of ways, but the preconceptions or mental state of their perceiver affect the interpretation. One never perceives signs neutrally: some interest is always at work shaping our point of view, and *Middlemarch* is very much concerned with the relative nature of points of view. In the above passage we see Dorothea's idealistic longings influencing her interpretation of Casaubon. There are numerous other examples of this in the novel, for instance Bulstrode's self-interested reading of signs in his interpretation of Rigg's selling him Featherstone's property: 'We are concerned with looking at Joshua Rigg's sale of his land from Mr Bulstrode's point of view, and he interpreted it as a cheering dispensation conveying perhaps a sanction to a purpose which he had for some time entertained without external encouragement' (Chapter 53). There is also the variety of interpretations of Featherstone's intentions in his will, which are shaped by the hopes and expectations of the people involved: 'But Brother Jonah, Sister Martha, and all the needy exiles, held a different point of view. Probabilities are as various as the faces to be seen at will in fretwork or paper-hangings; every form is there, from Jupiter to Judy, if you only look with creative inclination' (Chapter 32). In *Middlemarch*, both interpretations and points of view can be infinitely various.

Some signs are extremely equivocal in their meaning, which creates further difficulties of interpretation, though this seldom prevents self-interested conclusions being drawn. This is one reason why Featherstone's relations have trouble in interpreting his behaviour: 'She and Jane would have been altogether cheered (in a tearful manner) by this sign that a brother who disliked seeing them while he was living had been prospectively fond of their presence when he should have become a testator, if the sign had not been made equivocal by being extended to Mrs Vincy' (Chapter 34). The equivocal nature of signs is an important element in the novel. Since the mind plays an active role in discovering the meaning of signs, in order to read them correctly one must have a key. This point is made in *Felix Holt* but it is more appropriate to *Middlemarch*: 'But we interpret signs of emotion as we interpret other signs—often quite erroneously, unless we have the right key to what they signify' (Chapter 49). Both Dorothea and Lydgate acquire eventually the ability to interpret some equivocal signs at the expense of painful experience: 'Dorothea had learned to read the signs of her husband's mood' (Chapter 29); '[Rosamond] was keenly offended, but the signs she made of this were such as only Lydgate was used to interpret'

(Chapter 78). But Lydgate understandably misinterprets the reasons for Rosamond's agitation after Dorothea has surprised her with Ladislaw; he thinks it is the result of her hearing from Dorothea of his circumstances and difficulties when in fact it has been caused by something quite different. It is seldom easy to interpret signs in *Middlemarch*.

The most important factor in the misinterpretation of signs, however, is not so much their equivocal nature, though this is important, as the interests at work in the perceiver whose underlying desires may lead to imaginative distortion: 'We are all of us imaginative in some form or other, for images are the brood of desire' (Chapter 34). An obvious example of such misinterpretation is Lydgate's original view of Rosamond, which is produced by his own particular tastes and expectations with regard to women interacting with the equivocal signs she projects. He must eventually admit that he completely misinterpreted her nature: 'For the moment he lost the sense of his wound in a sudden speculation about this new form of feminine impassibility revealing itself in the sylph-like frame which he had once interpreted as the sign of a ready intelligent sensitiveness' (Chapter 58). Though Rosamond sets out to attract Lydgate, as she is eager to marry him, it is Lydgate who is most to blame for this mistake, since he sees in her what he wants to see and fails to notice signs of less attractive qualities. Rosamond does not consciously attempt to deceive him by pretending to be something she is not. The feminine role she plays is one she identifies with, and this is the type of woman to whom he is attracted and whom he believes he can dominate. But he discovers that underlying her feminine exterior there exists a will stronger than his.

With Dorothea it is religious idealism and her desire for knowledge that shape her interpretation of Casaubon and lead her to ignore or dismiss any signs which contradict it: 'She filled up all blanks with unmanifested perfections, interpreting him as she interpreted the works of Providence, and accounting for seeming discords by her own deafness to the higher harmonies' (Chapter 9). The Casaubon she sees is an imaginative construction of her own mind: 'Dorothea's faith supplied all that Mr Casaubon's words seemed to leave unsaid: what believer sees a disturbing omission or infelicity? The text, whether of prophet or of poet, expands for whatever we can put into it, and even his bad grammar is sublime' (Chapter 5). Critics of *Middlemarch* have perhaps not given sufficient emphasis to the intellectual scepticism clearly present in such a passage. It suggests that virtually all belief is subjective projection. For example, Bulstrode's belief in a providence which works for his own benefit and which makes him interpret signs egotistically is not a distorted faith or philosophy of life, but typical; 'He believed without effort in the peculiar work of grace within him, and in the signs that God intended him for special instrumentality' (Chapter 61). The narrator suggests that this philosophy is a way, like any other, of exerting human control over the world: 'it was as genuinely his mode of explaining events as any theory of yours may be, if you happen to disagree with him. For the egoism which enters into our theories does not affect their sincerity; rather, the more our egoism is satisfied, the more robust is our belief' (Chapter 53). George Eliot does not criticise Bulstrode's belief in providence because it is untrue or egotistic in its basis: she shows its vulnerability when it conflicts with his narrow self-interest, and he finds that his will refuses to submit to the providential ordering of events. Though a belief such as Bulstrode's is an egotistic construction, if adhered to it can discipline the ego and be the foundation for an ordered moral life. His faith in providence would have been a tenable though rigid philosophy of life if, like Nancy Lammeter in *Silas Marner*, he could have accepted events that favoured his self-interest and those that conflicted with it, like the appearance of Raffles, as equally providential. But when faced with ruin, selfish desire proves stronger than faith in providence, though he struggles hard to master the egotistic forces in his nature: '[he] had taken his selfish passions into discipline and clad them in severe robes, so that he had walked with them as a devout quire, till now that a terror had risen among them, and they could chant no longer, but threw out their common cries for safety' (Chapter 70).

Interpretation of signs is most difficult in the attempt to know another person, for it is here that signs are most equivocal and the interests at work in the perceiver are especially liable to lead to a distorted interpretation. This is shown by the following passage which refers to Lydgate's neighbours' judgements of him: 'For surely all must admit that a man may be puffed and belauded, envied, ridiculed, counted upon as a tool and fallen in love with, or at least selected as a future husband, and yet remain virtually unknown—known merely as a cluster of signs for his neighbours' false suppositions' (Chapter 15). The phrase 'cluster of signs' is particularly suggestive. It is not merely Lydgate who is 'a cluster of signs' which his neighbours interpret in various ways, depending on their particular interests. In almost all the relationships among the characters, each perceives the other as a cluster of signs, more or less equivocal, which he or she interprets, and their preconceptions influence their interpretations. I have already mentioned obvious examples: Dorothea's view of Casaubon and Lydgate's view of Rosamond. But one should notice that this operates in both directions. Dorothea and Lydgate are clusters of signs for Casaubon and Rosamond as well as the reverse. Both the latter characters have hopes and expectations which lead to distorted interpretations of their partners and to subsequent disappointment. There are many other examples of how characters' hopes or fears distort their interpretations of others. Sir James Chettam's strong desire to marry Dorothea makes him overlook obvious signs of her lack of interest and interpret other equivocal signs in his own favour: 'He thought it probable that Miss Brooke liked him, and manners must be very marked indeed before they cease to be interpreted by preconceptions either confident or distrustful' (Chapter 2). And again: 'Sir James interpreted the heightened colour in the way most gratifying to himself' (Chapter 3). A more important example in that it significantly affects the development of events in the novel is Casaubon's suspicious interpretation of Ladislaw's motives in returning to Middlemarch, which is conditioned both by his jealousy and by his doubts about Dorothea's feelings.

One of the interesting aspects of the relationship between Dorothea and Ladislaw is that many of its problems are concerned with the difficulty each of them has in interpreting equivocal signs and in avoiding making signs that are open to misinterpretation. The fact that he is poor and she is rich makes matters difficult: 'It should never be true of him that in this meeting to which he had come with bitter resolution he had ended by a confession which might be interpreted into asking for her fortune' (Chapter 54). Neither is really sure what the other feels and the situation of each makes it impossible to reveal unmistakable signs of love. Even when Ladislaw gives what he regards as a particularly clear sign of his love in his parting words on leaving Middlemarch, Dorothea is unsure whether he is referring to Rosamond or herself. This is partly because Mrs Cadwallader has influenced her mind by telling her scandalous gossip connecting Ladislaw and Rosamond. Her doubts prevent an unequivocal response on her part and he, thinking it impossible for her to misunderstand him, sees this as a sign that she does not love him. It is only after they have parted that his very last words convince her that it is she he loves: 'her consciousness had room to expand: her past was come back to her with larger interpretation' (Chapter 62). But even then she thinks they are inevitably divided by circumstances: 'She could no more make any sign that would seem to say, "Need we part?" than she could stop the carriage to wait for him.' Ladislaw retains his misinterpretation of her attitude.

Though she is convinced that he was not referring to Rosamond, the fact that 'she had at first interpreted his words as a probable allusion to a feeling towards Mrs Lydgate which he was determined to cut himself off from indulging' (Chapter 77), is an important factor in her later misinterpretation of the scene between him and Rosamond in which all the signs seem to her to point to his expressing love for Rosamond. But this situation leads paradoxically to their being brought together, since Rosamond later tells Dorothea that Ladislaw loves her, and Ladislaw himself feels he must see her again. Most of the barriers, then, are removed which had previously prevented them communicating their feelings, though even at this last meeting there is still difficulty in interpreting signs: 'It did not occur to her to sit down, and Will did not give a cheerful interpretation to this queenly way of receiving him' (Chapter 83).

It would be a mistake to believe, however, that all signs in *Middlemarch* are difficult to interpret. Some can be read quite easily: ' "You are very good," said Ladislaw, beginning to lose his diffidence in the interest with which he was observing the signs of weeping which had altered her face' (Chapter 21); 'Dorothea appealed to her husband, and he made a silent sign of approval' (Chapter 29). But interpretation is still involved in such instances. Sign and meaning are never identical in *Middlemarch*: the mind must constantly interpret.[3] George Eliot incorporates this into the human and social aspect of the novel by making the misinterpretation of signs responsible for some of the most dramatic situations, for example, Dorothea's misinterpretation of Ladislaw's relationship with Rosamond, which I shall discuss in more detail presently, and the belief of many people that Lydgate is implicated in the death of Raffles. In the latter case, 'in spite of

the negative as to any direct sign of guilt' (Chapter 71), almost
everyone is prepared to interpret the circumstantial evidence as
proving Lydgate's guilt. But though some interpretations are
wrong and can be shown to be wrong, George Eliot uses an image
derived from biology to suggest that any change in perspective
will lead to a difference in interpretation, thus again implying that
all points of view are relative:

> Even with a microscope directed on a water-drop we find
> ourselves making interpretations which turn out to be rather
> coarse; for whereas under a weak lens you may seem to see a
> creature exhibiting an active voracity into which other smaller
> creatures actively play as if they were so many animated tax-
> pennies, a stronger lens reveals to you certain tiniest hairlets
> which make vortices for these victims while the swallower waits
> passively at his receipt of custom.   (Chapter 6)

The problem of interpreting signs affects almost every aspect of
the novel. It is very relevant, for example, to the intellectual
interests of Lydgate and Casaubon, especially with regard to the
question of what constitutes an adequate or tenable theory both
in science and in other areas of life. Casaubon's 'Key to All
Mythologies' is an attempt to show that there is an underlying
Christian pattern present in the apparent diversity and disorder of
mythological data. But his manner of procedure does not permit
this theory to be tested against the otherness of reality since, as I
mentioned in the previous chapter, it involves 'a method of
interpretation which was not tested by the necessity of forming
anything which had sharper collisions than an elaborate notion of
Gog and Magog' (Chapter 48). Casaubon's 'theory of the
elements which made the seed of all tradition' has therefore no
scientific basis. Lydgate's work is similar in several respects to
Casaubon's. His theory of the existence of 'the primitive tissue' is
an imaginative creation to which he has a strong emotional
commitment; the search for 'that fundamental knowledge of
structure' which will 'help to define men's thoughts more
accurately after the true order' (Chapter 15) embodies the same
desire for order and meaning as Casaubon's quest for the key to
mythologies. But the difference is that Lydgate's theory confronts
the otherness of the world, or rather the otherness of the signs it is
trying to make sense of, and even if it fails, it can further the effort

of science to create a tenable theory which will allow the human mind to have a measure of control over reality.

Lydgate has no sympathy for interpretations and explanations which cannot be related to a scientific method. He is contemptuous of those who see some of his cures as near-miracles: 'But even his proud outspokenness was checked by the discernment that it was as useless to fight against the interpretations of ignorance as to whip the fog' (Chapter 45). At first it might seem that the novel is merely drawing an ironical contrast between Lydgate's scientific approach to the interpretation of signs in his intellectual life, an approach which involves rigorous testing, and his unscientific subjectivism in his personal relationships. In his relationships with women in particular, he is guided by subjective feelings alone, and since women arouse feelings in him that are limited in range and quality, he is strongly attracted by Rosamond's charms and fatally misinterprets her as a woman of warm, affectionate and submissive character who would suit his needs. His earlier resolve to 'take a strictly scientific view of woman' (Chapter 15) is forgotten. As a scientist, Lydgate can exercise control over his strong feelings by the necessity of submitting his theories to empirical tests, but in intense human relationships it is impossible to operate in terms of the formulation of theories which must be tested or verified. Lydgate, therefore, inevitably succumbs to his impulses when strongly attracted to women. Scientific method is no help to him in this area of life, and he has no alternative means of controlling strong impulse.

Though *Middlemarch* on one level is very much on the side of the scientific approach to the interpretation of signs, it also shows that this can be fully operated only under certain narrow conditions. In everyday experience it is impossible to apply anything like scientific tests of verification to all situations, particularly where human relationships are concerned, and it is one of the subtleties of George Eliot's position that she thinks it sometimes undesirable even to try. Feeling and intellect must attempt to deal with forms of experience in which complex and confused data have to be confronted immediately or in which there is little scope for testing or verifying judgements. After his first meeting with Dorothea, Lydgate concludes that such women 'usually fall back on their moral sense to settle things after their own taste (Chapter 10). Such an unscientific and subjective approach to experience will inevitably lead to mistakes, as

Dorothea's misinterpretation of Casaubon testifies. But the scientist Lydgate makes an equally disastrous mistake in his interpretation of Rosamond. With Dorothea, however, one also sees the value of trusting one's intuitive feelings and judgement, although this may result in an interpretation which is not submitted to tests or does not wait for verification. Her mistake over Casaubon is compensated for by the positive effects of acting on the basis of intuitive feeling on other occasions. For example, when Lydgate is almost universally felt to be guilty in the Raffles affair because this would seem to be the best interpretation of the signs, Dorothea's subjective conviction of his innocence makes her set out immediately to clear him of suspicion. Even Farebrother, who is something of a scientist, takes the view that the evidence suggests that Lydgate may be guilty, and holds back. Dorothea must eventually confront the facts of the situation, and on another occasion she could be wrong, but if she refused to act until she could verify her intuition that he was not guilty, she would not have been able to help him by the strength of her belief in his innocence. It is also only her faith in his integrity that overcomes his reluctance to tell his side of the story. If Dorothea had not acted as she did, he could have been completely ruined.

Another of Dorothea's important achievements is her success in breaking down Rosamond's egotism in their encounter when she pays her second visit to Lydgate's home. This has the completely unexpected consequence of making Rosamond be the means of bringing Dorothea and Ladislaw together, almost the only action she performs not motivated by narrow self-interest. In Dorothea's earlier determination to prove Lydgate's innocence, she chooses to trust a subjective feeling which makes her reject the interpretation of the situation that seems on the surface most likely to be true, and acts on the strength of her conviction without testing it in any way. Her action in going to see Rosamond for the second time is equally unscientific in its basis. It springs from a complete misinterpretation of what she sees in the course of her first visit, when she unexpectedly finds Rosamond and Ladislaw together. She interprets Ladislaw's behaviour to Rosamond as a sign that they are in love and sees this is a threat to Lydgate's and Rosamond's marriage, as well as the end of her own hope that Ladislaw loves her. In visiting Rosamond again, she not only possesses a false interpretation of what has taken place, but she also acts out of an intensity of feeling which is the product of her own particular crisis. But it is Dorothea's power of subjective feeling, even if it is mistaken about the nature of the situation, which makes a great impression on Rosamond. She at first interprets Dorothea's motives in the light of her own resentment, believing that Dorothea comes out of a desire to assert her superiority, and is therefore completely surprised by Dorothea's intense feeling and personal involvement. It is not so much what Dorothea says, or whether or not she has interpreted the situation correctly, that moves Rosamond as 'this strange manifestation of feeling in a woman whom she had approached with a shrinking aversion and dread' (Chapter 81). This undermines Rosamond's egotistic defences. Furthermore, Dorothea is unaware that Rosamond's preconceptions and expectations are making her interpret and respond to her words quite differently from the way she herself expects. Nor does she know that Rosamond is well aware of her involvement with Ladislaw, so that Rosamond is more interested in Dorothea's own feelings than in the content of what she says: 'she had no conception that the way in which her own feelings were involved was fully known to Mrs Lydgate.'

This scene is another illustration of George Eliot's superior artistic control in *Middlemarch*, for though Dorothea is acting morally in visiting Rosamond, we can still see the egotistic energy which is part of her character influencing her behaviour and reactions. This is in marked contrast to her earlier characterisations of Romola and Esther Lyon, who seemed in the final sections of *Romola* and *Felix Holt* to have completely transcended egotism. But with Dorothea, this artistic defect is avoided by showing the continued presence of the egotistic force of her nature even in the process of moral action.

I have tried to show that *Middlemarch* is written from a philosophical standpoint which assumes that any set of events, situation, or person can be interpreted in numerous ways, that a change in perspective will affect an interpretation, and that an individual's interests and preconceptions determine to a large extent his point of view. It might seem that this would lead George Eliot to be sceptical about the possibility of any genuine human understanding or contact, since there were such serious difficulties in the way of full communication. Could one ever be entirely sure one was interpreting a situation or a person correctly? But the scene between Dorothea and Rosamond shows that people can achieve intense contact on a level of human feeling even in the midst of misunderstandings and misinterpretations. Even if it is difficult, or perhaps impossible, to have complete knowledge of a situation or person and although one's interests necessarily influence one's interpretation in a way which may lead to distortion, this should not deter anyone from trusting his intuitive emotional reaction. It is this which can create bonds between people and break down even the most impenetrable egotistic barriers, as the Dorothea–Rosamond encounter illustrates. George Eliot recognises that Dorothea's impulsiveness has its dangers, but it is also responsible for all of her most positive qualities. Her ardent intensity of feeling in her encounters with Lydgate and Rosamond gives the latter characters such a powerful sense of connection with another human being that they are affected morally, even though Dorothea is limited by her lack of full knowledge and by a false interpretation.

II

The word 'expectation' is closely related to 'sign' and 'interpretation'. George Eliot, anticipating modern psychology, shows that expectations play a central role in determining the interpretation of signs. In *Middlemarch*, expectations are the most common means employed by the mind to impose order and structure on the data received by the mind from external reality. These expectations derive in part from one's preconceptions and in part from one's prior interpretation of signs. Almost all the characters in the novel confront their world with expectations, and almost all of them are 'disappointed' (another important word in the novel) in some degree. The particular interests of individuals encourage them often to interpret reality in a way which gratifies their hopes and desires. But reality resists such constructions: it remains quite indifferent to human desires. Those who are most frustrated by this are characters like Fred Vincy, whose 'irrepressible hopefulness' (Chapter 11) leads him to interpret the world in terms of a providence working for his personal benefit: 'What can the fitness of things mean, if not their fitness to a man's expectations?' (Chapter 14). However, reality frustrates his expectations on numerous occasions, notably in regard to Featherstone's money which he had looked forward to receiving 'with a too definite expectation' and must suffer 'a proportionate disappointment' (Chapter 23).

It is too simple a response to the novel, however, merely to criticise Fred and other characters for having such expectations. It is virtually impossible to lead any kind of ordered life without having expectations which structure one's experience. But as a result of human egotism, expectations tend to incorporate an individual's desires and hopes, and these become projected onto the world. Almost all the main characters are affected by this to some degree, and in consequence their expectations are often founded on gross misinterpretations of the world which lead on to further misinterpretations. They are thus bound to be disappointed eventually. Dorothea's experience of Casaubon at first confirms her expectations: 'Thus in these brief weeks Dorothea's joyous grateful expectation was unbroken' (Chapter 10). But after her marriage, her expectation encounters facts about Casaubon which are more difficult to accommodate: 'But the door-sill of marriage once crossed, expectation is concentrated on the present' (Chapter 20), and soon 'she was gradually ceasing to expect with her former delightful confidence that she should see any wide opening where she followed him.'

The breakdown of such an expectation can cause a serious crisis in a person's life: 'We are all humiliated by the sudden discovery of a fact which has existed very comfortably and perhaps been staring at us in private while we have been making up our world entirely without it' (Chapter 35). But such a breakdown can sometimes be liberating and proves to be so in Dorothea's case. It has the effect of making her feel she really sees Casaubon in himself for the first time, and this radically alters her attitude to him. She has had her first serious difference of opinion with him over his work and has been made aware of his egotism and want of feeling:

> But Dorothea remembered it to the last with the vividness with which we all remember epochs in our experience when some dear expectation dies, or some new motive is born. To-day she had begun to see that she had been under a wild illusion in expecting a response to her feeling from Mr Casaubon, and she had felt the waking of a presentiment that there might be a sad consciousness in his life which made as great a need on his side as on her own. (Chapter 21)

Though it can be disorienting when reality shatters an expectation, this experience can also create such an intense awareness of the otherness of a person or of the world that it can liberate one from the unconscious egotistic construction and distortion which is normally part of one's perception and judgement. For George Eliot, this can be an important stage in a character's moral growth, as it proves with Dorothea. Even as self-absorbed an egotist as Rosamond is affected morally by such an experience. The shock of Ladislaw's reaction after Dorothea discovers them together, and the later shattering of her expectation about Dorothea in her second visit, give Rosamond her most powerful experience of otherness, which has a significant moral effect on her, if only a temporary one.

Lydgate as a scientist believes he has his expectations under proper control. The scientific view of woman he is determined to take necessitates 'entertaining no expectations but such as were justified beforehand' (Chapter 15), and he is also 'impatient of the foolish expectations amidst which all work must be carried on' (Chapter 26). But outside of his scientific work, his expectations are as egotistic as those of most of the novel's other characters. His confidence in the power of his will and his 'vulgarity of feeling' lead him to entertain many expectations which are quite unscientific in their basis. He has, for example, 'a fearless expectation of success' (Chapter 13) which takes no account of the antagonistic forces he could encounter in Middlemarch or the possibility that the ambitions of others might interfere with his own. His expectations in choosing Rosamond as a wife are similarly ill-conceived, as he later admits: 'The first great disappointment had been borne: the tender devotedness and docile adoration of the ideal wife must be renounced, and life must be taken up on a lower stage of expectation' (Chapter 64). The fact that he possessed such an expectation about Rosamond says little for his discernment, and the expectation itself shows his low evaluation of the importance of both women and marriage. His earlier determination to be without 'personal expectations from Bulstrode' (Chapter 46), as Ladislaw puts it, rings rather hollow in the light of his later request and eager acceptance of money from him.

Bulstrode himself receives some shattering blows to his expectations. Raffles says to him: 'you didn't expect to see *me* here' (Chapter 53), which Bulstrode admits, and calls his finding a letter from Bulstrode 'providential'. This ironically calls in question Bulstrode's notion of providence. It was his belief in providence that had led him to base his life on the expectation that his conduct had divine justification, which the appearance of Raffles makes problematic. His own idea of himself and his deep-seated belief in his ability to dominate his world also suffer a severe shock when the reasons he offers Ladislaw for accepting his money are rejected: 'Mr Bulstrode had gone on to particulars in the expectation that these would work strongly on Ladislaw, and merge other feelings in grateful acceptance' (Chapter 61). Ladislaw's scornful refusal of the money constitutes a serious crisis for Bulstrode: his confidence that events will work out for his personal benefit and his belief that he need feel no guilt about the past, both of which are fundamental to his world-view, are shattered, and for the first time he feels himself defined by another's judgement of him.

The novel shows that for virtually all of the characters, expectations play a central part in their transactions with the world. There is a particularly interesting sentence which refers to Celia's surprise when she learns about Dorothea's engagement to Casaubon: 'She was seldom taken by surprise in this way, her marvellous quickness in observing a certain order of signs generally preparing her to expect such outward events as she had an interest in' (Chapter 5). This passage clearly reveals the relationship between the interpretation of signs and expectations, and shows how the interests of the perceiver affect the whole process. Celia receives a mild shock when she finds out that events have not unfolded as she was expecting. Other characters who project their hopes onto reality are more seriously affected when their expectations are upset. The most single-minded egotists find themselves repeatedly frustrated. Rosamond, for example, is disappointed when Lydgate turns out to be a less suitable husband than she had expected. More directly shattering is her disappointment at Lydgate's uncle's response to her letter requesting financial help; Lydgate was 'in total ignorance of her expectations' (Chapter 65). But even such a frustration cannot make much impression on her ego, and she succeeds in making herself out the aggrieved party. Her most intense disappointment is when Ladislaw upsets the expectation she has always held about her ability to dominate others and have her own way. Ladislaw's 'Don't touch me!' (Chapter 78) completely shatters this expectation and leaves her directly exposed for the first time to the reproaches of another, which undermines her own idea of herself and also makes her see with great immediacy another's pain, which affects her almost as much. She suffers her most serious crisis: '[she] was almost losing the sense of her identity, and seemed to be waking into some new terrible existence'. There is some parallel between this scene and the one in which Ladislaw rejects Bulstrode's offer of money. Bulstrode and Rosamond, two of the most self-centred and self-confident of egotists, have their most basic expectations about themselves undermined by Ladislaw. They are exposed to an experience which they cannot dominate by force of ego or construct to serve their self-interest.

Many other aspects of the novel are related to the theme of expectations. Featherstone's will in particular creates hopeful expectations in almost everyone concerned: 'Jane, the elder sister, held that Martha's children ought not to expect so much as the young Waule's; and Martha, more lax on the subject of primogeniture, was sorry to think that Jane was so "having". These nearest of kin were naturally impressed with the unreasonableness of expectations in cousins and second cousins' (Chapter 35). In the event, all of them must suffer the disappointment which results from unconsciously projecting one's desires or hopes onto reality and expecting the two to be identical. Featherstone has purposely kept his illegitimate son Rigg out of the picture so that he will 'frustrate other people's expectations' (Chapter 41). But Featherstone's own expectations are posthumously upset when Rigg sells Stone Court to Bulstrode, for whom Featherstone had had contempt because he was not a landowner: 'every one had expected that Mr Rigg Featherstone would have clung to it as the Garden of Eden. That was what poor old Peter himself had expected' (Chapter 53). Reality cannot be calculated on, even by people like Featherstone. The role of expectations in determining people's points of view is well illustrated in the following passage concerning Fred Vincy: 'tacit expectations of what would be done for him by uncle Featherstone determined the angle at which most people viewed Fred Vincy in Middlemarch' (Chapter 23). The spirit of the time is one in which expectations are tending to dominate realities, since the prospect of reform can generate 'millennial expectations' (Chapter 56).

Three characters succeed, however, in resisting the human tendency to allow egotistic hopes and desires to create foolish or selfish expectations: Mr Farebrother, Caleb Garth and Mary Garth. Mr Farebrother has some hope and expectation that Mary Garth may be willing to marry him, but when he learns his hope is unfounded, he accepts the situation and even acts to bring Fred and Mary together. Mr Farebrother is more scientific in his approach to everyday life than any other character in the novel. I have already mentioned this in connection with his attitude to Lydgate's involvement in the death of Raffles. In his relationship with Mary, he treats the possibility of her being willing to marry him as if it were a hypothesis; he then finds it being tested in his conversation with her in Chapter 52, and accepts its failure stoically without pleading his case or attempting to persuade her to change her mind. What makes *Middlemarch* a particularly interesting novel is that it reveals not only the advantages but also the limitations of this approach to life.

Caleb and Mary Garth are similarly in control of their expectations. Caleb is a man with strong roots who is very little motivated by narrow self-interest; in relation to Featherstone's property he has 'little expectation and less cupidity' (Chapter 35). Mary is a girl with a strong ego, but she is also able to see the world as independent of her own will and desires:

> There were intervals in which she could sit perfectly still, enjoying the outer stillness and the subdued light. The red fire with its gently audible movement seemed like a solemn existence calmly independent of the petty passions, the imbecile desires, the straining after worthless uncertainties, which were daily moving her contempt . . . having early had strong reason to believe that things were not likely to be arranged for her peculiar satisfaction, she wasted no time in astonishment or annoyance at that fact.   (Chapter 33)

But this does not mean that Mary confronts experience without any expectations, only that she is suspicious of those that would seem to be personally gratifying. Ironically, it perhaps makes her over-sceptical about Farebrother's feelings for her, though she must eventually recognise the signs of his regard: 'inevitably her attention had taken a new attitude, and she saw the possibility of new interpretations' (Chapter 57).

But there may be possible danger in Mary's kind of realism. The narrator comments that without her love for her parents and 'a well of affectionate gratitude within her' (Chapter 33), she could have become cynical. To be aware that expectations are human constructions and that reality is indifferent and neutral to the human interests which inevitably become a part of them, is a form of knowledge that could lead to cynicism or even nihilism. There are indications in the novel that George Eliot recognised such dangers. After the passage I quoted earlier: 'What can the fitness of things mean, if not their fitness to a man's expectations?' the narrator goes on: 'Failing this, absurdity and atheism gape behind him' (Chapter 14). Though this is primarily designed to satirise Fred's hopefulness, there is a suggestion that a breakdown of the belief that reality possesses an order which is meaningful to man and his hopes, could have such an effect. There is also an earlier passage relating to the expectation of Featherstone's family that he must leave his money to them: 'The human mind has at no period accepted a moral chaos; and so preposterous a result was not strictly conceivable' (Chapter 12). There is again irony in equating the term 'moral chaos' with Featherstone's leaving his property outside his family, but there is also the implication that to discover that reality is quite indifferent to human hopes and expectations could produce the feeling that life is a moral chaos.

There may be as much danger, then, in possessing Mary Garth's knowledge of the nature of human expectations and the indifference of the world as there is in believing that the world must respond to expectant hopes. But Mary's background and upbringing have given her a firm sense of self with which to face life, without either expecting it to gratify her desires or becoming cynical or despairing because the world remains other and neutral. She feels secure enough to act with resolution even in a world which she knows to be quite indifferent to her feelings. For example, she feels that to burn Featherstone's will would be to perform an act which contradicts the sense of right she has derived from her past. What provides her with a means of moral orientation is this sense of order underlying her own life, and not some reassurance of a humanly meaningful order in the universe which supports and justifies moral action. Even the fact that Fred has apparently lost ten thousand pounds as a result of her decision does not make her feel she did the wrong thing. But perhaps this is another reason why she chooses to marry Fred: 'Fred has lost all his other expectations; he must keep this' (Chapter 57).

It might seem at first that George Eliot is drawing ironical or sceptical conclusions from the fact that expectations, incorporating particular human interests or egotistic hopes, influence all interpretations and points of view. Can any interpretation or point of view claim to be true or objective in anything more than a relative sense if it is necessarily shaped by underlying human interests? But George Eliot's aim is not to communicate subversive relativism. She shows in the novel that human perception and cognition could scarcely function if expectations were eliminated from them; yet though this means that no point of view can be completely objective, that is no threat to a humanist philosophy. The novel suggests that it would be undesirable even to try to free expectations from the interests, hopes, and desires which inevitably become part of them. All human idealism requires such expectations. Even at a late stage in the novel, Dorothea's ardent feeling creates expectations, incorporating strong hopes and desires, which are clearly of great value. Her belief in Lydgate's innocence is an obvious example. Without her expectant faith in him, it is doubtful if he would have confessed to her: 'He hesitated a little while, looking vaguely towards the window; and she sat in silent expectation' (Chapter 76). One of her great qualities is that her idealistic expectations of people encourage them to try to live up to her ideal: she 'hold [s] up an ideal for others in her believing conception of them' (Chapter 77), and this has a particularly strong influence on Ladislaw. Though George Eliot is very much concerned to expose the egotism that underlies most expectations and to show how 'the irony of events' (Chapter 46) defeats them – and of course events could only be interpreted as ironical in relation to expectations about how they should turn out – she is not urging that expectations should be held in as detached and neutral a state of mind as possible. Her treatment of Dorothea makes this quite evident.

Dorothea's early religious idealism is vulnerable because she believes that the world possesses an order and structure which corresponds to her beliefs. Her hopes are inevitably disappointed, but this does not invalidate the feelings which underlie her beliefs. In her later development in the novel, she is able to preserve these feelings while discarding the theoretic religious frame. Her actions are the product of powerful hopes and expectations, though there is always the risk of being wrong. She could have been mistaken about Lydgate's innocence, for example, but this would not necessarily have devalued the feeling underlying her expectation of his integrity. Similarly her hope for a better society may be contradicted by events, but this does not invalidate it. She must be aware that reality can frustrate or disappoint her, yet at the same time not allow this to neutralise the expectant feelings which motivate her most ardent actions. Clearly, only a person of the highest spiritual stature can achieve this. In science also, it is impossible to proceed without expectations, which are not held in a neutral or detached manner with the bare minimum of subjectivity, but, as Lydgate's approach indicates, are expressive of great imaginative power and subjective construction. But the essential thing in science is to submit the theories based on them to the most rigorous tests of verification and ruthlessly discard those which fail the tests, no matter how great the disappointment involved. Properly controlled, then, expectations are both necessary and valuable.

III

I have tried to show that 'sign', 'interpretation' and 'expectation' are significant words in the novel. If the above discussion of their implications is acceptable, then clearly George Eliot is concerned with problems seldom associated with the Victorian novel. One might see some similarities between this aspect of *Middlemarch* and Henry James's preoccupations in his later fiction. One further point, however, needs to be considered. I have argued that the novel suggests that the human mind can only interpret the world and that its interpretation is greatly influenced by certain interests, preconceptions, or expectations. But does this not make it inconsistent with itself, for the narrator seems to have omniscient knowledge of the minds of all the characters and of everything that happens? If the novel is to be coherent, must the narrator not also be shown as an interpreter of the world?[4] It could be argued that it is a weakness of *Middlemarch* that George Eliot was unable to adapt the form of the novel to cope with those implications of its content that I have discussed, while, in contrast, James realised that the novel required a new form to deal with those problems.

I shall argue, however, that George Eliot tried to take account of this in the form of narration she adopted, though it has to be admitted that few readers have noticed this. J. Hillis Miller probably expresses the general view when he writes that the narrator in *Middlemarch* is 'an all-embracing consciousness which surrounds the minds of the characters' and 'a divine knowledge, sympathy, and power of judgement'.[5] But in my view George Eliot does not mean to suggest that the narrator's view of the world is God-like or the only one possible. Though it is not her intention, I think, to lay great emphasis on the narrator's role as interpreter, she means some of her readers at least to be aware that the narrator is interpreting and ordering the world of the novel.

One of the significant features of *Middlemarch* is that the narrator is constantly present before the reader in the first person, and far from being a neutral, objective observer, it is plain that the characters and action are being seen from the narrator's point of view:

> But at present this caution against a too hasty judgment interests me more in relation to Mr Casaubon than to his young cousin. . . . I protest against any absolute conclusion, any prejudice derived from Mrs Cadwallader's contempt for a neighbouring clergyman's alleged greatness of soul, or Sir James Chettam's poor opinion of his rival's legs. . . . I am not sure that the greatest man of his age, if ever that solitary superlative existed, could escape these unfavourable reflections of himself in various small mirrors.   (Chapter 10)

It is interesting that in the above passage we have the narrator expressing a point of view about the limitations of the characters' points of view. George Eliot must surely have appreciated this irony. The narrator is also referred to several times as an historian writing about what purport to be real people and real events; for example, Ladislaw and Mr Garth are said to have been known personally by the narrator. The narrative should then, I would argue, be seen as a construction by a narrator who is writing an historical novel and not as a neutral, 'objective' description of reality, just as an historian presents an interpretation of a period or of events and not the only account possible. The narrator makes it clear that the narrative is being constructed: 'I at least have so much to do in unravelling certain human lots, and seeing how they were woven and interwoven, that all the light I can command must be concentrated on this particular web, and not dispersed over that tempting range of relevancies called the universe' (Chapter 15). The reference to light in this passage calls to mind the pier-glass analogy at the beginning of Chapter 27 which compares the ego's structuring of events with the order given by the light of a candle to scratches on a mirror which 'are going everywhere impartially'. The reader is also informed that the narrator has other purposes in mind for the narrative in addition to telling a story: 'whatever has been or is to be narrated by me about low people, may be ennobled by being considered a parable. . . . Thus while I tell the truth about loobies, my reader's imagination need not be entirely excluded from an occupation with lords' (Chapter 35). *Middlemarch* is not then a novel which 'implicitly assumes that the world and the world as we are made conscious of it are one'.[6] George Eliot tries to make clear to her more discerning readers, perhaps, that *Middlemarch* presents an interpretation of the world by a narrator with a particular point of view and set of beliefs, and though there is no difference between George Eliot's philosophy of life and that of her narrator, her real self should not be identified with the narrator, who is treated, I think, as a persona of the author.

This interpretation of the narrator allows one to look at such matters as omniscience and coincidence from a different point of view from that of most critics. The narrator's penetration of the minds of the characters need not be seen as omniscience in a metaphysical sense but rather as a function of the narrator's role as an historical novelist who is free to shape and interpret the narrative and to reconstruct the inner lives of the characters. The narrator's 'omniscience', in other words, is an imaginative reconstruction and does not imply God-like knowledge. Barbara Hardy has used the term 'coincidence' to refer to parallels and connections between characters and events in the novel. But in my view this is misleading, since the word coincidence implies that chance or accident has created these relationships, that they are the consequence of the development of events in the external world. For example, she calls the juxtaposition of the deaths of Featherstone and Casaubon 'Perhaps the most interesting coincidence in *Middlemarch*.'[7] But there is no reason why these events, considered as historical happenings in the world of the novel, should have any relation to each other or significance, other than that the narrator sees parallels between them and structures the narrative to bring these out. If one can conceive of the events of *Middlemarch* being narrated from a different perspective, a possibility which the narrator's active role as the constructor of the narrative could put in the mind of the reader, there need not be any relationship between these two deaths. In other words, the parallel between these events is one created by the narrator: there is no 'coincidence' in the usual sense of the term.[8]

If this view of the narration and its functions is acceptable, then one can perhaps go even further in connecting the narrator with the problems raised in the novel about point of view and the interpretation of signs. The narrator clearly shows the egotistic distortion which enters into most of the characters' points of view, best illustrated by the pier-glass analogy I have already mentioned. But, as I suggested, one can draw a comparison between the narrator's structuring of the narrative and the ego's structuring of events which the analogy is designed to clarify. The difference between the narrator and the ego of someone like Rosamond is that the narrator is aware that the mind structures the world in the process of perception and cognition. Though egotistic interests inevitably affect point of view and interpretation of the world, the narrator clearly realises that it is necessary to have a point of view in order to make any judgement or commitment, or to find sufficient motive for action. The narrator says with reference to Mr Brooke that 'it is a narrow mind which cannot look at a subject from various points of view' (Chapter 7). But this attitude can be dangerous and leads Brooke to drift aimlessly from one point of view to another. He is unable to maintain a firm position on any subject and cannot act decisively. The danger of knowing the relativity of points of view is that it can lead either to the aimlessness of Brooke or even to complete scepticism. The opposite danger is exhibited by many of the characters: identifying one's point of view with reality and recognising no distinction between the two. The narrator must steer a path between these dangers: that is, be able to hold firmly to a particular point of view without confusing it with reality. This point of view is based on certain philosophical and moral assumptions; there is no pretence that it is 'objective' or the only one possible. George Eliot cannot consistently claim that her own view of the world as presented by her narrator is objectively true while those of her characters are only interpretations. The narrator also can only be an interpreter.

But though *Middlemarch* is written from a relativistic stand-point, George Eliot is anxious to show that an awareness of the relative nature of points of view need not lead either to scepticism or to the inability to hold firmly to a particular position. The narrator possesses this awareness and a strong moral commit-ment. George Eliot implies that even if it is invalid to justify a point of view by claiming that it is objectively or absolutely true and not merely an interpretation, it is still necessary to have one. The narrator's point of view is held with self-consciousness and a recognition of the assumptions underlying it. *Middlemarch* does not present us with reality as such, but with reality as seen through the medium of the narrator's mind; it is one interpretation of the world and the narrator is aware of this. The narrator, then, has two aims: to show that the ego can only interpret the world from a particular point of view and that no point of view can claim absolute truth, and also to show that such an acceptance of relativism need not lead to the lack of a strong moral response to experience.

9 *Daniel Deronda*

I

Introduction

The Romantic aspects of George Eliot's fiction I have discussed in previous chapters are especially important in her last novel, *Daniel Deronda*. For this reason it deserves a detailed and thorough analysis. It not only contains a greater number and a wider variety of Romantic egotists than any of her other novels and exposes the weaknesses and contradictions of their egotistic philosophies, but it also embodies the fullest expression of her own organicist Romantic position, one which attempts to reconcile many of the positive elements of earlier Romanticism with the radically anti-metaphysical views of later Romantic thinking. Her most important concern in the novel, I shall suggest, is to show that the later Romantic can overcome both mental and social alienation and find a sense of identity which is compatible with a humanist philosophy and the adoption of a social role.

The novel owes a good deal to *The Spanish Gypsy*. Several of the most important elements in the poem are treated anew in *Daniel Deronda*: the Romantic egotist re-emerges in the characterisation of Gwendolen Harleth and the Princess Halm-Eberstein; Deronda's situation in relation to the Jews resembles that of Fedalma with the gypsies; and Mordecai's ideal of Jewish nationhood is similar to Zarca's vision of gypsy nationhood. But *The Spanish Gypsy* is tragic in its outcome; all of its main characters suffer defeat. It seems likely that one of George Eliot's purposes in using material from her poem in her novel is to try to show that the tragic view of life she takes in the poem can be overcome.

The novel also returns to one of the main themes of the poem: how can an alienated individual find a sense of identity? Fedalma, though intellectually sympathetic to Zarca's vision, had felt unable to identify completely with her gypsy race. She suffered from alienating self-consciousness, which made her feel a sense of self-division. Though she decides that her first duty is to her race and Zarca's vision, there is no joy in her decision: 'I choose the ill that is most like to end/With my poor being' (p. 271). In her study of Deronda, George Eliot reconsiders this problem, and even makes it more difficult, for Deronda's alienation is partly the product of philosophical views which encourage relativistic thinking. The question implicitly raised by his characterisation is whether or not a strong and secure sense of identity is possible for someone brought up deprived of a sense of tribal consciousness, unable to accept metaphysical beliefs, and self-consciously aware of the asymmetrical relation between human thought and feeling and the world. Can such an individual overcome his alienation and, if so, how? *Daniel Deronda* is also more concerned than any of George Eliot's other novels with demonic forces which are a threat to the ego during an identity crisis or when the will loses control over energies within the self, as the novel's epigraph indicates:

> Let thy chief terror be of thine own soul:
> There, 'mid the throng of hurrying desires
> That trample on the dead to seize their spoil,
> Lurks vengeance, footless, irresistible
> As exhalations laden with slow death,
> And o'er the fairest troop of captured joys
> Breathes pallied pestilence.

Even an apparently pure character such as Mirah can be threatened by such forces.

Although *Daniel Deronda* is one of the most highly structured of George Eliot's novels, most critics have felt that it is marred by weaknesses in the Deronda 'half' of the novel. There seem to be obvious artistic dangers in incorporating plot elements from *The Spanish Gypsy*, which had been used as the basis of a tragic structure, into a novel which is non-tragic in its outcome, particularly as regards the development of Deronda. This perhaps suggests that George Eliot was determined to express a positive viewpoint in this novel, which she may have realised would be her last, and was prepared to risk the sacrifice of artistic values in order to show Deronda succeeding where Fedalma had failed. Of course, if she succeeded in restructuring in an artistically convincing way material which had previously seemed to her tragic in its implications, she ought to be given the greatest artistic credit for writing a novel that does not take a tragic view of life. But, as I shall try to show later, in order to show Deronda succeeding where Fedalma failed, George Eliot had to sacrifice a good deal of the potential of the character and to protect him by plot manipulation from situations of possibly great dramatic interest. In my view George Eliot had to pay an artistic price for Deronda's success.[1]

Another important artistic objection to *Daniel Deronda* is that it exhibits a lack of integration in its stylistic and formal aspects, that the Deronda 'half' reads like a romance which creates an artistic conflict with the Gwendolen 'half' in which George Eliot is at the peak of her form as a realistic novelist. But it is a mistake, I think, to see the novel as divided in this way into the romance and realistic modes. In George Eliot's defence it should be said that *Daniel Deronda* as a whole is something of a new departure in style. One detects, for example, some influence from the 'sensation' novel. An extended discussion of this would not be appropriate here, but perhaps it is close to the truth to say that George Eliot was attempting a novel closer in style to the romance tradition than anything she had done before, as the epigraph and the heightened language of much of the novel suggest, without however departing from a realistic mode in any deeper sense; that with the Gwendolen side of the novel she succeeded in integrating romance and 'sensation' elements with her earlier style of psychological and social realism, but with the Deronda side she failed to achieve this integration, mainly because of her determination both to show Deronda overcoming the problems that face him and to present a positive picture of Jewish life to an audience generally unsympathetic to Jews.

In terms of its philosophical structure, however, *Daniel Deronda* is a work of the greatest interest. I shall try to show that the structure of the novel is based on the conflict within the Romantic tradition which I have already discussed: that between the egotistic and organicist sides of Romanticism. Almost all the important characters can be related either to some form of Romantic egotism or to an organicist position.

The most extreme Romantic egotist in the novel in Deronda's mother, the Byronic Princess Halm-Eberstein, who refuses to recognise anything as superior to her own ego: 'I wanted to live out the life that was in me, and not be hampered with other lives' (Chapter 51). Her Jewish background and the situation her father forced her to accept are regarded as 'bondage' against which it is her right to rebel. Even love is rejected as a limitation on the ego. Like Armgart she is a great opera singer, but, for her, music is valuable only as a vehicle for her own self-realisation and, again like Armgart, when her will is unable to resist external forces, she maintains a defiant stance. She refuses to give way to the reality which is gradually overcoming her will, or even to acknowledge as valuable the feeling which urged her to reveal to Deronda his true identity. Such resistance to all external forces and claims she sees as the defining quality of her nature: 'It was my nature to resist, and say, "I have a right to resist"' (Chapter 51). Resistance allows her to feel that she can deny all prior definition and create her own purely personal sense of identity by an act of will. George Eliot's portrait of the Princess is one of her most objective studies of a Romantic egotist, since, unlike Armgart or Don Silva, the Princess is not shown repudiating her egotistic philosophy. The novel is content to reveal the sufferings and frustrations of her life and show how she is deprived of love and left isolated.

In complete contrast to the Princess and Romantic egotism stands Mordecai. He is no less a Romantic figure than she, but is an example of the Romantic as messianic visionary. His prophetic vision of a Jewish nation is clearly based on Romantic organicist principles. But the projective nature of his vision is stressed in his belief that another will come to carry on his work, though he is aware that his own imagination plays an active role: 'His inward need for the conception of this expanded, prolonged self was reflected as an outward necessity. The thoughts of his heart . . . seemed to him too precious, too closely inwoven with the growth of things not to have a further destiny' (Chapter 38). Mordecai belongs to an early stage of organicist Romanticism, since he expects reality to correspond to his innermost intuitions. For him there is a divine principle present in both the self and the world, but he is Romantic in believing that it is the subjective imaginative vision which is necessary to create value: 'They said, "He feeds himself on visions," and I denied not; for visions are the creators and feeders of the world. I see, I measure the world as it is, which the vision will create anew' (Chapter 40). His fervent nationalism is very much part of a Romantic tradition that would include such figures as Ernst Moritz Arndt and the Pole Mickiewicz.

While the Romantic egotist seeks identity through the elevation of the self, Mordecai urges the individual to identify himself with his race or nationality. For him, the only way for the individual to discover a true sense of identity and overcome alienation is to feel himself part of his social world, united with others in shared values and common roots. The man who rejects his nation 'is an alien in spirit, whatever he may be in form; he sucks the blood of mankind, he is not a man. Sharing in no love, sharing in no subjection of the soul, he mocks at all' (Chapter 42). This is the condition of the Princess and Lapidoth, Jews who reject and despise their racial and cultural traditions. It is also clear that Mordecai's vision of organic Jewish nationhood has more than a purely Jewish significance. The relationship he believes the Jew should feel with his race and heritage applies by implication to people of all nationalities and races.

Almost all the main characters in the novel are drawn either to some form of Romantic egotism or to Mordecai's organicist goal of a tribal identity. The conflict is exemplified in the two major characters, Gwendolen and Deronda. In the opposition between their personalities and the relationship that develops between them, the structure of the novel is worked out.

II

Gwendolen Harleth as Romantic Egotist

Gwendolen Harleth is George Eliot's most complex and interesting psychological study of a Romantic egotist. The fact that Gwendolen was partly based on Byron's grand-niece, whom George Eliot saw at the gambling tables of Bad Homburg when she was in Germany, suggests that she intended the character to be associated with Romantic egotism.[2] There are Byronic connections also in the language used to describe her, for example in her response to losing at roulette: 'she was in that mood of defiance in which the mind loses sight of any end beyond the satisfaction of enraged resistance; and with the puerile stupidity of a dominant impulse includes luck among its objects of defiance' (Chapter 1). She possesses the 'inborn energy of egoistic desire' (Chapter 4), feels 'the hunger of the inner self for supremacy' (Chapter 6), and believes that she has a 'right to the Promethean tone' (Chapter 24) when she is suffering. She is also determined that her will shall triumph over all resistant forces, even her own feelings of guilt when she accepts Grandcourt's proposal: 'No: it was surmounted and thrust down with a sort of exulting defiance as she felt herself standing at the game of life with many eyes upon her, daring everything to win much—or if to lose, still with *éclat* and a sense of importance' (Chapter 31).

The presence in her personality of demonic forces is stressed several times. We are told that observers see in her 'a trace of demon ancestry' (Chapter 7); Deronda thinks that roulette at Leubronn 'brought out something of the demon' (Chapter 32); and he later observes that 'there seemed to be at work within her the same demonic force that had possessed her when she took him in her resolute glance and turned away a loser from the gaming-table' (Chapter 35). But these forces in her are subjugated, particularly as a result of Grandcourt's mastery of her, and this creates the danger of an uncontrollable impulse overpowering her will. At times she feels that the demonic could take command of her whole personality and she longs for rescue: 'It was sometimes after a white-lipped, fierce-eyed temptation with murdering fingers had made its demon-visit that these best moments of inward crying and clinging for rescue would come to her' (Chapter 54).

A major difference between Gwendolen and the Princess is that the latter was able in her earlier life to find an outlet in art for the demonic forces in her nature, and in this she resembles Armgart. A speech of Armgart has particular application to Gwendolen:

> 'Poor wretch!' she says, of any murderess—
> 'The world was cruel, and she could not sing:
> I carry my revenges in my throat;
> I love in singing, and am loved again.'   (p. 75)

Gwendolen has no such form of sublimation, and the demonic side of her nature makes her capable of murder as a response to the frustrations of her life. She might have had sufficient talents to have been a great singer but her social situation and the low standards of her class have prevented any development of her potential. Even though 'She rejoiced to feel herself exceptional' she was 'nevertheless held captive by the ordinary wirework of social forms' (Chapter 6). Though *Daniel Deronda* concentrates more on studying character in considerable psychological depth and is less concerned with the detailed depiction of society than *Middlemarch*, the dependence of character on society is nevertheless clear. Deprived of any artistic outlet, the demonic side of Gwendolen can find expression only in a debased activity such as gambling.

But it is clear that Gwendolen resembles the Princess in several other respects. Resistance is a feature of Gwendolen's character as well as of the Princess's; we are told of 'her resistant temper', 'her resistant spirit' and her 'haughty resistant speeches' (Chapters, 13, 21). Mirah compares Gwendolen to Schiller's Princess of Eboli in *Don Carlos*, the kind of Romantic egotist the Princess resembles. Like the Princess, Gwendolen is also determined to have her own will and let nothing stand in her way: 'My plan is to do what pleases me' (Chapter 7). But she discovers the weakness of this philosophy in her relationship with Grandcourt; there are forces in the self which are stronger than the conscious will and these threaten to take control: 'This subjection to a possible self, a self not to be absolutely predicted about, caused her some astonishment and terror: her favourite key of life—doing as she liked—seemed to fail her, and she could not foresee what at a given moment she might like to do' (Chapter 13).

In addition, her constant exertion of will, not only to overcome external circumstances but also to master important elements in her own nature, creates a sense of self-division. In allowing her life to be ruled by will and impulse, she contradicts other feelings which are part of her nature. This creates a sense of guilt and insecurity and makes her feel vulnerable to the judgements of others; to resist such judgements she must exert her will even more strongly, which worsens her sense of self-division. She is caught up in a process which can lead only to self-alienation. She possesses no stable centre in her life which can direct her impulses and feelings; only what her will desires at any particular time or a sudden impulse operate on her as motivations. She has no notion of continuity of self which could help to direct her life.

The reason for this lies partly in her childhood and upbringing. Maggie Tulliver also possesses strong feelings and impulses, but she is fortunate in having a valuable relationship with her family in her early life at the mill. This provides a stable centre for her feelings and memories and prevents the wilful and impulsive side of her nature having the same scope for development as Gwendolen's. But Gwendolen has no experience of 'some spot of a native land . . . where the definiteness of early memories may be inwrought with affection, and kindly acquaintance with all neighbours, even to the dogs and donkeys, may spread not by sentimental effort and reflection, but as a sweet habit of the blood' (Chapter 3). She has been spoiled by her mother, deprived of the influence of a father or any settled life which would allow her feelings and memories to become attached to a particular place and particular objects. There is thus nothing objective to her ego to which feeling and memory can relate and which can help to shape and control the egotistic forces in her nature. Her natural egotism is allowed almost free expression, and being spoiled and brought up in a protected situation, she has no need to face a resistant reality.

Two events in her childhood are particularly important from a psychological point of view: her refusal to leave her bed and fetch her mother's medicine when her mother is in pain, and her strangling of her sister's canary when it interrupts her singing. These are impulsive acts of egotism which gain mastery over her other feelings. She is not lacking in sympathetic feeling, but, being spoiled and undisciplined, her sympathetic feelings have not been sufficiently developed to counteract wilful and impulsive egotism. Though she later feels she acted wrongly, her easy penances are insufficient expiation. Such acts are the beginning of her self-alienation; they are offences against the deep forms of feeling which are part of her nature, and her repressed guilt becomes the foundation of her later experiences of dread and terror. In allowing will and impulse of the moment to direct her life, she violates feelings and affections which are also part of her self. When she sees the dead face in the panel, this becomes a sign for her of her own ravaged inner self which finally proves to be stronger than her will. This incident is reminiscent of Piero di Cosimo's painting of Tito in his dread at seeing Baldassarre in Florence. Baldassarre becomes a sign to Tito of his violation of basic human feelings, feelings which he has tried to dismiss by analytic reasoning and by exercise of will. Both Gwendolen and Tito experience the sense of self-division and self-alienation to which their ways of life are necessarily leading.

But Gwendolen continues to allow her egotistic will to rule her life. This leads to one of her most self-alienating acts: accepting Grandcourt as a husband when she has quite spontaneously felt it would be wrong to injure another, Mrs Glasher, deliberately. She has to struggle hard against her feelings of dread:

> It was new to her that a question of right or wrong in her conduct should rouse her terror. . . . But here had come a moment when something like a new consciousness was awaked. She seemed on the edge of adopting deliberately . . . that it did not signify what she did; she had only to amuse herself as best she could. That lawlessness, that casting away of all care for justification, suddenly frightened her.
>
> (Chapter 28)

She senses a moral knowledge which is an integral part of feeling itself. In choosing to ignore this, she creates the foundation for the 'avenging powers' which later become present in her consciousness. The furies which attack her after Mrs Glasher's curse are the expression of the suppressed feelings which assail her consciousness when her will is no longer able to retain control.

Grandcourt's mastery of her also places her consciousness under great stress. Her egotistic energies become trapped within the self, and are perverted by her hate and fear into an intense resentment which arouses the temptation to surrender to the demonic forces in her nature. If she gives way to this, her self-division will become complete: 'Side by side with the dread of her husband had grown the self-dread which urged her to flee from the pursuing images wrought by her pent-up impulse' (Chapter 54). She becomes afraid of her own desires 'which were taking shapes possible and impossible, like a cloud of demon-faces'. This state of mind is responsible for her belief that she is guilty of murdering Grandcourt after his drowning. The conflict between her wilful and impulsive egotism and her moral feelings has finally produced the psychological crisis which has been threatening all through the novel.

Gwendolen is George Eliot's most artistically successful study of a Romantic egotist. She convincingly depicts the wilful and the moral sides of Gwendolen's nature, and creates dramatic situations in which the conflict between the two gradually develops towards crisis. Romantic egotism is shown as irreconcilable with a human identity. Gwendolen discovers in herself 'that murderous will' over which she has no conscious control, and experiences 'that new terrible life lying on the other side of the deed which fulfils a criminal desire' (Chapter 57). Instead of achieving her ideal of complete self-realisation, she has nearly created a monstrous second self which masters her will. Her demonic energy has almost transformed her into a demon. She is glad of 'a restful escape . . . after following a lure through a long Satanic masquerade, which she had entered on with an intoxicated belief in its disguises, and had seen the end of in shrieking fear lest she herself had become one of the evil spirits who were dropping their human mummery and hissing around with serpent tongues' (Chapter 64).

III

Acting, Gambling and the Self

The acting imagery in the last passage quoted is significant. Gwendolen in her devotion to the ego had been acting in a 'Satanic masquerade'. Almost all the characters who are drawn towards one form or another of assertive egotism are represented as actors or role-players. Acting is probably the main symbol in the novel of the ego's desire for power and dominance. It enables the egotist to be what he wants by assuming a role which is not conditioned by his past or by any pre-existing responsibilities or claims. He can also leave off a role if he becomes bored with it or exhausts its possibilities and assume another. Acting, then, is primarily used as a metaphor for the ego's desire to transcend the claims imposed by the past or the restrictions of the present and to realise itself in any way it chooses. It allows the egotist by an act of will to create his own idea of himself and to attempt to impose it on the world.[3]

As might be expected, acting is of crucial importance in the life of the Princess. The narrator comments on her speech to Deronda proclaiming her need for freedom:

The speech was in fact a piece of what may be called sincere acting: this woman's nature was one in which all feeling— and all the more when it was tragic as well as real—immediately became matter of conscious representation: experience immediately passed into drama, and she acted her own emotions. . . . It would not be true to say that she felt less because of this double consciousness: she felt—that is, her mind went through—all the more, but with a difference: each nucleus of pain or pleasure had a deep atmosphere of the excitement or spiritual intoxication which at once exalts and deadens.

(Chapter 51)

Though acting is adopted as a means of exalting the self, it can have the opposite effect of negating it. Since it is only a role that is being represented, one which can be assumed or discarded by an act of will, there is no depth in the Princess's feeling. It has no connection with her past, with any felt memories, but remains entirely on the surface. Role-playing is thus ultimately deadening, creating a 'double consciousness' in which part of her stands aside and observes her role-playing self. Instead of facing the real world, she lives in a world of make-believe. She says later of her decision to remarry: 'I made believe that I preferred being the wife of a Russian noble to being the greatest lyric actress of Europe; I made believe—I acted that part.' In choosing also to make herself what she wills by acting, she must deny herself any emotional commitment which might set up claims superior to the self. Even love must be rejected: 'I am not a loving woman. That is the truth. It is a talent to love—I lacked it. Others have loved me—and I have acted their love' (Chapter 53).

Gwendolen also has a great love for acting. She is never happier than when playing a part before others in order to win their admiration, most obviously when she strikes a pose at the gambling table. She enjoys her relationship with Grandcourt as long as she can play a queenly role: 'Gwendolen . . . found her spirits rising continually as she played at reigning. Perhaps if Klesmer had seen more of her in this unconscious kind of acting, instead of when she was trying to be theatrical, he might have rated her chance higher' (Chapter 28).

But she discovers numerous disadvantages in role-playing. In moments of stress the role can break down, leaving her the more exposed and defenceless. When she sees the picture of the dead face while acting the part of Hermione, she cannot prevent her repressed fears, with their basis in feelings of guilt, completely undermining her performance. If she cannot find a suitable role with which to confront experience, she is also vulnerable and powerless, as, for example, when Rex makes love to her. The opposite disadvantage is to find oneself trapped in an intolerable role. She cannot let it be known that she made a disastrous mistake in marrying Grandcourt. Her whole existence being based on choosing to do as she likes, she can neither repudiate her choice nor submit. She has freely chosen to marry him, and to let Grandcourt or anyone else know she wishes to go back on her choice and thus has been defeated by him would undermine her philosophy of life. She cannot give him or anyone else the satisfaction of knowing her will has been crushed, and so she must act out this pretence. But the price she pays is to be trapped in a hateful role, a situation Grandcourt relishes:

> Constantly she had to be on the scene as Mrs Grandcourt, and to feel herself watched in that part by the exacting eyes of a husband who had found a motive to exercise his tenacity. . . . And she herself, whatever rebellion might be going on within her, could not have made her mind up to failure in her representation. No feeling had yet reconciled her for a moment to any act, word, or look that would be a confession to the world.   (Chapter 44)

She even has to play the role of being satisfied to her mother, the person closest to her: 'To her mother most of all Gwendolen was bent on acting complete satisfaction' (Chapter 44). It is an ironical result of Gwendolen's role-playing that it makes her sense of identity so insecure that she can risk no serious confrontation with the judgements of others: 'In spite of remorse, it still seemed the worst result of her marriage that she should in any way make a spectacle of herself.' Having committed herself to impressing other people by acting, she now becomes the slave of her audience, forced to play a hateful part to prevent them seeing through her role to that vulnerable, fragile self she tries to deny. Her greatest humiliation would be to feel herself judged by others and to know that this judgement is true. Then she would be defined by others and lose the freedom to define herself. Even the pity of others is hateful as this is also a definition imposed from outside.

Paradoxically, acting as a means of self-realisation leads to a loss of identity. One does not create an identity for oneself but only in the eyes of others. In the actor or role-player himself, there exists a double consciousness in which he is aware of playing a role which is not the expression of what he feels to be his real self but exists apart from it. Eventually this can lead to an extreme sense of self-division. Again George Eliot is implying that only by cultivating continuity of self can one avoid this divided consciousness and feel sufficient inner security to be true to oneself despite the adverse judgements of others.

Even Grandcourt, contemptuous of almost everyone and apparently indifferent to the world, acts for the benefit of others. The pose of 'not-caring' which he adopts requires 'a world of admiring or envious spectators' (Chapter 48). Acting also enters into the passion of Lydia Glasher: 'There was a strange mixture of acting and reality in this passion' (Chapter 30). Mirah's father, Lapidoth, is an actor, a man of the theatre, a Tito-like role player who is prepared to adopt any role which is likely to further his interests. Eventually this constant acting has made him incapable of any of the most natural responses to experience. Every response lacks the reality of felt experience and seems as if it is being performed on a stage, as, for example, when he weeps after Mordecai's strong attack on him: 'As Ezra ended, Lapidoth threw himself into a chair and cried like a woman, burying his face against the table—and yet, strangely, while his hysterical crying was an inevitable reaction in him under the stress of his son's words, it was also a conscious resource in a difficulty' (Chapter 66). Though Mordecai's criticism has completely surprised him and broken through his prepared defence, he cannot prevent himself acting to serve his own interests and is detached even from the most powerful of emotional responses.

One of the most interesting actors is Hans Meyrick, a character seldom mentioned in discussions of the novel. He is an impulsive and capricious artist, who rejects the idea of a stable self in favour of a series of roles. As Mirah comments: 'all in one minute Mr Hans makes himself a blind bard, and then Rienzi addressing the Romans, and then an opera-dancer, and then a desponding young gentleman' (Chapter 37). Nothing is really serious to him, everything is a game. Even his two greatest concerns, art and love, are treated as such. His playful attitude to art is apparent in his discussion with Deronda of his Berenice paintings in Chapter 37, and Deronda thinks that even love will provide him only with another role: 'Already he is beginning to play at love; he is taking the whole affair as a comedy' (Chapter 52). Although Hans is not without affection or sympathy for others, he constructs their inner lives, as Deronda puts it, 'to fit his own inclination'. Even when he offends Mirah and apologises profusely, self-dramatisation and refusal to take any situation seriously are present: 'Even in Hans's sorrowful moments, his improvised words had inevitably some drollery' (Chapter 61). But when Deronda takes the lightness and sense of mockery in Hans's attitude as signs that he has no real designs on Mirah, he protests that he does love her.

His refusal, however, to take anything seriously, his treatment of life as a game in which he is imaginatively free to construct himself and his interpretations of others in any way he pleases is part of a larger strategy for confronting the world. He is an interesting development of the Romantic egotist. He does not believe in the kind of total self-realisation that the Princess strives for, nor can he take any external commitment seriously. Even if the self cannot find definition by complete identification with art or love or any set of values, the exaltation of the egotistic will into the supreme value is, for him, no alternative. The mockery that can be applied to the world and its values can equally be applied to the ego and its pretensions. Since he cannot create an identity for himself by identifying with any external set of values or ideas or by adopting a philosophy of self-realisation, he confronts the world by adopting a variety of self-mocking roles and prevents himself (unlike Tito) from being continually subject to dread and crisis when reality shatters a role, by taking neither his role nor the situation he is in with total seriousness: 'Hans was wont to make merry with his own arguments, to call himself a Giaour, and antithesis the sole clue to events; but he believed a little in what he laughed at. And thus his bird-like hope, constructed on the lightest principles, soared again in spite of heavy circumstance' (Chapter 61). One can see Hans as a later stage of Byronic egotism, the stage which is presented in Byron's *Don Juan*.[4]

There is an underlying nihilism in Hans's attitudes, one which is present in a different form in Grandcourt's desire for domination, Lapidoth's amoral pursuit of gratification, and Gwendolen's occasional feeling that since nothing matters, one might as well obey any impulse. Hans seems to have no belief in or respect for any values or philosophy. He takes nothing seriously because he thinks nothing is worth taking seriously. Since he cannot identify himself with anything beyond his own mind or will or even create his own value, his solution to the problem of identity is to allow his imagination the maximum scope in constructing roles for himself and situations in which to act out these roles. But he is well aware that it is his own imaginative construction that is most in evidence here, and therefore that there is no truth or objectivity in either the role he is playing or the situation in which he is acting. The only reality is the one he himself is conscious of creating.

In its own terms, this is a possible solution to the problem of identity, but George Eliot shows the price to be paid for it: the lack of any substantiality in Hans's life, the failure to form any deep relationships with people, since he constructs their inner lives for his own imaginative purposes, and the impossibility of being able to take anything seriously. The result is a life without any real joy or sense of purpose. Despite his determination to be light-hearted no matter what the circumstances, he is also more vulnerable to disappointment than he thinks; for example, when he realises that Mirah loves Deronda. For once he was 'out of humour with his lot, and yet bent on making no fuss about it' (Chapter 67). But he does not take long to recover from this set-back. He is last seen reflecting light-heartedly that if Mirah had loved him, she need not have feared the rivalry of Gwendolen.

In contrast to those characters who are enthusiastic actors and role-players, Deronda and Mirah have significantly an intense dislike of acting. When Sir Hugo asks Deronda if he would 'like to be adored by the world and take the house by storm' (Chapter 16), he replies that he would hate it. He had 'set himself bitterly against the notion of being dressed up to sing before all those fine people who would not care about him except as a wonderful toy'. Mirah's father forced her to sing and act on the stage, which she hated. He says of her: 'She will never be an artist: she has no notion of being anybody but herself', but he nevertheless made her 'rehearse parts and act continually' (Chapter 20). Her father's use of his actor's skill in his mimicry and mockery of Jewish life makes the world seem meaningless to her: 'Is this world and all the life upon it only like a farce or a vaudeville, where you find no great meanings?' Clearly, some of the characters, Lapidoth, Grandcourt, and Hans Meyrick, are of this opinion, but Mirah believes the greatest art contradicts this. Significantly, she 'knew that my acting was not good except when it was not really acting, but the part was one that I could be myself in, and some feeling within me carried me along'.

The question of what is proper and improper acting is related to two different views of art in the novel. There is one kind of art, exemplified by the Princess, in which self-display is the dominant feature. Art is used as a vehicle for the ego in its desire, as Sir Hugo puts it, 'to be adored by the world and take the house by storm'. Gwendolen aspires to be this kind of artist. But contrast Mirah's singing: 'She sang Beethoven's "Per pietà non dirmi addio", with a subdued but searching pathos which had that essential of perfect singing, the making one oblivious of art or manner, and only possessing one with the song' (Chapter 32). Here the artist serves art, instead of using it as a means of dominating an audience by force of ego. Mirah still sings, though her voice is not strong enough for her to make singing her career. But for Gwendolen, singing is valuable only as a means of performing, and she gives it up when she discovers that she is not good enough to be a performer. In her view, being unable to imitate excellence 'only makes our own life seem the tamer', but Deronda replies that 'We should have a poor life of it if we were reduced for all our pleasure to our own performances' (Chapter 36).

The apologist for art as something which the self should serve, and not use for egotistic domination, is Klesmer. Art for him is superior to the individual ego and can help to define the self. Thus one can see a parallel between Klesmer's concept of art and Mordecai's vision of the organic nation. Both offer the ego a means of definition in devoting itself to the service of a higher ideal. Klesmer tells Gwendolen that if she decides to commit herself to art, 'I will ask leave to shake hands with you on the strength of our freemasonry, where we are all vowed to the service of Art, and to serve her by helping every fellow-servant' (Chapter 23). Although the Princess was a great artist, art as such was not important to her, only the self-realisation that was possible through art. When she thought another singer was gaining precedence over her, she gave up singing and sought a new role in which her ego could reassert its dominance.

Acting is not the only activity symbolising the egotist's attempt to dominate his world. Gambling and, to a lesser extent, hunting are also important metaphors for this. Deronda, significantly, objects to both. His main objection to gambling is that it is a means of gaining from another's loss. But for the egotist, gambling represents the longing of the self to assert its mastery over the world and to succeed even against the odds, to place one's 'foot on the neck of chance' (Chapter 1). All of Gwendolen's most demonic tendencies are brought out in gambling. The excitement she feels when winning makes her imagine herself a kind of 'goddess of luck', and she feels confident that by sheer force of ego she can triumph over chance and circumstances: '[She] would make the very best of the chances that life offered her, and conquer circumstance by her exceptional cleverness. . . . She felt well equipped for the mastery of life' (Chapter 4). There is, however, another aspect of gambling, which emerges when Gwendolen is disillusioned with life after her marriage. Then it becomes an escape from boredom and ennui. She tells Deronda: 'I am going to justify gambling in spite of you. It is a refuge from dulness' (Chapter 35). The need to gamble, like the need to act, springs from a sense of alienation from reality which the self seeks to overcome. Larger implications are suggested in the presentation of the variety of European nationalities caught up in 'the passion of gambling' at Leubronn, as if this condition is threatening not just Gwendolen, but European civilisation as a whole.

Gwendolen is not the only character fond of gambling. The Princess's life has been one in which she has gambled with her ego in striving to achieve dominance and self-realisation, often sacrificing others in the process. Her gamble in marrying the Russian noble was not, however, successful, and like all habitual gamblers she finds she must lose eventually, for the world finally crushes the ego. Gambling imagery is used in connection with Grandcourt's secretary Lush. He thinks the odds are against Grandcourt marrying Gwendolen: 'I will take odds that the marriage will never happen' (Chapter 13). He also tries 'gambling in argument' with Grandcourt (Chapter 25). Hans Meyrick gambles on winning Mirah's love: 'I would rather run my chance there and lose, than be sure of winning anywhere else' (Chapter 37), though he claims no one but himself can be hurt by this and that he does not intend to despair if he loses. But the most dedicated gambler in the novel is Lapidoth. The narrator sees a demonic element in his gambling mania:

> The gambling appetite is more absolutely dominant than bodily hunger, which can be neutralised by an emotional or intellectual excitation; but the passion for watching chances . . . nullifies the susceptibility to other excitation. In its final, imperious stage, it seems the unjoyous dissipation

of demons, seeking diversion on the burning marl of perdition.   (Chapter 66)

Gambling, like acting, can create self-division because the self feels guilt at profiting from the losses of others. Gwendolen finally finds the psychological strain of this guilt intolerable, as she confesses to Deronda in telling him of her broken promise to Lydia Glasher not to marry Grandcourt: 'I wanted to make my gain out of another's loss—you remember?—it was like roulette—and the money burnt into me. . . . It was as if I had prayed that another should lose and I should win. And I had won. I knew it all—I knew I was guilty' (Chapter 56). The gambler finally and ironically runs the risk of self-alienation. Even if he wins, there is a sense of guilt because there is no relation between winning and desert, and others must lose in order that he win. Though chance and disorder may characterise events in the external world, there is a psychological need within the human mind to feel a sense of equilibrium between one's actions and one's deserts. Lapidoth, however, feels no sense of guilt at gambling with events and profiting if they work out in his favour, but he is almost entirely devoid of human feeling. Gwendolen, in contrast, does feel strongly that marrying Grandcourt despite Mrs Glasher's superior claim is wrong. Her wilful act in marrying him alienates her from her feelings and increases her sense of self-division.

It is Gwendolen's capacity for having such strong guilt feelings that prevents her becoming like Grandcourt or Lapidoth, probably the two most negative characters in George Eliot's fiction. When Grandcourt was young, he sought complete self-realisation in love, like Don Silva or Mrs Transome. But when his passion for Lydia Glasher burned itself out, this Romantic intensity of feeling becomes transformed into sadism. Only the pleasure of mastering others, 'his delight in dominating' (Chapter 30), can dispel the 'languor and *ennui*' (Chapter 12) of his life. Being 'without the luxury of sympathetic feeling' (Chapter 35), he suffers no guilt at making others submit to his will. Though Gwendolen resembles him in her desire to have her own will, she differs from him crucially in her capacity to feel.

She also resembles Lapidoth in some respects. Like him she loves acting and gambling, and desires self-gratification. She thinks she can exploit chance for her own purposes and, when events seem to be going against her, is prepared, as Mr Gascoigne puts it, 'to adapt herself to circumstances like a girl of good sense' (Chapter 24). These character traits, taken to an extreme, ultimately produce someone like Lapidoth. He is the kind of person all committed egotists risk becoming. He has gambled away almost all human feelings: 'Among the things we may gamble away in a lazy selfish life is the capacity for ruth, compunction or any unselfish regret' (Chapter 62). Self-interest has reached such a pitch as to cut him off almost entirely from feelings of guilt or susceptibility to the judgements of others. In a sense he has solved the problem of identity by refusing to possess a human identity at all. Only impulses and the desire for gratification motivate him, and all other considerations are ignored. He rejects any connection between his past self and his present self. Even his most personal memories, like those aroused by the inscription on Mirah's purse, can be viewed with detachment and neutrality: 'Lapidoth had travelled a long way from that young self, and thought of all that this inscription signified with an unemotional memory' (Chapter 62). Lapidoth is George Eliot's most extreme egotist, a man who has cut himself off from almost all human values and feelings and is utterly devoted to self-interest. He has virtually destroyed all human identity and become instead a kind of animal, adapting and adjusting to all circumstances in the gamble for gratification or survival. It is perhaps significant that he survives.

What saves Gwendolen from becoming a Grandcourt or a Lapidoth are the very feelings of dread and remorse which threaten to cause a personality crisis. These are evidence that part of her self is fighting to preserve her human identity. In Deronda's view 'her remorse was the precious sign of a recoverable nature; it was the culmination of that self-disapproval which had been the awakening of a new life within her; it marked her off from the criminals whose only regret is failure in securing their evil wish' (Chapter 56). But the price of retaining some form of human identity might be irrecoverable self-division and self-alienation.

Though Gwendolen leads a life dominated by ego and will, her susceptibility to feeling is apparent throughout. In her first response to Mrs Glasher's claim on Grandcourt, moral feeling strikes her with an immediacy almost as strong as her most egotistic impulses:

she acted with a force of impulse against which all questioning was no more than a voice against a torrent. The impulse had come . . . from her dread of wrong-doing, which was vague, it is true, and aloof from the daily details of her life, but not the less strong . . . and even apart from shame, her feeling would have made her place any deliberate injury of another in the region of guilt.   (Chapter 27)

This is a very clear example of what George Eliot regards as a valid impulse, one which is an expression of Gwendolen's whole self and not merely the product of the moment or an animal response. To act, then, in wilful contradiction to such a feeling by marrying Grandcourt places a great strain on her consciousness. Her partial awareness of the danger explains why 'a question of right or wrong in her conduct should arouse her terror' (Chapter 28). She cannot easily dismiss 'the most permanent layers of feeling'.(Chapter 29), and she confesses to Deronda that she 'can't help feeling remorse for having injured others' (Chapter 36). This potential for feeling prevents her going the way of Lapidoth and she preserves human identity.

This is true for the Princess also. She finally cannot resist the feeling which urges her to tell Deronda of his parentage. For George Eliot, the rejection of such feelings is a human betrayal: one becomes, like Lapidoth, almost beyond the pale of humanity. This is why Deronda can assert that his grandfather's vision, which has its basis in such feeling, is stronger than the egotistic will, for to reject what this feeling represents is to deny the human. Even the Princess, the most wilful of egotists, cannot finally resist fulfilling her father's wish; it was, as Deronda puts it, 'the expression of something stronger, with deeper, farther-spreading roots, knit into the foundation of sacredness for all men' (Chapter 53).

IV

Deronda: From Alienation to Identity

Despite the subtlety and psychological insight shown by George Eliot in her critique of the various forms of Romantic egotism in *Daniel Deronda*, it is arguable that this critique will be familiar to readers of her previous work, even though it is extended in scope and none of her previous egotists is as brilliantly characterised as Gwendolen Harleth. But where *Daniel Deronda* breaks new ground and is particularly interesting from a philosophical point of view is in its study of Deronda himself. Here George Eliot as a later Romantic expresses more fully than in any of her previous works her own organicist Romantic position. None of her other positive characters is, I think, as close to her intellectually as Deronda, and her deepest concern is to show that an advanced Romantic who has rejected metaphysical beliefs can discover or create a sense of identity which overcomes the most severe alienation and leads to positive social commitment and action. Few critics have judged Deronda to be an artistic success, but in some respects he is her most ambitious characterisation.

Though Deronda is completely opposed to all forms of Romantic egotism, despite having the Princess as a mother and accepting Lapidoth as a father-in-law, he himself has clear Romantic associations:

> And, if you like, he was romantic. That young energy and spirit of adventure which have helped to create the world-wide legends of youthful heroes going to seek the hidden tokens of their birth and its inheritance of tasks, gave him a certain quivering interest in the bare possibility that he was entering on a like track.   (Chapter 41)

He is also compared to Shelley at one point (Chapter 16), and the sense of inner suffering which is a consequence of his doubts about his parentage is likened to 'Byron's susceptibility about his deformed foot' (Chapter 16). Deronda, however, is a Romantic who has gone beyond any form of transcendentalism or any belief in a divine principle in either the self or the universe. He has reached an advanced stage of Romantic thinking and partly as a consequence of this, suffers from intense self-consciousness. He is subject to extreme alienation in two senses: he is intellectually detached from all forms of positive belief or commitment, despite his desire for a strong social identity which could shape and direct his life; and he experiences psychological alienation to such a degree that there is a danger of his losing any sense that he possesses a centre of self.

As with Gwendolen, George Eliot shows that his childhood

helps to account for his later personality. The most important of his early experiences is his sense of estrangement because of his belief that he is illegitimate. This makes him feel separate from Sir Hugo and the life in which he has been brought up, a very unhappy situation for someone so temperamentally disposed to be 'an organic part of social life'. His awareness that he does not fully belong is compared to 'the threatened downfall of habitual beliefs which makes the world seem to totter for us in maturer life' (Chapter 16). This has serious consequences for his later development, since it leads to intense self-consciousness and the suppression of his potentially passionate nature. But an implicit contrast with Grandcourt and Gwendolen is drawn in the following passage: 'his disposition was one in which everyday scenes and habits beget not *ennui* or rebellion, but delight, affection, aptitudes' (Chapter 16). His nature is one in which feeling is more predominant than the egotistic will. In contrast to Gwendolen and other characters, he does not respond to alienation by asserting his ego against the world in an effort to achieve a sense of mastery and domination. Rather, his intense feelings and sympathies become allied to his self-consciousness and suppression of self, and create a different form of self-alienation from that experienced by Gwendolen or the Princess. For Gwendolen, exertion of will and giving way to her strongest impulse of the moment create a sense of self-division which cuts her off from the potential for feeling which is also part of her nature. But for Deronda, extreme self-consciousness and his habitual suppression of personality make it seem that his feelings and sympathies do not centre on any self at all. Instead of acting to dominate the world by force of ego and strength of will, he *reacts* selfconsciously to experience and shrinks from any commitment which demands that he expose his personality. The word 'shrink' is repeatedly used to describe his responses.

From an artistic point of view it is unfortunate that George Eliot fails to dramatise convincingly the effects of Deronda's self-consciousness and suppression of strong feeling on his personality and behaviour. His alienation is presented mainly in descriptive terms by the narrator and is not made an integral part of his character. As a result he lacks dramatic life, in sharp contrast to Gwendolen. It seems likely that part of the reason for George Eliot's artistic failure with Deronda is that her main concern was not in exploring his condition, but in enabling him to overcome it. But this artistic failure should not lead to a neglect of the philosophical interest of his role in the structure of the novel.

The intense self-consciousness Deronda suffers from as a result of his belief that he is illegitimate encourages the development in him of a dangerously relativistic form of thinking: he feels mentally and emotionally detached from all forms of belief, and at times even his sense of self seems to disintegrate. We see an example of the latter experience after he has been rowing on the Thames: 'He was forgetting everything else in a half-speculative, half-involuntary identification of himself with the objects he was looking at, thinking how far it might be possible habitually to shift his centre till his own personality would be no less outside him than the landscape' (Chapter 17). Deronda's capacity almost to negate his own ego in such an experience is very closely related to the Romantic egotist's role-playing. Deronda's experience, like role-playing, calls into question whether or not there is any substantial centre to the self. But George Eliot does not go on to explore this implication of Deronda's character in depth; as I have said, her main interest is in his recovery. One of the effects of his relativistic thinking, however, is to create an analytic frame of mind which makes it impossible for him to believe or act, despite sympathising with many beliefs and causes: 'His plenteous, flexible sympathy had ended by falling into one current with that reflective analysis which tends to neutralise sympathy' (Chapter 32). Subject to such 'a reflectiveness that threatened to nullify all differences' (Chapter 32) and to 'oppressive scepticism' (Chapter 50), he fears the ultimate alienation of consciousness from concrete reality: 'he dreaded, as if it were a dwelling-place of lost souls, that dead anatomy of culture which turns the universe into a mere ceaseless answer to queries, and knows not everything, but everything else about everything—as if one should be ignorant of nothing concerning the scent of violets except the scent itself for which one had no nostril' (Chapter 32).

If one can achieve a strong sense of identity only by embracing a belief one feels to be true, then there seems no solution to Deronda's problem. His analytic mind has cut him off from such belief. He will remain 'a yearning disembodied spirit', since the thought of making a commitment in the face of reason disturbs him almost as much as the consequences of his alienation: 'he also shrank from having his course determined by mere contagion, without consent of reason; or from allowing a reverential pity for spiritual struggle to hurry him along a dimly-seen path' (Chapter 41). George Eliot's prime concern in her study of Deronda is to show the process by which he finally overcomes what seem to be insuperable difficulties that lie in the way of his committing himself to a set of beliefs and a course of action.

In *The Spanish Gypsy*, Fedalma embraces the gypsy cause, but this decision only creates sorrow and anguish for her. She is faced with a tragic choice between love for Don Silva and her duty to her race, with which she is unable to identify fully. If George Eliot had presented Deronda with a similar choice between love for Gwendolen and commitment to Mordecai's ideal of a Jewish national state, it is possible that the relationship between Deronda and Gwendolen would have possessed greater dramatic tension, and Deronda's decision to serve the Jewish cause would have been more problematic and therefore more interesting from an artistic point of view. That George Eliot was aware of this possible development of the novel and perhaps only reluctantly abandoned it is suggested by several references she makes to Deronda's being potentially capable of loving Gwendolen, for example: 'a man . . . hardly represents to himself this shade of feeling towards a woman more nearly than in the words, "I should have loved her, if——:" . . . he had never throughout his relations with Gwendolen been free from the nervous consciousness that there was something to guard against not only on her account but on his own' (Chapter 50).

But to have developed the novel in this way would have made it extremely difficult for George Eliot to have shown Deronda finding identity through joyfully committing himself to his Jewish race and the ideal of nationhood. She therefore prevents Deronda from falling in love with Gwendolen by arranging the plot so that he meets Mirah before encountering Gwendolen. One may feel that this is merely to avoid the problem she was concerned with in *The Spanish Gypsy*. In the poem, the intense love between Silva and Fedalma is seen in relation to the individual's sense of separateness from his society, or from any religion or set of values in which he can believe completely. Romantic love is the product of the alienated self's desperate search for meaning and value. But in protecting Deronda from such an experience of intense love, one to which his original condition would have made him extremely vulnerable if he had met Gwendolen before his involvement with Mirah and Jewish life, George Eliot can be accused of allowing Deronda to recover a sense of tribal identity too easily, without facing some of the most serious difficulties. In contrast to love for Gwendolen, Deronda's love for the conveniently Jewish Mirah can easily be accommodated in his acceptance of his Jewishness and his commitment to Jewish nationhood.

Mirah does, however, serve an important function in the novel. She also can be connected with a character in *The Spanish Gypsy*, for like Fedalma's servant, Hinda, she is a person who feels wholly at one with her race. She possesses the sense of tribal consciousness which Deronda so strongly feels he lacks, and she maintains this despite her father's attempt to uproot her from Jewish life. She feels at one with her people and thus can submit to what she regards as her duty without egotistic rebellion or self-conscious reflection. Observing her state of consciousness increases Deronda's tribal yearnings: 'she seemed to Deronda a personification of that spirit which impelled men after a long inheritance of professed Catholicism to leave wealth and high place, and risk their lives in flight, that they might join their own people and say, "I am a Jew" ' (Chapter 32). Deronda's love for her is as if Fedalma had fallen in love with a male equivalent of Hinda before meeting Silva. The conflict Fedalma feels between passionate love and duty to her heritage, which leads to her tragic situation, is absent from Deronda's experience.

Despite the artistic difficulties presented by such a character as Mirah, George Eliot is not content merely to treat her as representative of a tribal consciousness. Even she is not immune to negative egotistic forces, as is shown in her intense jealously when she believes that Deronda loves Gwendolen. In her difference with Mordecai over the interpretation of the story of the Jewish maiden and the Gentile king, it is suggested that she has received a disturbing insight into the inner self, one which the idealist Mordecai refuses to recognise. It is clear she does not accept his view that she has read too many plays which represent 'the human passions as indwelling demons'. (Chapter 61). She has become aware of the dangers of demonic forces in the self, which George Eliot believes are always a threat to human values, as the novel's epigraph suggests. But like Deronda, she values Mordecai's idealism too much to wish to disillusion him.

Deronda's love for a Jewish girl who feels wholly defined by her heritage, and the fact that this prevents him from experiencing a more intense form of love for Gwendolen, are important factors in his recovery of a sense of tribal identity. Another essential factor is his relationship with Mordecai. Both Mirah and Mordecai help to renew Deronda's spirit even though his intellect cannot accept their beliefs. Mirah sees some larger meaning in his rescue of her, but for him it was chance: 'It was my good chance to find you' (Chapter 32), and he regards his meeting with Mordecai and his involvement with the Jews as springing from this chance and its consequences, despite Mordecai's metaphysical interpretation: 'To me the way seems made up of plainly discernible links. If I had not found Mirah, it is probable that I should not have begun to be especially interested in the Jews' (Chapter 41); in his view Mordecai possesses 'illusory notions' on the subject. Even though Mordecai's belief that Deronda is Jewish is compared to a scientific hypothesis, only Deronda preserves the proper scientific scepticism towards the hypothesis until it has been tested: 'We must not lose sight of the fact that the outward event has not always been a fulfilment of the firmest faith' (Chapter 40).

But though Deronda is intellectually sceptical about Mordecai's prophetic ideas, he is able to draw on Mordecai's enthusiasm and emotional power to renew his inner self. His meeting with Mirah and his experience in the synagogue in Frankfurt have aroused his interest in Jewish life, and contact with Mordecai greatly develops this. He is able to feel an emotional attachment to one particular religion and cultural tradition instead of looking on all in a detached, relativistic frame of mind without preference. What first attracts him to Judaism is the intensity of feeling it arouses in believers: 'Mirah, with her terrified flight from one parent, and her yearning after the other, had flashed on him the hitherto neglected reality that Judaism was something still throbbing in human lives, still making for them the only conceivable vesture of the world' (Chapter 32). It is also suggested that, like Feuerbach, he sees the basis of all religion as feeling: 'since Jews are men, their religious feelings must have much in common with those of other men. . . . Still it is to be expected that a Jew would feel the forms of his people's religion more than one of another race—and yet . . . that is perhaps not always so.' What Deronda acquires is not belief in Judaism but a sense that it is more central to his life and feelings than any other religion. By being exposed to the power of Mordecai's personality and undertaking serious study of Judaism, Deronda finds a perspective to which he can devote his energies, a centre which can prevent his subjectivity becoming diffused, and around which he can build a firm sense of his own self.

It seems certain that without Mirah and Mordecai and the deep interest he develops in Jewish culture, the revelation of his own Jewishness would have meant comparatively little to him. He would have felt unable to identify with his race or Mordecai's ideal, just as Fedalma in *The Spanish Gypsy* could not recover a strong sense of gypsy identity. When she is confronted by the strength of Zarca's idealism, 'Resolve is strong', but it cannot be sustained:

> But soon the glow dies out, the trumpet strain
> That vibrated as strength through all my limbs
> Is heard no longer; over the wide scene
> There's nought but chill grey silence, or the hum
> And fitful discord of a vulgar world.   (pp. 278–9)

Deronda, however, has already developed a strong interest in Jewish religion and culture before his own Jewishness is revealed to him, and unlike Fedalma his consciousness is not divided by a conflict between love and duty. Though he refuses to accept Mordecai's ideas in a literal sense, he allows himself to empathise with the emotions underlying them, the feelings which the ideas represent in symbolic form: 'He felt nothing that could be called belief in the validity of Mordecai's impressions concerning him or in the probability of any greatly effective issue: what he felt was a profound sensibility to a cry from the depths of another soul; and accompanying that, the summons to be receptive instead of superciliously prejudging' (Chapter 40). He gradually outgrows his self-consciousness and reserve in the presence of Mordecai and lets him define a form for his tribal yearnings.

The complex nature of Deronda's relationship to Mordecai and his beliefs is especially apparent with regard to the theme of expectations, which is important in both this novel and *Middlemarch*. Before he forms any close relationship with Mordecai, Deronda had been longing for a confidant, and imagines someone who would ideally fit this role: 'But he had no expectation of meeting the friend he imagined' (Chapter 37). Earlier, in going in search of Mirah's family, he was 'without expectation of a more pregnant result than a little preparation of his own mind, perhaps for future theorising as well as practice' (Chapter 33). He is well aware that reality remains quite indifferent to the expectations and hopes which necessarily enter into human interactions with the world. But as I suggested in the previous chapter, too great an awareness of this can paralyse action and create a pessimistic view of life. The value of expectations as a means of arousing the motive for action and giving a sense of meaning and purpose to life, even though these expectations may prove to be mistaken, is expressed in this novel as well as in *Middlemarch*.

Mordecai is a man whose life is dominated by expectations, and this state of mind is made more intense by the knowledge that he cannot live much longer. In spite of 'overwhelming discouragements', his yearning and hope are not diminished but 'took rather the intensity of expectant faith in a prophecy which has only brief space to get fulfilled in' (Chapter 38). When he meets Deronda, 'the ever-recurrent vision had the force of an outward call to disregard counter-evidence, and keep expectation awake'. At first Deronda disappoints Mordecai's expectation by saying he is not a Jew, but when they meet on the river, Mordecai is convinced his expectant vision has been confirmed. But the projective nature of this is stressed: 'Obstacles, incongruities, all melted into the sense of completion with which his soul was flooded by this outward satisfaction of his longing' (Chapter 40). The need for confirmation of the expectation is so strong that all previous disappointments are forgotten: 'I expected you to come down the river. I have been waiting for you these five years.' For Deronda, this belief is based on an illusion, but he is extremely reluctant to dismiss it with rational scepticism. He realises the value of the feeling underlying the expectation and is determined to do nothing to disappoint it unless this proves unavoidable:

I suppose I am in a state of complete superstition, just as if I were awaiting the destiny that could interpret the oracle. But some strong relation there must be between me and this man, since he feels it strongly. Great heaven! what relation has proved itself more potent in the world than faith even when mistaken—than expectation even when disappointed? Is my side of the relation to be disappointing or fulfilling?—well, if it is possible for me to fulfil, I will not disappoint.

Though Deronda cannot believe in Mordecai's expectations, he makes use of the intensity of feeling they generate in Mordecai, something from which his own sceptical intellect has dissociated him. It is impossible for him to make an absolute commitment to Mordecai's ideas based on complete belief, but he allows Mordecai's fervent enthusiasm to sustain him. The same longing is present in both men, but in Deronda the longing is not projected into objectivity. Deronda's conscious awareness of projective thinking has in the past detached him from all beliefs or strong commitments and made him feel only separate and self-conscious; but Mordecai's projection of his longing into objectivity leaves him vulnerable when reality frustrates his human structuring. Deronda suffers a two-fold dread: 'a compassionate dread of discouraging this fellow-man who urged a prayer as of one in the last agony, but also the opposing dread of fatally feeding an illusion, and being hurried on to a self-committal which might turn into a falsity' (Chapter 40). On their own, both Mordecai and Deronda suffer greatly from the weaknesses of their forms of thinking, but together each complements the weakness of the other. Mordecai's strong feeling and enthusiasm support Deronda's sceptical, over-reflective consciousness, while Deronda's care in preparing Mordecai to survive disappointment if he is wrong about Deronda being Jewish, and his willingness to do all he can to conform to Mordecai's vision of him, support Mordecai. This leads to a happy conclusion for both. When Deronda finds he can fulful Mordecai's expectations he is overjoyed: 'It was his nature to delight in satisfying to the utmost the eagerly-expectant soul' (Chapter 63).

In a way Deronda gambles on Mordecai's prediction that he is a Jew turning out to be true, just as such characters as the Princess or Gwendolen gamble on events favouring their egotistic interests. One might object that Deronda has more than his fair share of luck in the novel. But his gamble is somewhat different. He is well aware that he can lose and is fully prepared for all the consequences of this. It is, besides, impossible to eliminate gambling from experience, even if only in a metaphorical sense, since any hope or expectation that precedes empirical testing is a kind of gamble in that it may be wrong and result in some emotional loss. But Deronda's 'gamble', his hope that Mordecai's premonition may be right, does not involve profiting from others' losses. The only people who could possibly be hurt are Deronda himself and Mordecai, and Deronda does everything in his power to protect Mordecai from being hurt if he is wrong. But the gambling of someone like Lapidoth is designed only to serve his own ends and involves the exploitation of others. Egotistic gamblers also tend to discount the possibility of failure, believing that their egos are strong enough to dominate the world or that the world must favour their interests. Thus it is usually a crisis for them if reality frustrates their hopes. In contrast, Deronda is prepared for disappointment.

However, in fulfilling Mordecai's expectation, Deronda finds that he must disappoint Gwendolen's. He is almost as concerned to protect Gwendolen as he is to protect Mordecai, but this proves impossible. Her expectations are stressed throughout the novel and they are repeatedly disappointed. She is forced to recognise 'how quickly might life turn from expectancy to a bitter sense of the irremediable!' (Chapter 35). But she feels little danger when Deronda is on the point of disclosing to her that he is a Jew: 'she felt the more assured that her expectations of what was coming were right' (Chapter 69). The revelation that he is going away and will marry Mirah is a crushing blow. She must come to terms not only with the otherness of the world but with the separateness of Deronda.

But the relationship with Gwendolen is also an important stage in the evolution of Deronda towards a tribal identity. In his efforts to help her overcome her alienation and to prevent her being engulfed by her inner demons, he becomes more aware of his own need for what he prescribes for her: 'Try to care for what is best in thought and action—something that is good apart from the accidents of your own lot' (Chapter 36). Critics tend to see this as priggish moralising, but Deronda himself, though in a different way, has as much trouble as Gwendolen in concentrating his sympathies. When he tells her that 'what we call the dulness of things is a disease in ourselves. Else how could any one find an intense interest in life? And many do' (Chapter 35), he is referring as much to himself as to Gwendolen. The boredom she at times feels with life is something to which he is also extremely vulnerable because of his over-reflective, detached way of contemplating the world and his 'shrinking' from experience. In recognising another's need for a larger aim in life and in his efforts to make this clear to her, Deronda discovers a deeper emotional awareness of his own similar need, and this is an important factor in his willingness to make a full commitment to his Jewish heritage and to Mordecai's ideal.

George Eliot retains something of Fedalma's dilemma in *The Spanish Gypsy* by making Deronda have to choose between Gwendolen and Mordecai, though in his case the choice is much less difficult: 'on the one side the grasp of Mordecai's dying hand on him, with all the ideals and prospects it aroused; on the other this fair creature in silk and gems, with her hidden wound and her self-dread, making a trustful effort to lean and find herself sustained' (Chapter 45). Though it can be argued that his rejection of Gwendolen has a beneficial effect in that it makes her aware of a wider world beyond her own ego and of her need to live without his support,[5] Deronda could not predict what the effect of his rejection of her might be. The break with Gwendolen is necessary no matter what the consequences for her, and he himself thinks these could be serious. He is in effect choosing a form of self-realisation in preference to a concrete, sympathetic responsibility which is in conflict with it. *Daniel Deronda* is a novel about which it is dangerous to come to simple conclusions. To say that it attacks self-realisation, gambling, and role-playing would be a crude over-simplification, since all of these in some form can be connected with Deronda. One has a duty to oneself, and this must be taken into account even if it means rejecting someone in need. Deronda is thus prepared to discard Gwendolen despite her need of his support, though it is not an easy decision for him. But the opposite decision was taken by Mordecai when he chose to remain with his mother and sacrificed his own dreams of serving the ideal of Jewish nationhood. There are no clear-cut rules or guidelines to resolve a moral problem of this kind. The individual can only make the choice which he feels is truest to his sense of whole self.

In choosing to be true to his racial heritage, not merely with his intellect but with his deepest feelings, Deronda achieves what had seemed beyond him previously, a sense of tribal identity. He says to his mother: 'But I consider it my duty—it is the impulse of my feeling—to identify myself, as far as possible, with my hereditary people, and if I can see any work to be done for them that I can give my soul and hand to I shall choose to do it' (Chapter 53). This is a particularly important passage. The phrase 'identify myself' is especially significant. Deronda feels the desire for a sense of Jewish identity, but it is he who chooses to identify himself with his Jewish heritage. For a Romantic consciousness like Deronda's, complete definition is impossible. He must choose his own identity since, for the Romantic, no role can be completely identified with the self.[6] His tribal identity is not something given either by race or by cultural heritage, but something chosen. But the choice is made joyfully, with his mind and feelings at one with each other. Instead of his previous 'shrinking' from direct contact with experience, this time impulsive feeling urges him to make this commitment. His relationships with Mirah, Mordecai, and Gwendolen have in various ways prepared his emotions and consciousness for this. There is no indication, however, that he has accepted the metaphysical beliefs of Judaism. The value of identifying with his Jewish race is that it allows him to overcome the alienation caused by his extreme self-consciousness and his previous relativistic way of looking at the world. But he says that he will not profess to believe in the same way as his ancestors, and it is implied that he regards Judaism and Mordecai's prophetic vision of Jewish nationhood as symbolic forms which express valuable human feelings and hopes, and not as truths in any objective sense.

Deronda's tribal identity, then, is fundamentally different from Mirah's or Mordecai's. Being a Jew is not for him an objective reality which completely defines him but a role he has chosen to play. But his role, unlike those of the egotistic role-players in the novel, is not chosen by will and ego in an effort to achieve dominance or mastery: it is the expression or realisation of what he feels to be his whole self and it embodies his deepest feelings, memories, and experiences. It even embodies feelings which transcend his personal existence, for he sees his desire to carry on the work of his grandfather as 'an inherited yearning' (Chapter 63). He has discovered a duty and an ideal which both his mind and his strongest feelings can assent to, and committing himself to them provides him with what George Eliot regards as an authentic form of self-realisation. It is possible, then, for him to overcome his earlier alienation without adopting a metaphysical position or rejecting advanced Romantic thinking. He remains an advanced Romantic, yet succeeds in reconciling this with a strong sense of identity that involves commitment to direct moral and social action.

Daniel Deronda must be judged to be one of George Eliot's greatest achievements, despite the fact that it is flawed by her failure to present characters like Deronda and Mordecai in a dramatically convincing way. But, as I have tried to show, Deronda is nevertheless one of her most interesting characterisations from a philosophical point of view. She succeeds in overcoming the pessimism that was present in the endings of *Felix Holt* and *Middlemarch*, as well as the tragic vision of *The Spanish Gypsy*, the work most directly related to *Daniel Deronda*, without altering her fundamental views. It could be argued that Deronda's decision to give up his English identity and to devote his energies to the creation of a Jewish nation-state reflects George Eliot's pessimism about the English situation. It seems to me, however, that pessimism about the spiritual condition of England is not the dominant note of the novel. Greater emphasis is given to the hope that even a race like the Jews which has lost its 'organic centre' (Chapter 42) and been dispersed over the globe can recover nationhood and national identity. Here one sees a parallel between the Jewish race and Deronda himself. As he is able to discover a centre for his life by committing himself to the ideal of Jewish nationhood and thus overcomes the mental 'dispersion' of relativistic thinking, so the Jews in recreating a centre, a nation state, will reverse the dispersal of their race and find national identity. And if such a revival is possible even for the Jews, it must also be possible for other nations, particularly the English whom George Eliot regards as akin to the Jews in several respects, but in possession of a centre of nationhood.

It is appropriate to end this study with *Daniel Deronda*, for in this novel George Eliot comes closest to creating a Romantic resolution by showing that Deronda is able to reconcile organicist goals with the acceptance of advanced Romantic thinking and with self-realisation, an aim one usually associates with Romantic egotism. Although Gwendolen's development remains problematic, it is suggested that her experiences and the influence of Deronda have helped her to outgrow her egotism. She is determined both to survive and to seek a better life for herself. In this last novel of George Eliot, then, there is some hope even for the Romantic egotist.

Notes

CHAPTER 1

1. See, for example, F. R. Leavis, *The Great Tradition: George Eliot, Henry James, Joseph Conrad* (London, 1948); Barbara Hardy, *The Novels of George Eliot: A Study in Form* (London, 1959); W. J. Harvey, *The Art of George Eliot* (London, 1961).
2. See, for example, George Levine, 'Determinism and Responsibility in the Works of George Eliot', *PMLA*, LXXVII(1962), 268–79, who argues that she is in fundamental agreement with John Stuart Mill about the relation between determinism and moral responsibility; Bernard J. Paris, *Experiments in Life: George Eliot's Quest for Values* (Detroit, 1965), who regards her as being very much part of a Comtean positivist tradition of thought; and Neil Roberts, *George Eliot: Her Beliefs and Her Art* (London, 1975) who sees her more broadly as a positivist in terms of her beliefs.
3. *Romanticism: The Culture of the Nineteenth Century*, ed. with an introduction by Morse Peckham (New York, 1965), pp. 15–16.
4. See preface to H. G. Schenk, *The Mind of the European Romantics: An Essay in Cultural History* (London, 1966), p. xv.
5. Morse Peckham, 'On Romanticism: Introduction', *Studies in Romanticism*, IX (1970), 220.
6. See U. C. Knoepflmacher, *Religious Humanism and the Victorian Novel: George Eliot, Walter Pater, and Samuel Butler* (Princeton, N. J., 1965), pp. 44–59, and Bernard J. Paris, *Experiments in Life*, pp. 89–113.
7. *The Essence of Christianity*, trans. George Eliot (New York, 1957), pp. 5, 13, 29–30. (Feuerbach's italics.)
8. *The George Eliot Letters*, ed. Gordon S. Haight (7 vols, New Haven, Conn. and London, 1954–5), II, p. 153. Hereafter referred to as *Letters*.
9. 'I have very little sympathy with Free-thinkers as a class, and have lost all interest in mere antagonism to religious doctrines. I care only to know, if possible, the lasting meaning that lies in all religious doctrine from the beginning till now' (*Letters*, IV, p. 65).
10. *Letters*, III, p. 111.
11. *Letters*, III, p. 231.
12. *Letters*, VII, p. 344.
13. *George Eliot: A Critical Study of Her Life, Writings and Philosophy* (London, 1883), p. 61.
14. *George Eliot: essai de biographie intellectuelle et morale 1819–1854* (Paris, 1933), especially p. 154.
15. *Letters*, III, p. 186.

16. *Letters*, VI, pp. 246–7.
17. George Eliot refers to Lewes working on Aristotle in a letter of 6 December 1861, and in her journal of 12 July 1863 she recorded that she was reading *Aristotle*, 'which gives me great delight'. See J. W. Cross, *George Eliot's Life As Related in Her Letters and Journals* (Edinburgh and London, 1885), II, p. 358.
18. *Problems of Life and Mind*, II, p. 3. This work consists of five volumes: volume I, *The Foundations of a Creed* (London, 1874); volume II, *The Foundations of a Creed* (London, 1875); volume III, *The Physical Basis of Mind* (London, 1877); volume IV, *The Study of Psychology: Its Object, Scope, and Method* (London, 1879); volume V, *Problems of Life and Mind* (London, 1879). I shall refer in future to these as *Problems*, I, II, III, IV and V. Lewes in his earlier life had been a great admirer of Shelley. See Roland A. Duerksen, *Shelleyan Ideas in Victorian Literature* (The Hague, 1966), pp. 139–49.
19. Michael Mason has argued that there was an important change in Lewes's thought some time between the late 1850s and early 1860s. See '*Middlemarch* and Science: Problems of Life and Mind', *Review of English Studies*, XXII (1971), 151–69, especially p. 159. Though I agree with this, I think one can discern the influence of Romantic thinking on Lewes's earlier writings, even when he was closest to Comte and Mill.
20. *Problems*, III, p. 339. (Lewes's italics.)
21. *The History of Philosophy: From Thales to Comte* (London, 1867), I, pp. 369–70. (Lewes's italics.)
22. *Problems*, II, pp. 86, 88.
23. *Aristotle: A Chapter from the History of Science* (London, 1864), p. 84.
24. *Aristotle*, p. 85. (Lewes's italics.)
25. *Aristotle*, p. 66. (Lewes's italics.)
26. *Aristotle*, p. 86.
27. *Problems*, I, p. 326. (Lewes's italics.)
28. *Problems*, I, p. 334.
29. *Problems*, II, pp. 317–18. This idea is also present in *Aristotle*: 'The hypotheses of atoms, and of an attractive force inherent in molecules, are beyond all reach of proof. They are metaphysical ideas, and find a place in Science simply because they facilitate calculations and the exposition of facts' (p. 92). The view that the atom was not something objectively real is to be found in several philosophers in the later part of the nineteenth century, such as F. A. Lange, Nietzsche, Vaihinger and Mach.
30. All quotations from George Eliot's works are from *The Works of George Eliot*, 20 vols, Cabinet edn (Edinburgh and London, 1878–80).
31. See Michael Mason's '*Middlemarch* and Science' for a more detailed account of the influence of Lewes's scientific ideas on George Eliot.
32. *Aristotle*, p. 90. (Lewes's italics.)
33. *Aristotle*, p. 91. (Lewes's italics.)
34. *Problems*, II, p. 388. (Lewes's italics.)
35. *Problems*, I, pp. 311, 312. (Lewes's italics.)
36. *Problems*, II, pp. 103–4. For an understanding of the context of Lewes's differences with Mill, see Mill's *System of Logic*, Book III, Chapter 14, Sections 1–2.

37. *Beyond Good and Evil*, trans. Marianne Cowan (Chicago, 1967), p. 24.
(Nietzsche's italics.)
38. For a detailed discussion of the nihilistic and egotistic side of Romanticism
and the variety of positive alternatives to it that emerged, see H. G. Schenk,
The Mind of the European Romantics, especially Part 2, 'Nihilism and
Yearning for a Faith', and Part 4, 'Romantic Enchantment'.

CHAPTER 2

1. Cross, *Life*, ii, p. 352.
2. *Letters*, v, p. 174.
3. Cross, *Life*, ii, pp. 332, 336, 344.
4. Cross, *Life*, ii, p. 386.
5. Miriam Allott, 'George Eliot in the 1860's', *Victorian Studies*, v (1961),
93–108, especially p. 97.
6. *Letters*, iv, p. 96.
7. *Dearest Isa: Robert Browning's letters to Isabella Blagden*, ed. Edward C.
McAleer (Austin, Texas, 1951), p. 178.

CHAPTER 3

1. For a detailed discussion of the Byronic egotist, see Peter L. Thorslev, Jr,
The Byronic Hero: Types and Prototypes (Minneapolis, 1962).
2. Page numbers are from the Cabinet edition of *Jubal and Other Poems*.
3. It is clear from George Eliot's letters that she was well acquainted with
Byron's writings. It is interesting that in 1869 she felt a renewed interest in
him and stated in strong terms her dislike of his work: 'Byron and his poetry
have become more and more repugnant to me of late years (I read a good
deal of him a little while ago, in order to form a fresh judgment)' (*Letters*, v,
p. 54).
4. *The Byronic Hero*, p. 123.
5. *History of Materialism*, trans. E. C. Thomas (London, 1880), ii, p. 254.
Lange thinks this is a complete misinterpretation of Feuerbach, and George
Eliot would obviously have agreed with him.
6. *The Nihilistic Egoist: Max Stirner* (London, 1971), p. 42.
7. *The Ego and His Own*, trans. Steven T. Byington (London, 1912), p. 215.
(Stirner's italics.)
8. *Beyond Good and Evil*, p. 203. (Nietzsche's italics.)
9. *Letters*, v, p. 448.
10. See *Letters*, iv, p. 301.
11. Cross, *Life*, iii, p. 43.
12. Page numbers are from the Cabinet edition of *The Spanish Gypsy*.
13. W. J. Harvey says of Middlemarch: 'The taproot of her vision . . . is her
concern with what we may call the transcendence of self.' See *Middlemarch*,
ed. with an introduction by W. J. Harvey (Harmondsworth, 1966), p. 14;
and Bernard J. Paris writes in *Experiments in Life*, p. 84: 'The great division
among George Eliot's characters is between egoists and those who approach
reality objectively . . . and the development of the action often hinges upon

or produces the education of the protagonist from egoism to objectivity.'
14. *Problems*, v, pp. 386–7. This passage is largely by George Eliot. A recent article by K. K. Collins, 'G. H. Lewes Revised: George Eliot and the Moral Sense', *Victorian Studies*, xxi(1977–8), 463–92, shows that George Eliot revised extensively and added material of her own to volumes four and five of *Problems of Life and Mind*. Collins actually quotes this passage to show how great her contribution was. See pp. 491–2. The phrase I have italicised was added by George Eliot.
15. Arnold Kettle, 'Felix Holt the Radical' in *Critical Essays on George Eliot*, ed. Barbara Hardy (London, 1970), p. 106.
16. *Problems*, i, p. 159.
17. *Problems*, i, pp. 305–6.

CHAPTER 4

1. *Twilight of the Idols; The Anti-Christ*, trans. R. J. Hollingdale (Harmondsworth, 1968), pp. 69–70. (Nietzsche's italics.)
2. *Romanticism in Perspective: A Comparative Study of Aspects of the Romantic Movements in England, France and Germany* (London, 1969), p. 220.
3. *The Essence of Christianity*, pp. 62–3.
4. *The Essence of Christianity*, p. 121.
5. *Essays of George Eliot*, ed. Thomas Pinney (London, 1963), p. 187. All quotations from George Eliot's essays are from this edition.
6. *Essays*, p. 373.
7. *Essays*, p. 374.
8. *Essays*, p. 379.
9. *Essays*, pp. 450–1. See also a recently discovered section of 'Leaves from a Notebook' entitled 'Feeling is a sort of knowledge', in Thomas Pinney, 'More Leaves from George Eliot's Notebook', *Huntington Library Quarterly*, xxix (1965–6), 364.
10. *Essays*, p. 166.
11. See, for example, Mill's *Autobiography* and his essay 'Thoughts on Poetry and Its Varieties'.
12. Wendell V. Harris, 'The Warp of Mill's "Fabric" of Thought', *Victorian Newsletter*, xxxvii (1970), 3.
13. *The Principles of Psychology* (London, 1870), i, p. 491.
14. Page numbers are from the Cabinet edition of *Jubal and Other Poems*.
15. *The Principles of Psychology*, i, p. 493.
16. *Problems*, i, p. 219.
17. *Problems*, iv, p. 145. This passage is largely by George Eliot. See K. K. Collins, 'G. H. Lewes Revised: George Eliot and the Moral Sense', pp. 484–5. Deronda compares his 'inherited yearning' to 'an inherited genius for painting' (Chapter 63), which calls to mind Lewes's analogy from music. It has been maintained by some critics that George Eliot believed in the inheritance of acquired characteristics. See Bernard J. Paris, *Experiments in Life*, pp. 207–8, and Neil Roberts, *George Eliot: Her Beliefs and Her Art*, pp. 46–8. In my view, this is a misinterpretation. Though she believed that

tendencies of feeling could be inherited, she would not, I think, have regarded these as the same as acquired characteristics. Paris believes Deronda inherits 'specific racial characteristics and a kind of racial unconscious . . . which need only the appropriate external stimuli to bring them to conscious fruition' (p. 207). But Lewes is extremely doubtful if such 'specific' characteristics can be inherited: 'Some writers who are disposed to exaggerate the action of Heredity believe that certain specific experiences of social utility in the race become organised in descendants, and are thus transmitted as instincts. With the demonstrated wonders of heredity before us, it is rash to fix limits to the specific determinations it may include; but the evidence in this direction is obscured by the indubitable transmission through language and other social institutions' (*Problems*, IV, p. 152). What Deronda inherits, I think, are tendencies of feeling which strongly attract him to the ideal of Jewish nationhood. A specific form for these tendencies of feeling must be socially and culturally supplied and it is a mistaken reading of the novel which assumes that only the Jewish cause could provide form for Deronda's inherited tendencies of feeling.

18. *Problems.*, IV, pp. 144–5.
19. *Problems*, IV, p. 143.
20. *Problems*, I, pp. 455–72.
21. *Problems*, I, p. 317. Compare George Eliot's view of the imagination in *Impressions of Theophrastus Such* (Cabinet edn), p. 197: 'it is worth repeating that powerful imagination is not false outward vision, but intense inward representation, and a creative energy constantly fed by susceptibility to the veriest minutiae of experience, which it reproduces and constructs in fresh and fresh wholes. . . . The illusion to which it is liable is not that of habitually taking duck-ponds for lilied pools, but of being more or less transiently and in varying degrees so absorbed in ideal vision as to lose the consciousness of surrounding objects or occurrences.'
22. *Essays*, p. 166.
23. *Essays*, p. 409.
24. For a fuller discussion of this and of George Eliot's relation to Darwinism, see my essay 'George Eliot, George Henry Lewes, and Darwinism', *Durham University Journal*, LXVI (1973–4), 278–93.
25. Laurence Lerner takes this view in *The Truthtellers: Jane Austen, George Eliot, D. H. Lawrence* (London, 1967), pp. 235–43.
26. 'The Authority of the Past in George Eliot's Novels', *Nineteenth-Century Fiction*, XXI (1966–7), 137.
27. *Letters*, IV, p. 104. (George Eliot's italics.)
28. *Letters*, IV, p. 97.

CHAPTER 5

1. See, for example, *The Political Thought of the German Romantics: 1793–1815*, ed. H. S. Reiss (Oxford, 1955).
2. On the influence of Ernst Moritz Arndt and others on Riehl, see Viktor von Geramb, *Wilhelm Heinrich Riehl: Leben und Wirken (1823–1897)* (Salzburg, 1954), esp. p. 124.

3. See, for example, Bernard J. Paris, *Experiments in Life*, pp. 193–204; Peter Coveney's introduction to the Penguin edition of *Felix Holt* (Harmondsworth, 1972); D. R. Carroll, '*Felix Holt*: Society as Protagonist', *Nineteenth-Century Fiction*, xvii (1962–3), 237–52.

4. See *Essays*, pp. 84, 90–1, 149.

5. 'Unlike the nationalist Herder, Coleridge was in no sense a relativist. . . . Unlike Herder, he did have a standard that applied in the last analysis to all States. . . . Herder argued that nations should be understood, rather than judged. Coleridge had no such notion.' David P. Calleo, *Coleridge and the Idea of the Modern State* (New Haven, Conn. and London, 1966), pp. 131–2.

6. *Essays*, pp. 293, 295.

7. *Essays*, p. 288.

8. *Essays*, p. 295.

9. *J. G. Herder on Social and Political Culture*, trans. and ed. with an introduction by F. M. Barnard (Cambridge, 1969), pp. 29–30. (Barnard's italics.)

10. 'The Social Organism', in *Essays: Scientific, Political, & Speculative* (Osnabrück, 1966), I, pp. 276–7.

11. *Letters*, vi, p. 53.

12. *Past and Present*, Book iv, Chapter 1.

13. See 'The Everlasting Yea' chapter of *Sartor Resartus*.

14. *The History of Philosophy*, ii, pp. 641, 651.

15. *The History of Philosophy*, ii, p. 585. Lewes refers here to 'one very dear to me' (clearly George Eliot) having influenced him in this view of Comte.

16. For example, Jerome Thale writes in *The Novels of George Eliot* (New York, 1959), p. 20: 'But Christianity in Hayslope is bankrupt, has lost all its dynamism and exists chiefly as a tradition rather than a force for shaping people's lives.' Also George R. Creeger writes of Dinah's sermon: 'She has effectively stated the position of the heart, yet what she has to say is largely ignored, or worse, received apathetically.' 'An Interpretation of *Adam Bede*', in *George Eliot: A Collection of Critical Essays* (Englewood Cliffs, N. J., 1970), p. 88.

17. 'In summary, Herder regarded the development of humanity…as the purpose of human existence.…In the development of humanity each nationality functions as an organic unit, and each branch of culture is the organic part of the larger unit.' R. R. Ergang, *Herder and the Foundations of German Nationalism* (New York, 1931), p. 111.

18. Page numbers are from the Cabinet edition.

19. George Eliot's own strong sense of English identity is shown in the following comment she made in a letter to Harriet Beecher Stowe: 'But we cannot bear now to exile ourselves from our own country, which holds the roots of our moral and social life' (*Letters*, vi, p. 246).

20. *J. G. Herder on Social and Political Culture*, p. 324.

21. For example, W. H. Riehl became an extreme nationalist and had some influence on the development of Nazism. See George L. Mosse, *The Crisis of German Ideology: Intellectual Origins of the Third Reich* (London, 1966), pp. 19–24.

22. For a discussion of George Eliot's interest in the Jews and Jewish culture, see

William Baker, *George Eliot and Judaism* (Salzburg, 1975).
23. Bernard J. Paris, 'George Eliot's Unpublished Poetry', *Studies in Philology*, LVI (1959), 541–2.

CHAPTER 6

1. Q. D. Leavis takes too negative a view of Silas's former religion when she writes in the introduction to the Penguin edition of *Silas Marner* (Harmondsworth, 1967), p. 16: 'the current form of religion, a Christian fundamentalism, has finished the effects of denaturing him by disinheriting him'. Even though Silas finds a new identity in Raveloe, continuity with his earlier life, which is not entirely without value, is still necessary.
2. See Thomas Pinney, 'The Authority of the Past in George Eliot's Novels', *Nineteenth-Century Fiction*, XXI (1966–7), pp. 131–47, and Neil Roberts, *George Eliot: Her Beliefs and Her Art*, p. 102.
3. Neil Roberts calls this concern of Mrs Tulliver 'absurd and even immoral' (*George Eliot: Her Beliefs and Her Art*, p. 102). The point is, I think, that even the materialism associated with the 'Dodson' characters cannot destroy the psychological need for continuity, and this need becomes projected onto material objects.
4. To be capable of choosing between conflicting sets of feeling implies that one must feel one's will is free to choose, which might seem to contradict the view that George Eliot is a determinist. It has been argued in an influential essay by George Levine that she was in general agreement with Mill on determinism and believed that 'morality and responsibility are wholly bound up in determinism . . . one overcomes the depressing effects of determinism by understanding it'. See 'Determinism and Responsibility in the Works of George Eliot', *PMLA*, LXXVII (1962), 278. However, it seems to me, that though she accepted the theoretical validity of determinism, she did not think it could be reconciled with practical life, that, contrary to Levine's interpretation, she took the view that people must continue to believe they possessed free will. This is strongly suggested in a short article entitled 'Moral Freedom', which appeared in print subsequent to Levine's study. See Thomas Pinney, 'More Leaves from George Eliot's Notebook', *Huntington Library Quarterly*, XXIX (1965–6), 365. The emphasis she places on 'practice' in this article, 'When once we have satisfied ourselves that any one point of view is hostile to practice', suggests that she may have accepted Kant's argument in his *Critique of Practical Reason* that belief in free will was a practical necessity.
5. It is interesting to compare Maggie Tulliver's decision to reject impulses she feels are irreconcilable with past duties and claims with Catherine Arrowpoint's decision in *Daniel Deronda* to marry Klesmer, despite her family's view that her duty to them should have priority. Her mother says to her: 'A woman in your position has serious duties. Where duty and inclination clash, she must follow duty' (Chapter 22). Though Catherine might appear to make the opposite choice to Maggie, there is no contradiction. Both are true to their sense of whole self in the choices they make. The values of Catherine's parents have no connection with her

feelings or memories: 'I am sorry to hurt you, mamma. But I will not give up the happiness of my life to ideas that I don't believe in and customs I have no respect for' (Chapter 22).

6. U. C. Knoepflmacher writes in *George Eliot's Early Novels: The Limits of Realism* (Los Angeles, 1968), p. 220: 'Notwithstanding George Eliot's identification of the overflowing river with those deterministic "laws" within and without the girl's psyche, the drowning is not tragic . . . she remains a figure of pathos, the prey of circumstances that are capricious and accidental. There is no causal connection between her flight and the destiny assigned to her.'

7. Cross, *Life*, III, p. 49.

8. George Eliot may have been influenced by Kant's view that one's duty as a human being requires resistance to nature. See *The Moral Law: Kant's Groundwork of the Metaphysic of Morals*, trans. H. J. Paton (London, 1964), esp. pp. 92–3.

CHAPTER 7

1. See M. H. Abrams, 'The Correspondent Breeze: A Romantic Metaphor', *Kenyon Review*, XIX(1957), pp. 113–30.

2. H. V. Routh, however, thinks this was Spencer's aim: 'But only the most self-confident representative of a self-confident age could imagine that the time had come to repeat the achievement of Thomas Aquinas. Yet such was the dream of Herbert Spencer's constructive imagination.' *Towards the Twentieth Century: Essays in the Spiritual History of the Nineteenth* (Cambridge, 1937), pp. 252–3. Richard Ellmann has suggested that there may be something of Spencer in Casaubon. See *Golden Codgers: Biographical Speculations* (London, 1973), p. 20. The recent evidence that has emerged of George Eliot's unrequited love for Spencer perhaps suggests that Dorothea's love for Casaubon incorporates something of her own early relationship with Spencer. See *The George Eliot Letters*, ed. Gordon S. Haight (New Haven, Conn., and London, 1978), VIII, pp. 56–7.

3. For a detailed analysis of the intellectual background to Casaubon and his work, see W. J. Harvey's essay, 'The Intellectual Background to the Novel: Casaubon and Lydgate', in *Middlemarch: Critical Approaches to the Novel*, ed. Barbara Hardy (London, 1967), pp. 25–37.

4. See the preface to H. G. Schenk, *The Mind of the European Romantics*, p. xv.

5. See Michael Mason's discussion of this in '*Middlemarch* and Science', p. 164.

6. Neil Roberts, *George Eliot: Her Mind and Her Art*, p. 165.

CHAPTER 8

1. Criticism of *Middlemarch* in recent years has shown an increasing interest in the aspect of the novel I shall be discussing, from a number of different viewpoints. See, for example, Michael Mason, '*Middlemarch* and Science', esp. pp. 161–9; U. C. Knoepflmacher, *Laughter and Despair: Readings in Ten*

Novels of the Victorian Era (Los Angeles, 1971), pp. 168–201; J. Hillis Miller, 'Optic and Semiotic in *Middlemarch*', in *The Worlds of Victorian Fiction*, ed. Jerome H. Buckley (Cambridge, Mass., 1975), pp. 125–45; Peter Jones, 'Imagination and Egoism in *Middlemarch*', in his *Philosophy and the Novel: Philosophical Aspects of 'Middlemarch', 'Anna Karenina', 'The Brothers Karamazov', 'A la Recherche du Temps Perdu' and of the Methods of Criticism* (London, 1975), pp. 9–69.

2. *The History of Philosophy*, I, pp. xlvi–xlvii. The aspect of *Middlemarch* that I shall focus on in this chapter probably owes a good deal to George Eliot's interest in Lewes's philosophical concerns. He also refers frequently to 'signs' in his writings.

3. Here I am in disagreement with Peter Jones's analysis of *Middlemarch* in his *Philosophy and the Novel*. He believes that George Eliot finally decided 'to settle for an essentially passive theory of perception' (p. 67), and he cites the pier-glass passage at the beginning of Chapter 27 as an important piece of evidence in support of his view. He argues that the narrator's statement that it is demonstrable that the scratches are going everywhere impartially implies a passive theory of perception since this seems to be presented as a statement of fact: 'if imagination is an inalienable aspect of all perception, then the observer is offering an interpretation of phenomena even when he judges it patternless' (p. 26). George Eliot seems to me to be perfectly well aware of this. As I have already said, for her all facts are interpretations. The narrator's point, I think, is that the best interpretation of the scratches (e.g. by several observers, in natural light, etc.) would be that they are not related in such a way as to form concentric circles, but exhibit no pattern. Both the view that the scratches form concentric circles and that they are going everywhere impartially are interpretations, but the latter is so overwhelmingly the best interpretation that it could be said to be a fact.

4. For example, Peter Jones objects in his chapter on *Middlemarch* in *Philosophy and the Novel*: 'The omniscient author appears immune from precisely those obstacles to knowledge encountered by her characters, and to which we are all alleged to be subject in everyday life' (p. 27).

5. *The Form of Victorian Fiction* (Notre Dame and London, 1968), pp. 83, 84–5.

6. Gabriel Josipovici, *The World and the Book: A Study of Modern Fiction* (London, 1971), p. 139. He considers this a basic assumption of what he calls the 'traditional' novel and he sees George Eliot as one of the most notable of 'traditional' novelists.

7. *The Novels of George Eliot: A Study in Form* (London, 1959), p. 120.

8. For a fuller analysis of the narrator's role in *Middlemarch* and George Eliot's fiction generally, see my article 'The Role of the Narrator in George Eliot's Novels', *Journal of Narrative Technique*, III (1973), 97–107.

CHAPTER 9

1. However, one should bear in mind Robert Preyer's argument that a narrow concern with artistic success or failure 'does not do justice to the *interest* of a literary work of any magnitude'. 'Beyond the Liberal Imagination: Vision

and Unreality in Daniel Deronda', *Victorian Studies*, xiv (1960 – 1), 53 (Preyer's italics.)

2. 'The saddest thing to be witnessed is the play of Miss Leigh, Byron's grand niece, who is only 26 years old, and is completely in the grasp of this mean, money-raking demon. It made me cry to see her young fresh face among the hags and brutally stupid men around her' (*Letters*, v, p. 314). See also Gordon S. Haight, *Géorge Eliot: A Biography* (London, 1968), pp. 456–7.

3. Discussion of acting imagery in *Daniel Deronda* from a different point of view can be found in Karl Kroeber, *Styles in Fictional Structure: The Art of Jane Austen, Charlotte Brontë, George Eliot* (Princeton, N. J., 1971), pp. 99–109.

4. In her journal of 23 January 1869, George Eliot records that she read 'the first four cantos of Don Juan' (*Letters*, v, p. 6).

5. David R. Carroll makes this point strongly in 'The Unity of *Daniel Deronda*', *Essays in Criticism*, ix (1959), 377.

6. George H. Mead discusses this implication of Romanticism in *Movements of Thought in the Nineteenth Century*, ed. Merritt H. Moore (Chicago and London, 1972), p. 63: 'The self belongs to the reflexive mode. One senses the self only in so far as the self assumes the rôle of another so that it becomes both subject and object in the same experience. . . . As a characteristic of the romantic attitude we find this assumption of rôles.' See also pp. 82–4.

Index